Betting on the Boy Next Door

Center Point
Large Print

Also by Melanie Jacobson and available from Center Point Large Print:

Kiss Me Now
Kiss the Girl
Kiss and Tell
Scrooge and the Girls Next Door
Cocoa Kisses

Betting on the Boy Next Door

MELANIE JACOBSON

CENTER POINT LARGE PRINT
THORNDIKE, MAINE

This Center Point Large Print edition
is published in the year 2025 by arrangement with
Melanie Jacobson.

Copyright © 2023 by Melanie Jacobson.

All rights reserved.

The text of this Large Print edition is unabridged.
In other aspects, this book may vary
from the original edition.
Printed in the United States of America
on permanent paper sourced using
environmentally responsible foresting methods.
Set in 16-point Times New Roman type.

ISBN: 979-8-89164-542-4

The Library of Congress has cataloged this record
under Library of Congress Control Number: 2025930445

To Jaymee
Besties rule

Chapter One
SAMI

It's past midnight when I open the trunk of my car and toss in my gym bag with the combat boots, torn prom dress, and fishnets. I stand there for a minute, calculating. My parking space is in front of our condo, and all the windows are dark. That's good; the odds are lower I'll get caught sneaking in by my roommates—but they aren't zero.

I've thought about this all the way home: what is my cover story? I washed my hair thoroughly, but I can't be sure I got out all the glitter until I see it in the morning. It's hiding under a beanie right now, so that will help.

I only need to get past my roommates on the first floor, and I'm safe. But I've never been out this late after a gig before, so I've never had to think of an excuse. What if one of them asks me where I've been?

I won't tell them the truth. I don't tell anyone the truth. Well, except my grandma. But she wouldn't judge.

Maybe . . . a midnight supply run to the twenty-four hour superstore. I find one of my reusable grocery sacks and put in some random things from the trunk: an unopened bottle of motor oil, my car first aid kit, a flashlight, and a softball from the time I told Ruby I'd join her city league team but then remembered how much I suck at sports.

I look at the lumpy bag. It's not completely convincing, but it's the best I've got.

I close the trunk with a soft click and let myself in through our patio door.

The house is quiet. I slip off my shoes and sneak up the stairs. No one opens their bedroom door to see who it is or what I'm up to.

I dart into my room and shut my door, leaning against it with a sigh of relief. I let the bag of fake groceries slide to the ground. I have *got* to come up with a better excuse for next time.

Which is tomorrow.

Great.

There's a word for a person who is as obsessed with bacon as I am: addict.

Lots of people think they love bacon; they *like* bacon. Loving bacon is if you get captured by terrorists who try to torture secrets from you and everything fails: waterboarding, sleep deprivation, playing "Macarena" twenty-four/seven for weeks.

Then one day, they cook bacon and say you can have a piece if you tell them all your secrets. So you do, starting with the time you walked across the stage at high school graduation with toilet paper stuck to your shoe to the time last week when you got in your roommate's car at the grocery store, except you realized thirty seconds later it was actually a middle-aged woman you'd never seen in your life and you just changed her radio station.

Or that's what I did, anyway. The toilet paper thing. Then the car thing. It was awkward. She almost pepper sprayed me.

I haven't given any information up to terrorists yet though. Mostly because they haven't offered me bacon.

So when the smell of bacon frying curls under my bedroom door on Saturday morning, New Year's Eve, I follow my nose into the kitchen more predictably than one of Pavlov's dogs.

Ruby, one of my three roommates, smiles up at me. "Morning, chica. Figured it would be you in first."

"Bacon," I mumble.

"Coming up. But also, someone's moving in."

The condo next to us has been empty for nearly two weeks. The previous owner, a family with two young kids, sold it to move to Atlanta when the wife got a new job. But as I shuffle over to our patio sliding doors, I spot the moving truck. I slide the door open and poke my head out. There's some low-key clatter as two guys in company jumpsuits bring down a sofa and manhandle it through the low gate next door.

"Sit out there," Ruby says. "Bacon and omelets coming up. Tell me when the movers come by with something new."

"What have they brought in so far?" I ask, settling into one of the wicker patio chairs. I glance at Ava's parking space, which is empty. She's at her lab, no doubt. She doesn't have to be. Neither of us has to work weekends. For her, it's because the lab has normal business hours. For me, it's one of the perks of being the RN at a nursing home. My job is to oversee the licensed vocational nurses and certified nursing assistants, and since I outlasted the previous night shift RN, I got to move to days six months ago.

"A mattress. King size. Metal mattress frame. That's it. It was the first thing off the truck."

I squint, trying to think through my pre-coffee brain cloud. "Could be a couple. Or a tall guy."

Ruby nods. "Going to have to see the headboard."

A new neighbor in the Grove is a big deal, especially one right next door. The condos form a square, the front doors facing into a courtyard with a pool and community barbecue areas. The back of each condo has a patio and a small grassy yard with a low iron fence, separated from the parking lot by a sidewalk, plus a balcony hanging over it from the second-floor bedrooms.

It means we all get to know each other well.

There's no space between yards; they run along the sidewalk in an unbroken row. We always see neighbors if we hang out on the patio. We're also always bumping into each other at the mailboxes or the pool or the shared gym and game room.

I know everyone in our complex at least by name, and most of them are owners, so there isn't much turnover. I've been here since about six months after Ava bought it and she and Ruby moved in. Madi was only two months behind me.

This is only the third new neighbor we've gotten since we were the new neighbors two years ago, and our tiny yard's location by the parking lot means we get to judge the new residents' goods before the rest of the complex.

The movers walk past, and I call into the house to Ruby. "Next piece coming off."

She comes to stand at the door as we watch them wrestle the headboard out next. "Black leather, king-sized." She thinks for a few seconds. "Tall single male."

"Sounds right."

Over the next forty-five minutes, Ruby and I eat and watch more furniture pass and cement our guess. Dark walnut bedroom furniture, a large office desk, a flat screen TV approximately seventy-two inches, leather sectional, overstuffed and dark brown, a recliner, stainless steel fridge, and lots of boxes.

The movers come off the truck with a Traeger smoker.

"That's it. Single guy," I declare. "For sure."

As best we can tell, the neighbor himself hasn't made an appearance. We've guessed anywhere from mid-thirties and never married to a fifty-something divorced guy, but there's no way to be sure.

"Where's Jessica Fletcher when you need her?" Ruby asks. Jessica Fletcher is the heroine of an old TV series called *Murder, She Wrote*. It ran in the eighties, but it's Ruby's comfort watch on Netflix. I think Ruby Ramos would love to be the lead in her own series of cozy mysteries. If we have a murder in the Grove, Ruby will solve it way before the police do, using a slightly parted curtain and the wrong brand of cat food in the kitty dish as her only clues.

By the time the movers finish, nothing else has sailed past us to contradict our conclusions. The neighbor on our other side, a retiree named Mrs. Lipsky, appears on her balcony and stares down at us with a quirked brow, and we give her the lowdown.

"Single guy," Ruby calls up. She lays out her evidence, ending with, "It looks like he bought everything on a furniture showroom floor that looked like dude stuff."

Mrs. Lipsky nods and disappears.

Once the truck pulls away, we settle into our

Saturday routines. Ruby works at the library some weekends, but she's off today, and she leaves around noon to do something with her boyfriend, Niles. She doesn't say what, but if I had to guess, it's probably something like listening to a timeshare presentation to get a steak dinner. Niles is very big on freebies and bargains.

I wait until she's gone before I text my bandmates. None of my roommates know I'm in a band because . . . I don't know why. Because they'd insist on coming to my shows, and I'm not ready for that. This music is totally different from the singer-songwriter stuff I did in college. I don't know how to explain the drastic shift.

Meet at Wingnut's? I press send.

I'm sure it wakes up half of them even at noon, but the "K" responses roll in over the next five minutes. Satisfied, I head out to my car to fetch the gym bag holding my alter ego clothes so I can swap them out for a different stage outfit. Am I the only one in the condo lying about where I'm going all the time? Probably. It wouldn't surprise me in the least if Madi turned out to be an undercover agent or something wild—she's so vague about so much of her life—but somehow, I think I'm the only one living a secret rock star life.

Wannabe rock star, anyway. Tonight is another show in a small venue on the way to world domination. Or at least steady gigs.

I'll have to wait until tomorrow to get the dirt on any new neighbor sightings, but I've decided: the top-of-the-line smoker and huge TV screen scream recently divorced middle-aged man.

I'm sure he's nice, but I doubt I'm missing much.

Chapter Two
JOSH

I end the call from the moving company informing me that all my belongings have been moved into my new place. I'm now the proud owner of the first real estate I've purchased with my own money, a two-bedroom condo in the Clarksville area of Austin.

I push back from my desk in the overly somber law offices at Brower and Moore. Even though it's a Saturday—New Year's Eve, no less—I'm by no means the only attorney working. At least a dozen other associates occupy their offices. The grind is real.

I never want to be the first person to leave, but I've already put in four billable hours this morning and checking out my new place is a good enough reason to split early on a Saturday.

I pull the new key I acquired this week from my work bag. It still has a paper tag on it with the unit number, as if I'll forget. I make the drive in fifteen minutes—a big reason I bought it—and I turn into the numbered parking space for my unit. It's right in front of my patio, which is completely empty except for my smoker. I'll have to ask Reagan to look for patio furniture for me. My sister loves doing that kind of stuff, and I couldn't care less about it.

The patio next to mine is full of wicker furniture with bright cushions and lots of plants. It borders another yard with a tiny terrier-type dog, yapping loudly. Its face looks very intent, but it's like having a Muppet bark at me. "You aren't scary," I tell him when I climb from my car. "Sorry, bro. Keep trying."

I could enter through my back patio, but I want to go through the front door for the "Welcome Home" experience, so I take the breezeway on the other side of the yappy dog's yard. It opens into the courtyard and the pool hiding beneath a cover. Not only do Austin winters get cold, it's a humid cold that knifes at every bit of exposed skin on bad days. Those days mean chapped lips and skin, forcing me to google crap like "face lotion for dudes." This type of lotion is called *moisturizer*, which sounds inappropriate on a work browser.

At the door labeled "22," I pull out my key. It's satisfying, hearing that jiggle of a knob I've paid for. I open it and pause on the threshold to take in Reagan's handiwork. The last time I saw this place, it was empty. Austin property is hot enough that real estate agents don't even have to stage a place to get top dollar. That's why—even though I don't have any school loans—I had to work for three years to save up enough for a down payment that left me with a mortgage I can afford.

It had been in turnkey condition, which was a major selling point for me because I don't have time to oversee a remodel. It'll be my first time not having a roommate, so I had to furnish the whole place too. Reagan chose my furniture to work with the light gray walls, and now a leather sectional goes with the only two pieces of original furniture I contributed: my TV and my recliner.

I text her.

JOSH: It's manly enough.
REAGAN: You're welcome.

She follows that with an eyeroll emoji.

I cruise through the rest of the small first floor, poking my head into the half bath which Reagan has supplied with hand towels and soap, the kitchen where she's put white dishes in sets of four, and the tiny pantry, which only has three unopened boxes of Peanut Butter Cap'n Crunch sitting on a shelf.

I smile and text my sister again, this time with a cereal bowl emoji and a thank you.

She didn't have to do that. She didn't have to do any of this. I was grateful to her for finding good deals on furniture, but she said it was fun scouring warehouses for model home furniture sell-offs. And I know the only reason she got the dishes is because she was afraid I'd bring over a couple of mismatched plates and cups from my apartment.

She'd be right. But having matching dishes makes me feel as mature as holding the key to my own place does.

I go upstairs, stopping at the smaller bedroom first. I'd asked the movers to put all my office furniture in it so I can work at home when I need to. It's there. I'll need to rearrange it some, but it's good enough for now.

In the larger bedroom, my bed is set up but bare, so I take a few minutes to open the box marked "linens" and make up the mattress before collapsing on it and staring at the ceiling.

"This is mine." A small smile forms on my face.

Damn, that sounds good.

I sit up and say it louder, catching my reflection in the mirror of the closet door. "This is *mine*. This is *my* house."

I grin. Still sounds good, so I stand up and shadowbox at my reflection. "Mine, mine, mine. I did this." Pretty soon I'm jumping on the mattress, the slightly vaulted ceiling giving my six-foot frame plenty of clearance.

I want to do all the homeowner things. I jump down from the bed and go in search of the thermostat so I can change it, no matter what it's on already. I find it and bump it down a degree just because.

I close all the blinds and strip naked, then walk back through every room of the house. These are the things you get to do in your own house that you can't do with roommates. Or at least, you can't if you want to stay on good terms.

I get dressed again because changing the temperature actually made it kind of chilly, then sit on my new leather sofa—which proves to be comfortable—and try to think of other "it's my house now" things I can do.

Mail. I can check mail. There won't be any yet, although it's set up to forward from my old apartment. But I should find out where the mailboxes are.

I dig my keys from my pocket and make a guess that the mailboxes are probably at either end of the complex. I pick the end closest to me to try, and I'm standing there studying the unit numbers on the boxes when an older woman joins me.

She has a parrot on her shoulder.

"Hello." She has a raspy smoker's voice.

"Hello," the parrot echoes.

"I'm Enid Lipsky. You must be new here. I don't recognize you. Did you just move into number twenty-two?"

"I did. I'm Josh Brower. It's nice to meet you."

"You live next to the girls," she informs me. "Four of them. Couple of them are too sassy, but every one of them is prettier than the last. Are you single?"

"Married to my work," I say. She has strong matchmaker energy.

"Well, we guessed older when we watched your stuff come in this morning. You're young."

"Twenty-nine," I offer.

"Are you the new neighbor?" another female voice asks.

I turn to see a girl my age—maybe a little younger—walking toward the mailboxes. She's pretty. Dark hair, olive skin that could be selling face lotion on billboards.

Mrs. Lipsky answers before I can. "Josh. Twenty-nine and married to his work." She locks her box and turns to leave.

"Thanks, Mrs. Lipsky," the girl says, smiling.

"Sexy bastard!" the parrot squawks as Mrs. Lipsky turns the corner into the courtyard. I hear her mutter something to him, but I don't catch it.

The girl's smile grows to a grin at the parrot's catcall. "Mrs. Lipsky rescued Ahab from a tiki bar in Galveston. His manners aren't great. I'm Ruby, by the way. I'm in number twenty-one."

"Josh," I say, then feel stupid because Mrs. Lipsky already told her my name. "Uh, the sexy bastard."

She laughs. "Twenty-nine and married to your work. I got it all, I think. Welcome."

"Thanks."

"What kind of work are you married to?" she asks as she opens her mailbox.

"Paperwork." That feels like ninety percent of my job.

She points to her chest. "Librarian. Not single. But all my roommates are, in case you and work decide to have an open relationship."

"I'll keep that in mind."

"Will you have any roommates?"

"Just Bernice. We'll share a room. She'll be here tomorrow. I'm using the small bedroom for an office."

"Oh."

She looks slightly disappointed to learn about Bernice, my temporary red tail boa. I'm snake-sitting for one of my old roommates who's out of the country for two months on some oil job. But I don't clarify because I'm not looking to date right now. I've got way too much to prove at the firm before I can even think about it.

"Well, it's nice to meet you," Ruby says. "Sometimes when you make a big move, you don't realize all the stuff you need, so holler if we can help with the basics."

"Thanks, Ruby. That's nice of you."

She waves and leaves, and when I finally open my mailbox, I'm surprised to discover a card inside. I pluck it out and smile at Reagan's handwriting on the front with a postmark from yesterday on it.

I lock the box and walk back to my place, laughing when I pull out a card with a toddler in Star Wars underwear on the front. Inside, it reads, "Congratulations on your big boy pants!" Reagan signed it, "Love you, little brother."

It means a lot, coming from her. She's three years older, and she's been the perfect kid, meeting and exceeding our parents' high expectations. I have . . . not. Which is why I have to outwork everyone at the firm; it might be the only form of atonement my dad will understand.

An hour later, I'm setting up my desktop computer in my office when a knock calls me downstairs. I open the door to find Ruby there.

"Hey, neighbor," I say.

"Hey, Josh." I like that she says my name like it's the hundredth time she's used it. She's a comfortable personality. "I talked to Mrs. Lipsky, and we're throwing a patio party on Monday night to welcome you. Does that work? Will you be around?"

"Um, yes. But a patio party?"

"The four units on this side all come out on our patios, bring food, open all the connecting gates, and wander back and forth and talk. The neighbors you haven't met on your other side are Hugo and Jasmine. They're artists, and they're in for the party. We're thinking at six?"

I'm usually still at the office, but I say, "Sounds good. I'll see you then."

After I close the door, I place a delivery order for some basic groceries, including chips and queso for the patio party. I make a note to get some Torchy's Tacos delivered on Monday too so I can make a good impression.

Not that it matters too much. Unfortunately, these days my house is somewhere to sleep in between hours at work.

Chapter Three
SAMI

I pull into my parking space behind the Grove after a Sunday morning thrifting run. Usually, thrift stores are crowded on the weekend, but in a party town like Austin, I was banking on some relaxed New Year's Day browsing, and I got it. Didn't find anything good, but that's okay; no matter what else happens in a day, I can always count on my reserved space as a bright spot. The parking in our complex—which sometimes borders on demolition derby between 5 and 6 PM—is its only real drawback, which is why I was convinced to move in with the promise of a designated spot.

I walk into our condo and hang my purse by the door. Madison is sitting in front of the TV, watching *Sight Unseen*.

"Hey, bestie." She says it on autopilot, not taking her eyes from the screen.

"Don't watch that," I tell her. It's a reality show about couples who get married without seeing each other.

"I can't look away. You get that I made out with this guy the other day, right?" She points to a medium-cute guy on the screen who is fixing to meet the girl he chose face-to-face.

"You mean six months ago?"

Madi glances over and blinks her lash extensions at me. "Same difference." With a toss of her perfect caramel highlights, she turns back to the TV.

"How many times have you watched this?" I ask her.

"Lost count," she mumbles.

Ruby appears from the hallway. Madi is a very carefully cultivated kind of knockout. Ruby Ramos is the kind of understated gorgeous that takes your breath when you finally notice, and she has no idea.

"Hey, bestie," Ruby says, heading to the kitchen.

"Hey. How was New Year's?" I ask. "You and Niles have fun?"

"Yeah. We watched the CNN countdown and watched the ball drop." She continues to the kitchen, and Madi and I make faces at each other.

The worst, she mouths. She means Niles, and I nod. What a twerp.

"What about you?" I say aloud.

Madi shrugs. "Always a good night for tips. Made rent for the whole month already. What did you do?"

Made fifty bucks for playing a gig at a tiny club where no one cared because we went on after midnight and they were already drunk. Aloud, I say, "Went to a movie with a couple of work friends."

A door opens down the hall and my fourth and final roommate, Ava, makes an appearance. She's dressed in jeans and a lime green sweater that's the perfect color for her red hair and pale complexion. We're all obsessed with her hair; it falls below her shoulders in fat curls. She says curly hair is annoying, and we take turns threatening to beat her.

"Hey, bestie," she says, stopping at the end of the hall and leaning against the wall.

"Can't believe you're not at work," Madi says.

Ava slides her hands into her pockets and strolls the rest of the way into the living room. "I don't want another official roommate meeting."

Madi smirks. "So now you're just hanging out here, wishing you were at the lab anyway?"

Ava plops into an armchair. "I didn't say that."

Ruby walks out from the kitchen. "Do I have this right? Madi worked on New Year's Eve, Sami went to a movie with work friends, and you"—she points to Ava—"did what last night?"

Ava picks at her jeans. "Stayed home."

"And did what?" Ruby presses.

Ava's jaw firms in a stubborn line. "Watched an octopus documentary. And I *liked* it."

Ruby makes a disgusted tsk. "¿Neta? You know what I was doing at midnight last night? Kissing my man. When's the last time any of you did that?" She holds up her hand as Madi starts to answer. "I'm talking about a boy you go out with more than once."

Madi shuts her mouth. None of us points out that we'd make the same choices between kissing Niles and our actual New Year's Eve plans.

"I'm waiting," Ruby says. "I mean it. When's the last time any of you had a New Year's Eve that was so pathetic?"

"I'll take 'what is freshman year' for a hundred, Trebek," Madi says.

"He's dead," Ruby says. As a librarian, she is physically incapable of letting inaccurate information go unchecked.

"'What is freshman year?' for a hundred, host-of-the-week," Madi says without changing her tone.

We all lived in the same dorm at the University of Texas as freshmen, and we've been friends ever since. The dorms had been closed for winter break, but we'd all gotten restless at home after Christmas. When our group chat blew up with whining about how boring our New Year's Eves had been with our families, we all accepted Madi's invitation to crash at her parents' giant house for the rest of the break while they were in Europe or something.

"That's right," Ava says. "Freshman year." She plucks up the remote in front of Madi and turns off the TV.

"I was watching," Madi says.

Ruby snorts. "You could recite that episode. We need a bestie meeting."

Ava draws herself into a ball in her chair and eyes Ruby over her knees. These meetings only happen once or twice a year, and the last time, it was an intervention because we had to kidnap Ava for a long weekend in October when she'd worked eighty hours a week for three months straight. She's a genetics researcher and super into her work. *Too* into it.

Ruby disappears into the kitchen and comes back with a pack of Goldfish crackers. She curls up in the other corner of the sectional, opening her snack and rooting in it noisily. Loudest librarian ever.

"What are we meeting about?" Madi asks. She scoops up the remote and drops it down her shirt, like Ruby and I would even flinch at fishing it out. "I'll watch as much *Sight Unseen* as I want."

"Your love lives are sad," Ruby says. I think being a librarian also makes her a hardcore romantic. "Why?"

"I'm too busy," Ava says.

"Boooo," Ruby says. "You practically live in that lab. By *choice*."

Ava's eyebrow shoots up. "Do you know how many world-changing things are growing in my lab? Why wouldn't I want to be there?"

"I'm on Ava's side," I say. "Also, men are the worst, and I don't want one." I've held this opinion since a rough breakup with my college boyfriend a couple of years ago.

"There are good guys out there," Ruby argues. "Look at Niles."

I can feel Madi and Ava fighting the same urge I have not to exchange glances with each other. It's not that Niles is a *bad* guy. He's just not the kind of guy anyone with two personality cells to rub together would ever date. None of us can figure out why Ruby is with him.

But we all hold it together and say nothing about NilesQuil, as we call him when Ruby isn't around.

Ruby isn't done. "I'll prove it to you. How about a bet?"

"That Niles is a good guy?" I ask, confused.

"No. That doesn't need proving." There's merciful silence from Ava and Madi. "I'm good at matching," Ruby continues. "That's my gift in the library, right? I can match anyone with the perfect book. For their mood, for their forever favorite."

"That's true," I concede. She's constantly bringing books home from work for us, and she hasn't been wrong yet.

"I also do it with people," Ruby says.

This is undeniable. She's the reason we all intersect. I'd drifted across the hall in the dorm, drawn by her and Ava's laughter for countless late-night UNO and gossip sessions. Then Ruby had collected Madi when they'd bonded over kicking the boys out of the dorm lounge and watching the first season of *The Crown*, eventually turning at least half of our floor into royal watchers.

She can also put together the perfect mix of people for a barbecue or work team. She intuitively gets which people will click. Which, once again, leaves us all baffled about why she's with NilesQuil.

"So, you're betting . . . what?" Madi asks. "That you can find Sami a man?"

"A man that she would want?" Ava clarifies. "Because books are not men. Austin men are not *Austen* men, you know?"

"Nice one." I high-five Ava. "But she's right, Ruby. You really want to bet me you can find me a guy I'll like?"

"Yes," Ruby says calmly. "That's what I'm saying."

My eyes narrow. "Name your terms."

"I'll bet I can find you true love by New Year's."

"What are the stakes?" I ask. "I want to win something good."

"You get true love. That's all you get, but it's not nothing."

"But what do *you* get if you find me a boyfriend?" I ask, narrowing my eyes at her. There's something almost sly about her expression.

"From you? Your parking space."

We all gasp.

"How dare you?" I press my hand against my chest. "It is the one constant good thing in my life."

"And it's constantly one of the worst in mine. I'm tired of Armageddon every time I want to park my stupid car," Ruby says. "I don't want to be on the frontlines of the Grove parking wars anymore."

Madi, who also doesn't have assigned parking, snaps a few times in agreement.

"No way," I say. "I'm not giving up my spot."

"You're saying you'd take a good parking spot over a guy?" Ruby asks.

"Duh."

Madi and Ava nod in agreement, which only makes Ruby lift her chin and narrow her eyes, the way she does when she's going in for the kill in *Scrabble*.

"We're not talking just any guy here," she says. "We're talking the love of your life. The kind that makes you dream of babies and suburbs."

"Not my thing," I tell her. I've got big dreams, and being a wife and mother are low on the list. I want that someday, but dangling a potential fiancé does nothing for me right now. Not after my last almost-engagement.

Ruby studies me, eyes alert. "What kind of guy would it take then?"

"To give up my parking space?" Not going to happen, so I can name the impossible. "The perfect man. Excellent taste in clothes and music, no corporate types, a dimple, a respectable-looking outside wrapper with a bad boy streak. Must love puppies, travel, rain, and eighties movies. Must hate golf. He's got to be an excellent cook, a big reader, know all my favorite podcasts, and make me laugh. Frat bros are a no."

"Is that it?" Ruby asks, her tone drier than the last roast Madi made.

"No," I say, enjoying this now. "He should also hate long walks on the beach, dream in Technicolor, speak three languages, and think Texas football is overrated."

Madi and Ava burst out laughing. There is no guy in Austin who could meet the last criterion.

"Fine," Ruby says. "I accept your terms."

I quit grinning and straighten. "Wait, what? I didn't agree to anything."

"Yes, you did. I said to describe your ideal man. You did. And I will now find your ideal man in exchange for your parking space."

I blink at her a couple times then shake my head, my smile coming back. "Okay, Ruby. Bet's on." My list was made up to mess with her, which means I'm doubly sure to keep my parking spot. "You'll have one whole year." *To find the man who doesn't exist,* I add silently.

She smiles. "I won't need it."

Ava leans over to Madi and whispers, "She looks scary."

Madi only nods with wide eyes.

Ruby shakes her head. "You should be scared, because after I win this bet with Sami, you two are next."

"You sound like a creepy Bond villain," Madi complains. "Dr. Plotty-Pants."

"I prefer Señorita Amor," Ruby says. "And we need to nail down some conditions. First, you must give any matches I come up with a true and honest try."

"Sure." She won't find anyone who will rise to the level of sacrificing reserved parking.

"You have to go in with an open mind," Ruby insists. "You have to be willing to give them more than a date or two. If it's not going to work after a first date, you'll have to give me good reasons why. I need to know that you're keeping yourself open to this process."

"I have no reason to agree to this," I say.

"Because I'm good, and you know you'll lose your parking space," Ruby says.

"Won't happen." I'm positive.

"Then take the bet." Her eyes gleam with a challenge.

"You really don't have a reason not to," Ava says. "And honestly, I think it would be good for you."

Madi nods.

I roll my eyes. "This is so stupid. Fine."

"If you even *think* you're in love, it counts, even if you haven't said 'I love you' out loud by New Year's."

"No way," I say. I'm not concerned about losing but it's always smart to hedge your bets. "We both have to say 'I love you.' " *Easiest bet ever.*

"Fine. But you can't *not* say it just to keep your parking space." Ruby gives me such a confident smile that it shakes me for a second until I remember all the bad dates I've been on since breaking up with Bryce.

"I'm in," I say. I'm keeping my permit.

"The bet is on," Ruby says. "The countdown begins at midnight."

Chapter Four
SAMI

"You're up," Ruby informs me from the sofa when I walk in the door around five. Band practice had run long, but we'd dialed in one of our original songs, and I'm feeling good about performing it tonight.

"For what?" I ask.

"The bet. I found a guy for you."

Is she kidding? It's only been three days! "Did you make me an app profile or something? That's a loophole. We should have stipulated that these have to be dates with people you know."

"It *is* someone I know, and it's someone you're going to get to know at the patio party."

I pause with my foot on the bottom step. "The new neighbor?" I'd gotten her text about the party.

"Josh," she confirms. "And remember, you have to be open-minded about this."

I walk back into the living room and sit on the coffee table. "Tell me what you know."

"Very cute," she says. "Joey's height." She measures all men against her brothers' heights, so that makes Josh around six feet. "Possible workaholic. Short haircut but a beard. The kind that's more scruff."

"I like the beard part."

"You'll like all the parts," she says. "Very fit. Dark blond. Pretty eyes. Maybe dark blue? But long lashes. Great smile. Possible dimple."

"Just one?"

"Just one."

I groan. I'm a sucker for a dimple, and she knows it. "Are you even sure he's single?"

"Unconfirmed," she admits. "He mentioned something about Bernice but also said he's married to his job. But I'll get it out of him tonight, and if he's single, you better be ready to mingle."

I stifle a sigh. "I've only got a couple hours. I need to leave at 8:00."

"Open mic?"

I nod. I tell the girls that I'm doing folk stuff at small open mic nights like I did in college, and they always beg to come, but I always insist I'm not ready for them to hear me yet.

It's a lie. The open mic part. And the small part. But it's true I'm not ready for them to hear me yet. They will not be expecting to see me in a plaid mini skirt and Doc Martens, channeling my inner Hayley Williams, my rock inspiration. With her band, Paramore, making a comeback, it's a good time to carve out my place as the lead singer for Pixie Luna.

"That's fine," Ruby says. "Just make sure you spend a decent chunk of time talking to Josh before you take off."

"Deal." What's it going to hurt? I haven't been on a real date in a few months. If this works out, great. And if it doesn't—maybe we'll have some slightly awkward coming-and-going moments here and there, but it's not that big a deal.

Over the next forty-five minutes, Ava and Madi filter in, and Ruby informs them that she's found a guy for me. By six, we're all out on the patio with our snacks of choice.

"Make sure you sit in the seat closest to his patio," Ruby says.

"Duh," I say.

"Looking forward to this." Madi waves her open bag of popcorn, like she's here for the show.

"Feels a little on the nose," I say.

She answers with a loud crunch.

Mrs. Lipsky comes out on her patio carrying Migos, her personality-deficient Yorkie.

"Where's Ahab?" Ava asks.

"He's on one today," Mrs. Lipsky says. "He's watching *Wheel* and swearing at Pat Sajak."

We all nod like this is normal, because for Ahab, it is.

Hugh and Jasmine pop out next, calling their "Hey, y'all" from the other side of New Guy's porch. "We've got beer and lots of cold Diet Coke," Jasmine says.

"I'm making cookies," Ruby announces, and there's a cheer from both sides of us. Ruby makes an excellent chocolate chip cookie.

"New Guy is late," Madi notes just as we hear his back sliding door open.

"Sorry," a deep voice says. Josh steps into view, and three sets of eyebrows on our patio go flying up—including mine.

Josh is a fine-looking man. Like, if we saw him at a bar or club, one of us would turn to the others and say, "He is fiiiiiiiiiine."

"Is it too late to call dibs?" Ava says under her breath so he can't hear her.

"Yes," Ruby says. "I've got a different plan for you."

Ava looks intrigued and nervous at the same time.

"I was trying to follow up on a food order so I can contribute," Josh says, stepping into the glow of his porch light so we can see him even better. "Oh, there it is."

A middle-aged man carrying an insulated Door Drop bag is weaving through the parking lot, and Josh calls, "Delivery for Josh?"

The man stops and looks at his phone. "Two dozen Torchy's Tacos?"

"That's me," Josh confirms, and Hugh and Jasmine cheer again as Josh takes his food and settles it on top of his smoker. He doesn't have patio furniture yet, and Ruby, always observant, walks over to our shared fence with one of the teak folding chairs we keep for company.

"Use this," she says.

"I can just pull out one of my kitchen chairs," he says.

"Take it," I tell him. "It's used to being outside."

"Thanks." He accepts the chair and settles it before going to open his gate, which Hugh promptly wanders through.

"Our friendship can be bought," Hugh tells Josh after he introduces himself. He selects a taco from the box Josh extends. "Transaction complete."

Josh turns to us next. "Pork, steak, or veggie?"

Ruby nudges Ava, who steps forward. "Veggie. I'm Ava. Nice to meet you."

"Josh." He hands her a couple of tacos. "Nice to meet you too."

Ruby makes sure I'm the last one to get my tacos as she and Madi make their choices, Madi introducing herself as well.

It's my turn, and I step up, suddenly not remembering if Ruby told him she was trying to fix us up, or if only I know that. I'm not usually awkward. Quiet, sometimes, with new people, but not awkward. But not knowing if Josh knows Ruby is matchmaking causes a brain fumble.

"Um, steak? And pork."

"Nice to meet you, Steak and Pork." He hands me my tacos. "I'm Josh."

I'm glad it's too dim for him to see me blush. "Friends call me Sami. With an I."

"Short for Samuel, I'm guessing?"

My lips twitch. *Okay, cute boy. You got jokes. I see you.* "Yes. Steak and Pork Samuel Webster, Sami for short."

I try to ignore Ava's soft snort and the loud crunch of Madi's popcorn. I would like to retreat, but I feel their eyes on me almost like a shove forward, so I clear my throat and try not to be an idiot. "So where did you move from?"

"Most recently, North Loop. But I grew up in Austin."

"Nice. I'm from Hillsboro." I watch him closely for a reaction, but his expression doesn't change. Hillsboro has a redneck reputation, which is fine for most Texans, but sometimes Austin people jump to snap judgments. He's passed the test.

"Haven't been there," he says.

Mrs. Lipsky has marched into his yard for her taco. "You know Clarksville?"

I use this as an excuse to melt back from the fence and rejoin my roommates.

"What do you think, Steak?" Madi asks.

"Shut up," I mutter, mainly because Mrs. Lipsky is super nosy, and I want to hear the details. She jumps right in after requesting steak tacos.

Mrs. Lipsky: Did you go to school here?
Him: Yes.
Mrs. Lipsky: Major?

Him: Psychology.

Mrs. Lipsky: What do you do?

Him: A boring job.

Mrs. Lipsky: Like what?

Him: Too boring to talk about.

Mrs. Lipsky: Not psychology?

Him: Not psychology.

When she's convinced she won't get too much more out of him, she takes her tacos and goes to chat with Hugh and Jasmine.

Josh settles into his chair and turns toward us. He looks like he's about to ask me something when Ruby steps out of the house calling, "Cookies!"

She walks toward us with a plate that smells like childhood and home—if I'd had a mom who had time for baking.

"Cookies?" she asks Josh, stopping to let us scoop up a few.

His eyes light up. "Yes, please," he says with a boyish smile.

Shoot, Ruby is right; he has a dimple. That's plus one for Josh.

Honestly, I don't have a ton of time in my schedule between full-time nursing and my rock goddess ambitions, but it wouldn't be the worst thing in the world to go out a few times with a hot neighbor.

I did promise to make a real effort in this bet, so I hold up my cookie like I'm offering a toast as Ruby steps out of our gate and moves down to the other neighbors.

"Cheers to cookies," I say.

He's close enough to lean over and tap his cookie to mine. "I'll eat to that."

We eat in silence for a minute, and when my cookie's gone, I clear my throat. "So you've been here for a whole two days. What do you think so far?"

"What's not to like?" he asks. "Everyone is so friendly."

"The Grove is a pretty chill place to live," I agree. "I mean, people do get in your business sometimes, but not in a bad way."

"Just the Texas way?"

"Checking up on you, making sure you're eating right and cheering for the correct teams." I nod at the Torchy's Tacos box. It's an Austin institution. "You've got the eating right part down."

He holds up his hand, index and pinky fingers up, the rest folded, in a gesture that anywhere else would mean "rock and roll." But in Texas—especially in Austin—it means "Hook 'em, horns," the University of Texas cheer for our Longhorns.

"Hook 'em," I say. But I make a note that it's minus one for Josh, and he's back to zero. Do I love UT football? Yes. Do I watch every game and cheer? Yes. But he's already handed me my first out based on the list I gave Ruby. I'd been mostly joking, but it's always good to identify your exits.

"You went to UT?" he asks.

I nod. "Graduated three years ago."

"Seven years for me."

So he's around twenty-nine. I like that. It's a respectable age gap.

"You didn't seem to like Mrs. Lipsky digging into your business." I tilt my head and study him. Anyone who's grown up in Texas—or anywhere in the South—should be used to the Mrs. Lipsky types.

"It was no big deal." He takes a swallow from his beer. "It's just that women of a certain age feel duty-bound to get me married and settled, and the fewer details I give them, the less ammunition they have."

"Commitment-phobic?" It could upset Ruby's plans.

He pauses like he's really weighing it out. "I don't think so," he concludes. "I just don't have time for a relationship right now."

"Same," I say.

"Why are you smiling?"

I hadn't realized I was, but he's right; a half smile is tugging up half my mouth. The correct answer is, *Because I was disappointed when you said you had no time for a relationship and laughing at myself for being disappointed.* What

I say is, "I don't know. Post-cookie glow?"

"Fair. Anyway, even if I had time to date, it's tough. I have standards."

This rubs me the wrong way. "Like what?" *Big boobs, bigger hair, tiny waist?* It's every other Texas bro's wish list.

He wrinkles his forehead for a few seconds. "Clean criminal record," he finally says. "That might be it."

Ah. I fight another smile. "What if she has a record but it's for something noble? Like she got arrested at a protest for a cause she believes in?"

"Hmm . . . what was she protesting?"

"The . . . return of the McRib sandwich."

"Because she's vegan?"

"Because it's nasty."

"Worthy cause. I'd pay her bail and get a tattoo of her inmate number."

"Where?"

He doesn't miss a beat. "Toss up between my tongue and my stomach, since those are the two things she would have been protecting from the McRib."

I grin. "You're all right, new guy."

"What about you?"

"I'm all right too."

He rolls his eyes. "No. Coupled up? Single with standards?"

"Single with a busy schedule."

A nod. "I hear that. So barring your schedule, you have no standards?"

I snort. "Why do I have a feeling you're a lawyer?"

He tilts his head. "I don't know. Why do you?"

I meet his eyes for a couple of seconds, studying him. Ruby's right about his eyes too. I can't quite tell in the dim light what color they are, but his thick lashes and strong eyebrows make them striking.

I take another bite of my taco and settle back into my seat.

"Well?" he asks when I finish my taco without saying anything else. "No verdict?"

"On what?"

He shrugs. "The tacos. The weather." A beat. "Me."

"Yes, verdict," I say slowly. "You're a lawyer. And yes, I have standards."

"Do you have a no-lawyer rule?"

We've moved from joking to flirting. Is he checking to see if I'm actually open to dating him? This makes my stomach flutter. Even on a porch with my three gorgeous roommates, he's paying attention to *me*. Who knows, he might be dumb enough to try to make a move on all of us over time, but that'll be his problem. We don't ever date each other's exes. But also, maybe he won't. Maybe he's interested in a petite blonde who goes full alt-rock by night.

"I don't have a no-lawyer clause. My standards are lower than that. Right now, I'd say my only cutoff is that someone can't already be collecting his social security checks."

He gives me a quizzical look.

"I'm an RN at a nursing home," I explain.

"How is it possible that two of us reasonably attractive people aren't killing it on the Austin dating scene?" he asks.

"Maybe it's because you called me 'reasonably attractive.' I guess it's nicer than saying I'm a solid six."

He's taking a drink from his beer when I say this, and he splutters. I smile. "There's nothing wrong with being a six, but I'm objectively at least an eight." Maybe I'd be a nine with two more inches on my height and chest.

"I was just trying to be modest about *myself*," he says. "You are clearly an eleven."

I smile. "Nicely done."

"It's a scale of twenty, but you're welcome."

That makes me laugh out loud. I don't have time to think of a good comeback before Jasmine calls his name and he gets up with a smile for me before he goes to chat with his other-side neighbors.

Ruby shoots me a "how'd it go?" look. I give her a neutral face, like "Fine, I guess." She nods. I eat three more cookies and chat with Mrs. Lipsky about her dog's tooth decay for a while longer before I excuse myself to go inside and get ready for our show.

I love the costume part of each night where I slip out of my normal person clothes and into my rock goddess outfits. I always do this in the car or at whatever club we're performing in. There's no way I can walk out of the house in a thrifted prom dress and combat boots without the girls asking questions. Someday I'll tell them. But for now, this alter ego is just for me and the hundreds of Austin music fans I share it with.

It's a complicated balancing act involving spreadsheets. For real. I keep one to track which outfits I wore to which shows so I don't repeat at a venue. I have five main outfits I work with. Besides the prom dress and plaid mini skirt get-ups, outfit three is a pair of pleather leggings from Walmart and a UT shirt, arms ripped off, neckline cut out, worn over a mesh tank top and knotted at the waist. The rock star wardrobe is rounded out by a knee length peasant dress, and the final outfit is a pair of black hot pants with a black and white striped shirt, generally worn with red Converse high tops.

There will come a time when we've played a venue more than five times and I'll have to either mix and match or scour the sale racks and thrift stores again for a new look. But five is about right for weaving the clothes into my closet and drawers without the girls wondering what kind of cosplay is going on when they come into my room to borrow stuff.

Outfits matter, of course. But even more important, fronting a rock band is about attitude, and I have plenty of that onstage. I can use all the things I don't say to the family members of patients who rarely show up but only complain when they do as if to offset their neglect. All the CNAs that call out sick because they don't feel like coming in. The angry calls from stressed-out people who are shocked that we have a waiting list at our facility and can't take their relative immediately.

All of that gets channeled into the performance, the driving guitar riffs, the wild drums. It's probably why I don't boil over at work; performing a couple of nights a week is my release valve. If I could get more gigs, I'd perform even more.

The lyrics, though, are about something else. Anger I'm still working out for things a long time ago. And sometimes newer hurt.

So, therapy, basically. But with costumes. And crowd surfing.

My reserved spot is in the aisle behind the sidewalk spots, so if I go the long way around to my car, I don't have to walk past everyone still on their patios and deal with a dozen goodbyes. Slipping out quietly so no one notices is what my grandma calls an Irish goodbye. You tell everyone bye or no one bye. No one is easier. I only like a spotlight when I'm onstage.

As I put my trusty Honda in reverse, I glance in the rearview mirror at the glow of their patio lights. Then I turn my attention ahead, turn up the classic rock on the radio, and begin the shift into Lady Mantha, lead singer of Pixie Luna.

Chapter Five
JOSH

I'm going to like living at the Grove. It may end up being *too* social for someone with a schedule as busy as mine, but the neighbor party was cool. I've had worse neighbors than a condo full of cute girls.

I glance at the time on my dashboard as I start my car in the dark work parking lot. Seven o'clock. It'll probably be the earliest I get home this week.

I pull into my parking space back home fifteen minutes later after debating whether to stop by my gym or hit the one at the Grove. I might as well check it out. A quick change into workout clothes and a short jog across the complex later, and I'm stepping into the community gym. It's small but it has the basics, and there are only two other people there, which is the main advantage over my other gym.

I recognize one of them, the girl on the treadmill. Sami. I make sure I spell it with an *i* even in my head. She's running pretty fast and wearing a look I recognize, one that means she's hit the zone, her eyes slightly unfocused while her brain is elsewhere. Based on the sweat on her flat stomach and well-defined back, I'd guess she's been at it for a while.

A free weight bench catches my eye and I position it so that I'm not staring at her, although it's hard to avoid in a mirrored room. Still, I put in my own earbuds and get to work. My gym will be better for leg days, but I can get in a pretty good upper body workout here.

I've finished my bicep curls and moved to triceps dips on the bench when Sami enters my field of vision. She's breathing pretty hard, and as she takes a swig from her Hydroflask, she notices me and nods, too busy drinking to stop and say hi.

Respect.

"Hey," I say. "You left the neighbor party early the other night." I'd wanted to pick up our conversation, but when I turned from Hugh and Jasmine, she was gone.

She swallows and takes a deep breath, like she's trying to even out her rhythm. The movement draws my eyes to her chest for a split second, but I flick them back to meet hers so I'm not That Guy. It's enough to gather critical information. Pink sports bra, camo leggings, and she wears them both well.

I fight to keep eye contact even though I'd like to gather more data.

She shrugs. "Had things to do. Sorry I bailed."

"You should be. Mrs. Lipsky got lightly sloshed, and—"

"Sang an inappropriate limerick with Captain Ahab?"

I grin. "Guess you've heard it before."

She smiles back. "She swears Ahab taught it to her, but I don't believe her."

"Anything else I should brace for with Mrs. Lipsky?"

"As far as drunk and disorderly goes, the dirty ditties are the worst of it."

"Thanks for the insider info." I like Sami's vibe. She holds her own space like she's comfortable with it. "You done for the night?" I ask. I can't decide if I want her to stay so we can talk more or leave so I can work out and not worry about making weird faces.

"Yeah. I'm going to head home and crash with Netflix."

"Sounds like a good plan."

"It'd be better with a scandalous parrot, but that's life."

I laugh. "What happens if Ahab outlives Mrs. Lipsky?"

She gives me a concerned look. "No one told you?"

"No one told me what?"

"Whoever lives in unit twenty-two at the time of Mrs. Lipsky's passing takes possession of the devil bird. That's you."

"I must have missed that in the paperwork."

"Congratulations," she says. "Ahab is the

highest-maintenance resident in the Grove. And remember where I work? I know about high-maintenance residents."

She's funny and she's fast. I like it. Friendly but not flirty. She has the vibe of someone who likes good company and will be good company. Maybe that's why I say, "Want to tell me about Ahab over dinner sometime? Maybe tomorrow?"

She opens her mouth, and I'm almost positive she's going to say no, but she pauses. "Sure," she says instead. "I'd be down for that."

"Seven o'clock okay?" It's the absolute earliest I can leave my office without walking into an avalanche of work the next morning.

"That's fine. You know where to find me."

She waves and walks out of the weight room, giving me a glimpse of a small but bright green butterfly tattoo on her shoulder blade. The door closes behind her, leaving me and a woman about my mom's age working on the rowing machine. I didn't think she was paying any attention, but she glances up and catches my eye, then gives me a brief nod, like *well done*.

Maybe. Sami seems pretty cool, but there's something about her—an aloofness—I can't put my finger on. She's funny enough to make me want to spend a little more time figuring it out, and that's more interested than I've been in anyone in months. But even though I'm often a patient guy, my life isn't built for me to spend time unraveling mysteries, even when the packaging is cute.

I flash back to her leggings and revise. Sexy. The packaging is sexy.

I'll see how tomorrow goes. Maybe there's something. Maybe that something will be friendship. Maybe we're meant to be neighbors and nothing more. That's fine. Bernice and I have a good thing going. Sometimes another woman only messes things up.

Chapter Six
SAMI

"Present yourself for inspection," Ava calls up to my room.

I roll my eyes in my closet mirror, but I head down the stairs to where the girls are lounging in the living room. All three heads turn toward me when I hit the bottom step.

"You pass," Madi announces.

Josh and I hadn't exchanged numbers, but he had stopped by this morning after I'd already gone to work and left a message with Ruby that he was thinking we could walk down Lynn Street and get some dinner.

We'd all interpreted that to mean casual with sensible shoes.

Not that sensible has to mean boring. I glance down at my cheetah print Vans slip-ons. I have an impressive collection of printed Vans to wear with my plain scrubs. It entertains the residents at Sunnyside. I've paired them with bootcut jeans and a fitted black sweater.

"Class with sass." Ruby points at my shoes. "It's practically your brand."

"I try," I say.

"But you don't," Ava says. "That's why it works for you. It's effortless."

"And fricking annoying," Madi adds. She spends a looooong time curating every outfit she wears.

"Thank you and I'm sorry."

"Proud of you for going on this date," Ruby says.

"It's not exactly a sacrifice. He seems pretty cool. But no getting your hopes up," I warn her when she grins.

"A chance is enough." She's sitting on the sofa next to Madi, and she tucks her feet beneath the blanket they're sharing. One of the *Real Housewives* is paused on the screen. "It's like I tell patrons when I'm trying to convince them to try a new author I know they'll love. Give it three chapters, and if the writer can't hook you, you're free to drop it."

"What chapter am I on with Josh?" I ask.

"Chapter one, the neighbor party," Madi says.

Ava nods. "Chapter two was the weight room."

"That means tonight is chapter three," Ruby says. "But he'll hook you. I can feel it. I'm not wrong about these things."

"Annoyingly, you are not," Madi mutters.

I frown. "Should I feel nervous about that?"

"Do you?" Ava asks, her scientist mind always observing and gathering data.

"No. Maybe that's a bad sign."

"No, ma'am." Ruby says it like I'm a preschooler she caught coloring in a library book. "You will not start by talking yourself out of this or overthinking it."

"Yeah. That's *my* specialty," Ava says. "Find your own."

"I'm not overthinking," I say. "But it's been a while since I was on a date, and I feel like I should be more . . ." I trail off with no idea how to finish the sentence.

"Excited? Are you not excited?" Ruby sounds concerned, like this is the first real threat to her plans that she's heard.

"I think I am. I've been looking forward to it all day."

She smiles and relaxes against the couch. "That's good."

"I'm not the expert," Ava says, "but maybe you aren't nervous about this because you both already click. Does that even make sense?"

I shrug. "How about I just roll with it?"

"That," Madi says.

There's a knock on the door, and I glance at the wall clock. It's 7:00 exactly. That's good. He'd lose a jillion bonus points if he were late when he lives next door.

I open it and smile. "Hey, Josh."

"Hey, Sami. You ready?"

He's wearing faded jeans and a white hoodie under a black jacket. Simple, classic. He looks good. Literally the wholesome boy-next-door, but my rock-and-roll heart craves a clean-cut good boy now and then.

"Ready." I reach for my black peacoat while he greets the rest of the house.

"It's pretty cold," he says. "We can drive if you want."

January in Austin is brisk. We might get into the low sixties in the day, but at night, the temperatures drop into the forties, and it's a bitey forty, the humidity in the air sharp in the cold.

"It's okay. I like to walk." We're not going far anyway.

We wave to the roomies and head out, turning onto Lynn to take us toward the restaurants and shops.

He tucks his hands into his coat pockets and smiles over at me. "Walkability is one of the main reasons I bought my place, but I have a feeling I might appreciate it more in May than I do right now."

"For sure. But it's not like it snows, so if you can man up for a few minutes, you'll survive."

He grins. "Challenge accepted."

It's only three blocks from the Grove to all kinds of restaurants, bistros, and bars. The girls always ask me why I don't perform in any of them, and the answer is because these are *small*. We only perform at a handful of live music venues, ones that showcase rock. Places like the

Galaxy and other local cafés are intimate and acoustic.

Josh asks me about the best places to eat, and we decide on pho. Warm soup feels perfect for a cold evening. I like that it's super casual too. I don't know what our vibe with each other is yet, but an upscale place would have made me nervous no matter what.

"So, you're a nurse," he says when we're settled in a booth, each with a steaming bowl of pho. He picked steak and tripe, and I give him points for adventurousness. "Do you like your job?"

"Yes," I answer, but I hear the question in my own voice.

"But..."

I shake my head. "I love the patient side of things. I never saw myself doing geriatric care, but in a way, it makes perfect sense. I'm pretty tight with my grandmother. But I'm the care manager too. I don't really like doing that stuff."

"What does care manager mean?"

"Administration." I shrug. "I end up overseeing and delegating routine things like blood pressure checks or administering meds, but I don't get to do it much myself. I have to hire the nursing assistants and orderlies. And order medical supplies. I don't like doing that either."

"So your ideal day as a nurse is hanging out in

an old folks home all day and talking to the old folks?"

"Pretty much."

He nods. "I like old folks. I get it. And your job sounds important."

I raise an eyebrow. "That's not how most people feel about it. Some people think I'm a glorified candy striper."

"A what?"

"A candy striper? It means volunteer."

He blinks at me. "I wouldn't draw a line from 'candy striper' to nursing home volunteer if you gave me a million dollars and a map."

"It's an old term," I say. "I never really thought about it before. That's what I was called when I volunteered at the hospital when I was in college."

He pulls his phone out. "I'm not being rude. I'm looking it up." He taps out a search and then scans a few sentences. "I guess back in the olden days, volunteers wore pinafores with red-and-white stripes that reminded people of candy canes."

"I didn't know that, and I can't believe I've never stopped to figure it out." He's tapping on his phone again. "Now what are you looking up?"

"I have no idea what a pinafore is." He reads for a second then looks at me. "Do you know what a pinafore is?"

"Some kind of dress?"

"An apron. Did you wear an apron when you volunteered?"

I shake my head. "We wore these blue work shirt things that kind of looked like lab coats."

"So candy striping has nothing to do with aprons or candy?"

I don't know why this is so entertaining, but it is. Maybe it's because it's such a surprise to see a lawyer admit straight-up that he doesn't know an answer and go looking for it. Although . . .

"I teased you about being a lawyer the other night, but you never confirmed it."

"I didn't."

When he doesn't say anything else, I smile. "So you are."

"I didn't confirm it."

"Right. But you would have denied it if you weren't."

"Would I though?" He leans forward and rests his chin on his hand. "You can't think of any other jobs I might not cop to?"

"CIA." My eyes widen. "Oh, I get it. You're working undercover."

"What if that were true and you figured it out on your second guess?"

"You'd be pretty bad at your job."

"Probably."

I pluck a shrimp from my bowl with my chopsticks and chew it, thinking. "Got it," I say. "Stripper."

He spits a tiny bit of broth out and grabs a napkin to dab at his mouth. "Had to give it up. No sense of rhythm. I only got pity dollars."

I somehow doubted that would be true if he'd actually stripped. I'd paid attention in the weight room. You could bounce a quarter off that—never mind.

I tsk. "No sense of rhythm?"

"What is your face saying right now?" he asks. "It's saying 'dealbreaker,' isn't it?"

"I like to dance. Lack of rhythm is a tough one."

"But the stripping is fine?"

"I don't judge," I say. It's a lie. I'm very judgy.

"So this is a safe place for confessions?"

My jokes are flowing as easily as they do with my roommates. There's a distinct difference though; there's an undercurrent of energy buzzing between Josh and me. It's a constant hum, an attunement to everything about him. He must be wearing a cologne made of pure pheromones.

"Judgment-free zone," I say.

"Good. Then I'm a lawyer."

I frown.

"Aha," he says, with a slight smile. "Some judgment after all."

I shift my face back to neutral. "Do most people judge you for being a lawyer?"

"Probably better to say they make assumptions."

I sit back and spin some noodles between my chopsticks. "An undercover stripper lawyer. You win for most unique job."

"You should hear about my clients."

I smile at him as I spoon up more pho. "I'm done teasing now. Tell me about your job for real. Are you prosecuting bad guys? Defending the innocent?"

"Way more exciting. Corporate law," he says with a wry smile.

My shoulders tense slightly, but I try not to let my expression change. I've developed a recent allergy to corporate types. I wasn't kidding about that part of my Ideal Man list. But Josh is not my ex, Bryce the Weasel, and I need to give him his own chance. "Tell me about the glam world of corporate law."

"I don't get to do any of the glam parts. Whiskey lunches and golf course deals are for the partners. And I kind of hate what I do now, but that's normal for junior associates. I'm at Brower and Moore, so it'll take a while, but they bribe us to stay every year with the promise that we'll get to do interesting stuff eventually. And a bonus sometimes."

"Brower and Moore. As in that giant building downtown?"

"Yeah."

"You're a skyscraper penthouse kind of lawyer. Wow." This is not getting better.

He snorts. "Try 'mid-level drone.' Maybe I'll work up to the penthouse someday."

At least he's not trying to make his job sound like a bigger deal than it is. "Is that what you want? Skyline domination and your name on a building?"

He shrugs but watches me carefully. "I don't *not* want it."

"Why law? Why that firm?" I can almost hear my mother's voice in my head. *He's perfect, Samantha. Stable. Ambitious. Handsome. Figure out how to lock this down.* Even her imagined voice makes me feel claustrophobic, and I've lost my appetite. I set my chopsticks down.

"Allow me to introduce myself again," he says. "I'm Joshua Steven Brower, Junior."

"Ohhh." He doesn't have to connect the dots for me to realize it's the same Brower on the downtown skyscraper. "It's the family business."

"I definitely got the job because of who my grandfather and father are." He keeps his voice pleasant, the same light tone he's had all night, but I can sense the slightest tension beneath it.

"I was just thinking it explains why you chose law, but it sounds like a sore spot."

His lips thin for a fraction of a second before he's back to smiling. "Sorry. It's a good job. Don't mean to sound weird about it."

It's a lot of money and a lot of pressure, I'm betting. You don't have to know about old Austin families and their high expectations to figure that out, but I do know about those things. It's a drag to find out it's his background. He's a cool guy. If I were a different girl with a different ex . . . maybe it wouldn't matter. But it does.

I lean forward, hands tucked beneath my knees. Like I tell my patients, best to rip the Band-Aid off. It's time to shut this down. "Why did you ask me out, Josh?"

Surprise flashes across his face followed by confusion. "Because."

I give him a second to adjust. "Because why?"

"You're cute?"

"Is that a question?" I can't help teasing him, even if he is absolutely not the guy for me.

"No, Your Honor. That's a statement of fact. You're cute."

"Still looking for a motive here, counselor."

"I wanted to. I didn't think about it that hard." He sounds cautious now, like he senses a trap being laid. "Am I in trouble?"

"In trouble," I repeat. "No. Not in trouble, exactly. Can I tell you a few things?"

"Sure," he says, and it's the most uncertain he's sounded so far.

"I was a cheerleader in high school. Does that surprise you?" It shouldn't. Everyone assumes a petite blonde in Texas cheered.

"No. It also wouldn't surprise me if you weren't."

"How about the fact that I pledged Pi Phi?" It's the most prestigious sorority at UT, known for its enormous philanthropy and even bigger parties. It's the destination sorority for girls interested in becoming fixtures of post-college Austin society.

His eyebrows go up at this. "That's impressive. I'm a Fiji."

And that's the problem. I hold back a scoff. Fiji—Phi Gamma Delta—is the most elite UT fraternity. Pi Phi is the most elite sorority, and it carries weight with anyone who knows it. It takes money and connections to pledge, and I was the rare pledge who had neither. But the kind of people being a Pi Phi carries weight with are not my people. Not anymore.

I don't even want to explain. Josh isn't going to see the water he swims in, and I'm not here trying to undo his worldview. I came for a cute boy and pho. I got both. But I'll only be back for more of one of them, and Josh doesn't have enough scallions.

"I'm full," I say. "Are you okay if we head back?" I smother a yawn to underscore the point.

His eyebrows have knit together more tightly with each passing minute, and now furrows line his forehead. "Is something wrong?"

"No. Just not as hungry as I thought I was, and I have to work early tomorrow." *Yes, you are exactly like Bryce, and I'm not making that mistake again.*

"Okay." His tone is polite. Not cold but definitely reserved. Good. He read me right.

We walk back without talking much. A couple of comments from him on the weather. A couple of vague replies from me. When we get to our front doors, we say goodnight and go inside, no hug, no invitation or hint that we should do it again soon.

For once, it's Ruby on the sofa, not Madi, and she straightens and smiles when I come in.

"How was it?"

I shrug and hang my purse, jacket, and scarf on my peg. "He's Bryce 2.0."

Ruby's face falls. "What? No. I didn't get that vibe from him at all."

"You know the Brower building downtown?"

"That big silver one?"

"Not only is he a lawyer there, he's a Brower. A scion. Scions are ugly cars and worse people."

"Scion just means descendant," Ruby says, because of course she does. "That means literally every person on earth is bad."

"I mean the fancy kind. Heir to an empire and all that garbage."

I don't need to explain this to Ruby. She was there for the rise, fall, and wreckage of my relationship with Bryce. All the girls were.

She slumps against the cushions. "Bummer. He seems so down-to-earth. No rich brat vibes. Sorry, bestie."

I plop down beside her and rest my head on her shoulder. "It's okay. Just be prepared to give up on my parking space." I give her a consolation pat on the leg.

She slaps a remote in my hand. "We're only a week into the new year. I've got plenty of time. Sad girl gets to pick the show."

"I'm not sad." She reaches for the remote, and I hold it out of her reach. "But I still claim picking privileges."

I go with a reality show about a tattoo shop. Madi would complain, but Ruby doesn't mind. She finds everything fascinating. It's one of my favorite things about her. Only Ava and I have tattoos, and I think I'm the only one who toys with the idea of getting more, but Ruby gets as sucked into the strange art of tattooing as I do.

I snuggle into the sofa with her. So maybe the boy next door isn't my future-husband true love. But true-friend love with besties is a pretty good consolation prize.

Chapter Seven
JOSH

"Son, I need you to take out a client tonight."

I grimace. It's not mature, but my dad can't see me.

"I can't, sir." I don't call him "Dad" in the office if I can help it. I don't like to remind my coworkers of how I got this job. It's more nepotism than they know. I didn't get just my *job* because of my family name. I screwed around in college and my grades weren't impressive, so despite my almost-perfect LSAT score, it took some string pulling to get me into law school. And those strings look exactly like fat donations to the school's endowment.

Worse, I didn't take the first two years of law school seriously either, scraping by with the minimum effort. It took even more "strings" to keep me in the program, and I didn't pull it together until . . . well, unexpected loss gives you perspective.

I'm lucky they gave me the job, even after I turned into a model student my final year. That was only enough to lift me from bottom to middle of the class with only two semesters to try to turn things around. But it had also earned me the respect of all my third-year professors.

Too bad I had yet to earn the same from my father.

"It wasn't a request." His voice is firm. "Zed Pro Tech is looking to bring their business over, and that's two million in annual billing. They need white glove treatment, and they're looking for someone young to take out their directors. I'll handle their C-suite, but you need to take out the younger guys on the team. And girl," he adds. "Three people total. Find a wingman and handle it. Be up here in fifteen."

And he hangs up.

I massage my temples, trying to rearrange my workload so I can be out of the office by 6:30 to take these guys—and lady—to dinner. If I can get them back to their hotel by 9:00, I can work some more at home and not fall behind. Any further behind, anyway. This job is always about playing catch-up.

I turn in my chair and glance at the other offices, trying to think who I should grab and take with me. This is a political choice whether I like it or not; I have to think about who is on the partner fast track but who also doesn't get on my nerves.

Lauren, I decide. She'll balance out the overwhelming bro vibes when corporate males get together, and she's good socially.

I poke my head into her office. "Got a minute?"

She waves me in and finishes up something on her computer before smiling at me. "What's up, Josh?"

It's a small thing, but I like that she calls me by my name. A lot of the associates—mainly ones who belonged to fraternities in college—call me Little Brower. I hate it but smile like I don't. They'd do it even more if they knew it bothered me.

"Management wants me to show the younger members of the Zed team a good time. We need a wingman when we take them out to dinner. You want in?"

"Sure," she says. "What time?"

"Want to come upstairs with me and iron it out?"

She nods. She's no dummy. Being a team player only greases the track for her, and face time with any of the partners is always a bonus. Thirty minutes later, we're back downstairs after meeting with the Zed associates and making a plan for the evening. They've requested the Austin nightlife experience, so I'll be googling to figure out what that is. It's been a minute—or three years since I started at the firm—since I've had a regular "nightlife." I don't know what's hot right now.

"Steak and live music?" Lauren says. "How about you pick the restaurant, I pick the music venue?"

"Deal."

In my office, I buckle down to meet my most pressing deadline. I can't believe I'm having to go out twice in one week. Hope tonight goes better than pho with Sami. It had been fun until she flipped a switch and it wasn't. If I weren't working seventy-plus hours a week, I might take the time to figure her out. There's something about her that I can't put my finger on, something that makes me want to know more.

But I don't have time for complicated people puzzles on top of the legal ones I deal with. Maybe something happens between other versions of us. Another time, another life.

I push her out of mind and focus on the contract in front of me. This is the here and now.

Lauren shoots me a look across our small table on the mezzanine at the Continental Club, a legendary jazz spot. We secured it with a Ben Franklin-sized "donation" to a server. The Zed team, John, Will, and Amber, seemed to like dinner at III Forks, a high-end steakhouse, and they look like they're enjoying the music now, but it's hard to say. They were polite through dinner, and they're polite now.

I lean forward to be heard above the music. "How do you like Austin so far?"

Will holds up his beer and tips it toward me. "Good vibe, thanks."

Still polite. Maybe they aren't easily impressed? I decide to scratch below the surface. "You like jazz?"

John smiles. "We have to say yes, right? Or we sound uncultured."

Interesting. He's got some whiskey in him and it's loosening his tongue. "So you *don't* like jazz?"

He shoots a fast look at Amber and shrugs. "Sure."

That's a no. It's my turn to exchange glances with Lauren. She studies our guests for a few seconds then leans forward. "Sounds like you're not having the experience you want. How can we fix that?"

That's why Lauren is perfect for this kind of thing. She can read a room, and now she's pivoting to signal that flexibility is how we do things at Brower and Moore.

Will, John, and Amber trade looks before Will leans forward. "What do *you* do when you go out in Austin? Do you get fifty-dollar steaks and hang out at jazz clubs?"

"Nope," I tell him. "I'd order brisket at the counter at Interstellar with my friends and watch basketball."

"I'd still be listening to live music, but not this," Lauren says.

"That's more what we were hoping for if we're being honest," Amber says. "A place that gives you paper towels with your meal and a dive with a local band."

Lauren nods. "We let the power of the corporate card go to our heads."

Will smirks. "Trust me, if I can charge the company for a fifty-dollar steak, I'm charging the company for a fifty-dollar steak. We get it."

Lauren smiles back. "We can't do dinner over, but I have an idea if you want the Austin indie music experience."

The other three look at each other, and Amber nods. "Totally."

"Crimson," Lauren says, looking at me. "There's a newer band playing there—Pixie Luna—but I heard them last month at Vito's, and they're worth catching again. Kind of indie punk. Really good."

"Sounds dope," Will says, and only the laidback way he says it saves him from looking stupid for saying "dope" when he's a six-figure corporate bot. But I'm beginning to suspect none of them are corporate bots.

"Let's do it," I say. A hit of adrenaline surges through my veins. One of the best things about being in Austin is the live music scene. I used to love hitting all kinds of bars and dives to hear new bands. Some would break out in a big way later, and it was cool to hear them before they blew up. I loved the feeling of being in a room with people and sharing the experience of letting music and lyrics wash over us. Mood altering and totally legal.

"We're going to be overdressed," Lauren warns. "But you'll get the real Austin experience."

We're in business casual: no suits but all of us are in work slacks, the men in collared button-down shirts, Amber and Lauren in shirts that would look good under blazers.

"Preps who are slumming it," John says. "Works for me."

Crimson is only two blocks down on Congress, so we walk, and it's the most relaxed vibe we've had all evening, like we've all agreed to be people now instead of employees.

The sound is leaking out of Crimson before we even get to the door, and I smile when we have to hand over cash and get our hands stamped to go in. There's a stirring in my blood, the excitement of being on the verge, waiting for the door to open and the sound to boom out. It's been literal years since I had this rush. Four, at least. I didn't know how much I missed it until now, standing here with the bass vibrating my sternum.

"Feels like college again," Amber says, grinning.

"Came at a good time," the bouncer says. "They just started their set, and they're good."

Crimson isn't the kind of place with mezzanine seats and table service. We press into the crowd, and Lauren calls to me over the hard-driving drums, "Hey, plow through them, big guy."

I'm not exactly built like a linebacker, but I'm the tallest in our group, so I take the lead, gently bumping people to make a path for us through the crowd. When we reach the middle, Lauren taps on my shoulder to indicate that's good enough.

"I can't believe it's so crowded on a Thursday right after New Year's." I have to lean down so she can hear me.

"I can. Listen."

It's a five-piece group, a female on vocals, and she has my attention immediately. Her intensity is unreal, like if you could see her energy, it would be five times her actual size. She's short with a slight frame, her bright pink hair up in two buns, a glittery pink mask covering the top half of her face so we can only see her jaw and full pink lips. Strong feminine vibes, but she's wearing combat boots and prowling the stage like she'll stomp the first person who looks at her wrong.

I dig it.

And her voice . . . it's so much bigger than I'd expect from someone that petite. It's like watching a surly Tinkerbell open her mouth but a big Kelly Clarkson voice comes out.

"Wow," I say.

I glance at the rest of the group. Will's already bouncing, moments away from jumping along with the rest of the crowd as a chorus about little rich boys tears from the speakers, and I laugh.

She might as well be singing about me, but the band's energy is undeniable, and by the end of the chorus, we're all jumping.

They play an eight-song set, and it doesn't slow down. We've worked our way closer and closer to the front, like we all share the unspoken need to be as inside the sound as possible.

"Last song," the singer calls out. The crowd groans but she laughs at them. "Shut up and find us on Soundrack," she says into the mic. "But later. Right now, we rock!" And there's a new explosion of sound as they surge into their heaviest number yet, and the crowd pulses again.

Her performance is theatrical, and when it builds to the bridge, she turns and flings herself back onto the crowd who catch her and pass her from hand to hand. The guitarist takes center stage and tears it up as the lead singer crowd surfs, gesturing to the crowd to return her as they near the next verse. She's just gotten to us, and John, Will, and I reach up to help her along, but I freeze in shock.

She's wearing a shirt with thin straps, and one of them crosses a tattoo on her shoulder blade.

A tattoo of a butterfly on a flower, identical to the one I saw on Sami in the weight room at the Grove on Monday.

She lands back on the stage, and I press all the way to its edge, ignoring the protests of the people around me. I stare up at her, hard, trying to see if that's really her under the pink hair and mask. It has to be. That's a distinctive tattoo, and she's the right size. But I'm still not sure until her eyes lock on mine, and for the tiniest second, she freezes. Then she's off again, and I back up from the stage, sure now.

It's her. And I've got questions.

Chapter Eight
SAMI

I come off the stage into the waiting arms of my bandmates who hug, noogie, or ruffle my hair, depending on who it is. We crow, whooping and high-fiving, but there's an extra edge to my adrenaline, a spiky anxiety as I calculate how fast I can get to him and tell him to keep his mouth shut.

"Killed it!" That's Rodney, the drummer. For him, it's practically a monologue.

"Man, that felt so good," I say. There aren't enough high fives for this feeling. "You guys were so tight."

"And you, mighty-mite." The bassist, Luther, shakes his shaggy brown head. "You transcended, man. I watched a bona fide rock goddess up there."

"Good show, y'all," a mellow voice says behind us. I turn to find the lead singer of Night View standing there, easily recognizable by his trademark blue bangs. They're the biggest band on the Austin indie scene right now.

"Thanks, man," Luther says. "Looking forward to hearing your set tonight."

The Night View singer shakes his head. "Giving us a tough act to follow."

A couple more Night View guys are behind him, and they smile as they brush past us to set up. The drummer pauses. "You play with us at Krewe in a few weeks. Looking forward to it."

"Same, man," Jules, our guitarist, answers.

When they're out of sight, I open my mouth in a silent scream. Rodney gives a faint smile, Luther grins, and Jules gives a fist pump.

"Sami?"

I stiffen at the sound of a different male voice calling me. Guess I won't have to track Josh down because he's come looking for me.

"That's you, isn't it? Sami?" But he doesn't sound uncertain.

I blink behind my mask, frantically looking for a way to play this off, when our rhythm guitarist emerges from the bathroom at the end of the hall.

"Yo, Sami!" Wingnut calls. "You slayed!"

I wave my hand in acknowledgment even as my last chance to keep my secret identity disappears. I turn to Josh with a weak smile. "Hey, Josh. What are you doing here?"

He's in office clothes and sweaty, beads of it glistening on his forehead, his hairline damp, his sleeves rolled up. "Clients wanted to check out the live music scene. Didn't expect to see my neighbor tearing up the stage."

He's smiling, and I want to be chill about this,

but I'm in an awkward position. I'm not even sure how to approach the situation, so I choose head on and pull him to the side.

"Hey, so only my band knows my real identity," I tell him. "Even my roommates don't know, and I'd like to keep it that way."

His eyebrows go up. "Okay."

"You won't tell them?"

"I won't tell them. But why don't you want them to know?"

It's a complicated answer, and one I don't expect to make sense to anyone else. Even if I wanted to explain, the crowded backstage of a small club isn't the place to do it. I shake my head. "Tell you later." I gesture to the guys behind me. "We need to pack up. See you around?"

He nods but doesn't make a move to leave as we start gathering our amps and instruments. After I finish winding one of the speaker cords, I sense a change, a prickling that disappears from between my shoulder blades. I glance over my shoulder; he's gone.

The tension seeps out of me, and I join in the chatter with the rest of the band. Well, except Rodney, who just smiles now and then. We relive our set and talk about what we want to tweak. But mostly we talk about the highlights. It's the first time since we started playing together eight months ago that everything gelled, and that's a high I can't explain to other people—or even to other solo musicians. I already want to chase it with the next show.

Back when I was doing open mic nights, singer-songwriter style, I had fleeting tastes of what it could be like when my music resonates with other people. But those were a shadow compared to this. Tonight was a technicolor experience, and I can't go back to sepia.

My mom needs me to be sepia because it makes her feel safe. Bryce the Weasel needed me to be sepia so he could shine. But tonight, I was glitter and growl and manic energy, and there will be no turning back.

We store our equipment in our practice space, the pool house behind Rodney's McMansion. Or his parents' McMansion. Actually, given that it's on two acres, it's just a regular mansion. It's perfect because we can't bother any neighbors there, even if it's a bit of a trek from my part of town. It's worth it for the free space.

It also has the benefit of a shower I can use to rinse out my pink hair. It's the cheap spray stuff you find in the stores at Halloween, but it washes easily, and I don't have to explain to my patients—or my roommates—why I have pink hair.

My hair is still damp when I get home after 11:00. I'm still amped from the show, and I need time to come down, so I decide to sit out on my balcony and let it air dry for as long as I can stand the chill. That way, I don't wake anyone up with a hair dryer.

My balcony overlooks the parking lot, but the Austin skyline shines in the distance. The view is a fair trade for Ruby getting the bigger closet.

I wrap my comforter around me and settle into my cheap plastic deck chair, leaning back to prop my legs on the railing and replay the night. I'm running the final song through my head, wondering how I missed Josh in the crowd, when the sliding door for his balcony rattles, and a few seconds later, he steps out.

He reaches high above him and stretches. He's in joggers and a T-shirt now, and a strip of skin shows between his shirt hem and waistband. I should let him know he's got an audience in case he doesn't want one. But in a few seconds. I'm liking this view too.

"Hey," I finally say.

He drops his hands and twists my way. "Hey, Sami. Didn't see you. Hang out here much?"

I give a tired tilt of my head to the doors behind me. "That's my room. So yeah, I come out here a lot. Especially after shows. Decompress."

"That was something." He pauses, then adds softly, "A good something."

"Glad you enjoyed it."

He leans against the wall and crosses his arms

like he's settling in for a chat. "Want to tell me about the secret identity?"

Not really. I let my head fall against my chair. I want to stay in the quiet, enjoy the glow, and not chase it away by talking about it. "You're out here kind of late." We're creeping toward midnight.

"Night owl. Always have been. Came home and got some work done to knock down my to-do list for tomorrow."

"Two of my roommates were asleep before you left Crimson, and you came home and worked?" I shake my head and nestle farther into my comforter.

"Me? What about you? Did you work a full shift today?"

"Yeah."

"And then you went out and played a concert?"

"Different kind of energy."

He nods and rolls slightly so his back is against his wall. "Need to get a chair out here," he says lazily after a while.

"These are five bucks at the grocery store."

He laughs. "I'll keep it in mind."

This time in the quiet, I hear other sounds beyond the rush of adrenaline in my head. A distant bark. An even more distant siren. The soft hoot of an owl.

"Look," I say. An owl flies past, caught for the briefest second at the edge of the light cast by the parking lot bulb. "That doesn't happen too often."

"That's a barn owl." His voice is soft but sure.

I glance over at him. "You a birder?"

He shakes his head. "My grandfather. But you pick up things."

It's quiet for another minute except for small sounds. A closing car door on the back side of the complex. A muffled yip from inside Mrs. Lipsky's apartment.

"Josh?"

"Yeah?"

I take a deep breath. "I don't want to explain what tonight was. And I don't want you to say anything to the rest of the girls."

There's a slight pause, followed by an easy, "Okay."

I stand and pull my comforter around me. "Night, Josh."

And I go inside, taking my secrets with me.

Chapter Nine
JOSH

On Tuesday, I swing by my place around dinnertime to grab a document. I run into Ruby getting out of her car as I reach mine.

"Hey, neighbor," she says. "Haven't seen you around."

"Probably because I'm only here long enough to sleep. In fact, I'm running back to the office now."

She winces. "One nice thing about the library is predictable hours."

"Just one?"

She shrugs. "Plus hundreds of thousands of books."

"Right, that."

"It's a pretty good perk. So, how'd it go with Sami the other night?"

I rest my arm on the roof of my car. "She didn't tell you?"

Ruby smiles. "I want your version."

"It was fine until it wasn't. We were talking and laughing, and then we weren't. A switch flipped. I'm not sure what happened. I don't think she was thrilled about my family, but I'm not sure why. We're not a political dynasty or anything, so people don't generally hate us the way they do some Texas families on reflex."

"Who's your family?"

"I'm a Brower."

"Like . . ."

"The dorm? And the giant law firm? Yes. That was my grandfather."

"Ah."

"That's a very dense 'ah.' Packed with meaning."

"Yes."

That's all she says. "You're not going to tell me more?"

"Not for me to tell."

"Did one of my ancestors curse one of hers or something?"

She shakes her head. "Nothing like that. She's had a rough time with . . . uh, some people. She probably doesn't love the idea of hanging out with other people that remind her of those people."

I smile at her. "Next time I bump into her, I'll report that you kept her secrets like a box of discovery documents opposing counsel doesn't want me to find."

"Please do," she says. "Then she'll keep telling them to me. She's got some she's holding out on."

She gives me a small salute and heads toward her place, and I watch after her for a moment. Something about her expression makes me wonder if Lady Mantha is less of a mystery than

Sami thinks. But maybe that's because it's the only other secret I know Sami keeps.

An hour later, my dad walks into my office.

My eyebrows go up. He needs something. When he's ordering me to do something as a partner, I get called up to his office. When he wants to talk me into something I don't have to do, he comes down to my office. I don't know if he even realizes he does it.

He takes the seat across from me. "How are you?"

"Great. What's up?" I can read him when he's being cagey like no other associate in this firm can ever hope to.

"Just checking in."

Absolutely not true. But if he wants to work up to it, I'll grant him the runway. "I'm good. All settled in the condo." That I paid for by myself. Besides the hours I put in at work, it's some of the most solid evidence I can offer him that I'm not still a screwup. But he hasn't asked to come see it.

Even now, he only grunts, his mind clearly somewhere else.

My disappointment is so routine that it's barely a hiccup in my day. I push it aside. "Can I help you with something?"

His thumb drums the arm of his chair. "The Reillys are coming to town."

I stare him down for a couple of seconds then shift my attention back to my monitor. Now I understand his nervous drumming. I make it a point to say yes to my parents whenever they ask for something, but I'm not doing this.

His hand stills. "JP mentioned looking forward to seeing you."

I keep my eyes on the monitor without actually seeing it. "No, Dad." He can't ask me this as my boss, and I'm reminding him of that.

"He's bringing Presley with him—"

"No." Brower and Moore has handled Reilly Industry's litigation for thirty years. John Paul Reilly and my dad were college roommates, and Presley, his daughter, is my age. Our parents used to joke about marrying us off. Presley never took it as a joke. She has it in her head that we're meant to be; therefore, JP does too.

"It's just dinner," my dad argues. "We always go to dinner with them."

"You're right. I'm overreacting. Let's go, and you sit next to Presley so she can grab *your* thigh under the table all night."

"I'll make sure you don't sit by her."

I snort. "She has tentacles, not arms. Presley finds a way."

"Josh, come on."

I meet his gaze, wordless.

He blinks first and sighs. "All right. I'll think of an excuse for your absence."

"Tell her I can't stand her. That should do the trick." He would never be that rude to someone, and he frowns. "I'm kidding, Dad."

"I don't like you speaking of her that way."

"You're not a fan either."

He can't deny this. "Doesn't mean you need to badmouth her."

This time I blink first. "You're right. Sorry, Dad. If there's anything else you need, you've got it. But not this."

He doesn't look happy about it, but after a moment, he slaps his hands on his thighs and stands. "No dinner with the Reillys, but that doesn't get you off the hook for Sunday."

"Wouldn't miss it." Only a dummy would miss a Brower Sunday dinner when Gramps smokes a brisket.

He leaves and I work a few more hours until my eyes feel gritty. Then I head home, listening to an economics podcast to start downshifting my brain toward sleep. It's past 11:00 when I step out of my shower, tired but not sleepy yet.

I slip outside to get fresh air. Sami is sitting on her balcony.

"Hey." I haven't seen her since the first time we both ended up out here a few nights ago. "Another show tonight?"

She shakes her head. "No. Trying to wind down from a regular day."

"I came out here hoping to see an actual night owl like last week, but you'll do."

She's in sweats and thick socks this time, her hands buried deep in her hoodie pocket. "You sweet talker."

"They don't call me Mr. Moves for nothing."

She looks over at me, a smirk on her face. "Who calls you that?"

"Just me. I call myself that."

"How often do you do this?"

"In my mirror every morning. 'Hey, there, Mr. Moves. Looking good.' Sometimes I do it in court but only during emergencies because it makes the bailiffs nervous."

She clears her throat, and I think she's hiding a laugh. "What kind of court emergency requires you to call yourself Mr. Moves?"

"If I'm losing, basically. I give myself a pep talk. 'Make some moves, Mr. Moves.' Stuff like that."

"Works for you pretty well?"

"So far, never. I've been jailed twice for contempt of court, but I went to jail *confidently,* so you know what? Yeah, it did work." This time she does laugh, and I smile in the dark. Maybe it's knowing I have no chance with her that makes it easy to let my goofy side out, or maybe it's that it's late. Either way, I like hearing her soft laugh.

"Fine, I'm lying. Corporate attorneys never have to go to court. Why are you still winding down at almost midnight? Stressful day?" I ask.

Instead of answering, she stands and turns toward the other side of her balcony; when she straightens, she's holding a plastic chair like hers.

She walks to the railing nearest me and holds it out. "Got you something."

I reach across the space between us and take it. "You didn't have to do that."

She sits back down in her matching chair. "I know. You owe me five dollars."

She's hard to read but her voice is dry enough that I think she's joking.

"Can I pay in installments?"

"Nothing smaller than quarters."

"Deal. I'll check my sofa cushions tomorrow for my first payment." I sit and shift around. "It's a good chair."

She nods.

"You didn't answer my question," I say. "Tough day?"

She's quiet long enough for me to decide she's ignoring me when she finally sighs. "Yeah."

"Tell Mr. Moves all about it."

"Can I tell Josh instead of Mr. Moves?"

I heave a huge, annoyed sigh. "Fiiiiine." I smooth my hand over my face like a mime would. "Just Josh here."

"Hey, Josh."

"Hey."

"Today sucked."

"What happened?"

She tucks her chin into her hoodie, burrowing. "We lost a resident."

"Like . . . they had dementia and wandered off?"

"Like they're old, and eventually, if they're lucky, everyone dies of oldness."

"That must be the hardest part of your job."

"Sometimes it all feels hard."

"Doesn't sound like you get used to losing them." I pause. "That probably sounds ignorant. I don't know what normal is for a job like yours."

"It's normal *and* you don't get used to it, if that makes sense. It happens three or four times a month. But some losses are harder than others. This was a hard one."

"Were you close to them?"

"Her name was Mrs. K." She probably can't give her full name for privacy reasons. "She only has one son, and he never visits. Visited." She pauses like she's adjusting to the past tense. "Just paid for whatever Medicare didn't cover, I think. No grandkids. She was shy, so she'd go to the activity lounge whenever we had visiting performers or movies, but she didn't interact with the other residents much. She declined pretty fast in the last couple of months and quit coming out at all, so then her only contact was me and the CNAs."

"Sounds sad."

"Those are the worst ones. The lonely ones. Because it feels like I might be the only one who will notice they're missing, so I feel . . ." She breaks off and sighs again. "I don't know. It's different than the residents who have lots of family."

"Do you feel like you have to remember them because no one else will?"

A long silence, then a soft, "Yeah."

I don't know what to say, but I want her to know I'm listening. "That's a lot to carry."

"Is this where you tell me it's not my job to carry it?" Her tone is a borderline dare.

"No. This is where I say I respect that you do."

She's quiet again. It's strange to think that this is the same firecracker I saw tearing up the stage a week ago. Not that either is better or worse. Lady Mantha is so different than the girl next door that they're hard to compare.

"What about you?" she asks after we've been quiet for a while. "Do you like your job?"

I rub my jaw. "I shouldn't have to think about this question so hard every time someone asks it."

"It seems like something a person knows. You like it or you don't, right? Like black licorice. There's no in-between. You can't *kind of* like it." The words are impatient, but her tone is mild.

"I like parts of it, dislike others. Depends on the day on which way the scales tip."

"How about today? Do you like your job today?"

I flash to my dad's drop-by. "No. Today is not a day I like my job."

"Why not?"

"Lots of pressure to be a rainmaker. Long hours. Sometimes the worst parts of frat culture find their way to the office. Pressure to prove that I'm good because I'm a nepo baby."

"Kind of a lot to unpack there, bellboy."

"It's a lot to haul around."

"What's a rainmaker?"

"Someone who brings in business for the firm. Attracts a lot of clients. Bills a lot of hours."

"Guess that explains the long days."

"Yeah. Because part of signing new clients is networking, which has to be done out of the office—"

"Like at live music shows?"

I smile at her, not sure she'll see it in the dim light. "Only when they're headlined by a punk rock pixie."

"I want to get angry at you for calling me that, but people seem to think it's cute when I get mad. And you might say that I'm cute when I'm mad out loud. Then I'd have to stab you. Or push you off the balcony."

"Pixie? Sorry. But it's in the band name."

"No. Punk rock. I'm rock and roll."

"What's the difference? I kind of know, but I'd love to hear it from a musician."

She blows her lips out. "Vibe. Complexity.

Melody. Harmony. Fuller sound. Should I keep going?"

"No, I got it. Rock and roll pixie."

"Rock Goddess is fine."

"Yes, your worshipfulness."

"Good boy. So that night was networking?"

"Kind of, yeah. Wooing. Giving a prospective client every reason to sign with us or make them glad that they already did." I scoot my chair so I can lean on the railing facing her. "It's usually not as fun as that show was. You're really good. Now can I ask why you do it as a secret identity?"

"The Sami portion of this discussion is over. We're on Josh Brower, Heir and Scion, now."

"It's not as interesting as Rock Goddess."

"I'll decide that. You said work is stressful because you have to bring in business and bill lots of hours. That explains the late nights. What about frat culture?"

"Maybe it's bro culture," he says. "The constant competition. I don't know. I like the work, mostly. Sometimes I wish I could do it without the rest of the noise."

"At least you get paid well for it."

"Yeah." I get paid extremely well compared to most jobs, especially a nurse. "Sorry. I usually don't whine about my job because I get that it's obnoxious."

"I asked you. I like hearing about other people's jobs."

"Then can I complain about the stupidest part of mine?"

"Bring it on."

"When my dad decides to be my dad instead of my boss and guilts favors out of me that he wouldn't ask another associate for."

"Like . . ."

"There's this girl . . ."

She gives a soft groan. "This won't end well."

"Let me back up. There's this family we've known forever. My dad and their CEO were college roommates. We've represented his company since he started. He has a daughter my age, and our parents used to joke about marrying us off when we grew up."

"Only now they're not joking?"

"Only my parents were joking, and her parents never were. And neither is she. My parents—my mom especially—brings it up sometimes in a you-should-think-about-it kind of way, but mainly because she was hoping—" I break off. For a while, she'd hoped that getting into a serious relationship would settle me down. Reform me.

"Hoping what?" Sami prompts.

I've been trying to put my past behind me for four years now. I don't drag it up lightly. I shake my head. "Doesn't matter. Anyway, this girl, Presley, she's persistent. And her dad likes her to have what she wants. So he always brings her with him to Austin when he's here for business. My dad was trying to talk me into dinner with them tomorrow."

"Sounds awkward." Her voice is sympathetic.

"It is."

"Does she know you're not into her?"

"I've told her I only want to be friends, but she laughs and says I'll come around or something."

"That's . . . disrespectful." She's leaning on her railing too, so we can see each other easily.

"I hadn't thought about it that way. Feels more tone deaf than anything."

"And there's no chance you'll change your mind?"

"Definitely not."

"Because . . . ?"

I shrug. "We don't have much to talk about. That's a dealbreaker." Presley is pretty. More than pretty; she's got Texas beauty queen vibes because that's what she is. Second runner-up in Teen Miss Texas. But that's almost the problem. She's so polished from all her pageant training that it's hard to have a real conversation with her. She answers questions based on who she's with; even her favorite teams shift to appease whoever she's around.

She's smart. Very smart. And articulate. No doubt about any of that. She can speak intelligently on almost any subject, but it's always adapted to her audience.

"That doesn't bother her?" Sami asks. "Or does she have a thing for awkward conversations?"

"First off, I'm not sure she's even noticed we don't have that much in common because she does most of the talking. Second, you're the last person who should be throwing shade over awkward conversations."

"Me? Why? Does this conversation feel awkward to you?" She sounds so surprised that I laugh.

"Aren't you the rock goddess who chatted with me all the way to pho and then quit talking?"

"Oh. I forgot about that." She straightens and stretches. "I'm finally getting sleepy. Good night, Josh."

It's been good, sitting out here with her again, and even though sleep is calling me too, I don't want the conversation to end. "Hey, Sami?"

She pauses, halfway through her sliding door. "Hmm?"

"Could we try pho again sometime?" Whatever misfired that night seems to have fixed itself.

A short pause. "I don't think so, Josh."

Then she disappears inside, leaving me to wonder how I misread her so completely again.

Chapter Ten
JOSH

A notification on my computer Thursday morning informs me that my dad has added a meeting in his office after lunch.

I hit the intercom button on the desk phone. "Anne? Do you know what this meeting with my dad is about?"

My secretary gets up and walks to my door. "Nope. Just said to put fifteen minutes on your schedule."

"Thanks." I consider this for a moment as she goes back to her desk. He had dinner with the Reillys last night, but if this is about them, it must be business related for an office summons. Or maybe it's something totally unrelated?

I decide not to sweat it, but within a minute of arriving at his office, I realize I should have been sweating it the whole time.

"Had dinner with the Reillys last night."

"How did it go?" I ask.

"Have a seat, son."

This is the first hint that I'm not going to like this conversation, and as I take the chair opposite him, I feel like a pawn being moved on a chessboard.

"Presley kept asking about you," my dad says.

"That's nice of her."

My dad gives me a level look. "How about if we cut to the chase?"

There's not much point in subtext or dancing around stuff when you know each other so well.

"Hit me," I say, brushing nonexistent lint from my slacks.

"It was an issue that you weren't there. More of an issue than I expected it to be," he says. "You know how JP is about her. When she was so disappointed that you hadn't made it, the rest of the dinner was . . ." He pauses and thinks. "Stiff. I got the sense that he was holding it against me. An undercurrent of resentment. That's not normal between us."

That's true. My dad's friendship with JP is so long-standing that it's always felt like its own thing, outside of their work arrangements or anything else.

"Thanks for running interference for me," I say.

"They're in town through the weekend. I need you to come to dinner tonight. At the house. I offered when the mood felt so weird last night. I thought it would give me a chance to reset a bit with JP. Get us back to normal. But you're going to have to be there. It'll be too hard to explain why you're not at a *family* dinner."

"Dad . . ."

He holds up his hands. "I know. I'm not

asking you to propose marriage to Presley. But I'm telling you that as your managing partner, I think this matters on the business side. And as your father, I'm asking you to help me navigate a relationship with an old family friend that feels off at the moment."

It's a double whammy. There's no way I can say no. "Sure, Dad. I'll be there. But I'm not going to lead Presley on."

"Wouldn't expect you to, but maybe JP was offended when you didn't show, and this will fix that. Then you can have whatever conversation you need to have with Presley so it's not an issue again."

"I've already had this conversation with Presley. She didn't listen."

"Son, you're a moot court champion. Use your skills."

I roll my eyes. Winning a law school mock trial my final year and handling Presley have nothing to do with each other, and he knows it. "Fine."

"Dinner at 7:00." He turns back to his computer, a clear dismissal.

I take the stairs back to my floor to burn off some of my annoyance. It would be one thing if I was ghosting Presley, but I'm not. I've told her—as kindly as I could—that I'm not interested. I don't know how to make it any clearer.

I stew about it the rest of the day, and when

I leave around 6:00, plenty of other people are still working even though the firm technically closes at 5:00. There's no such thing as being truly off the clock if the client's retainer is big enough.

At home, I climb out of my car the same time as Sami is unlocking hers to leave.

"Hey," she says, smiling.

I haven't seen her since our Tuesday night balcony chat. I've taken to checking my balcony every night before I go to sleep on the off chance she's out there.

"How's it going?" I ask. "Show tonight?"

She shoots a glance at her place, as if to make sure none of her roommates overheard me.

"Sorry," I say, lowering my voice.

"I've got rehearsal. Show tomorrow."

"Nice."

She nods and gets into her car, and I walk into my condo feeling stupid. *Nice?* That was a meaningless response. I could have turned that into a question to keep the conversation going. *Where do you practice?* Or at least I could have said something marginally less idiotic. Even just *Cool.*

But somehow, when I'm around Sami, I feel like the funniest version of myself half the time and the cringiest version the rest.

I switch into something for dinner at home with old family friends who are kind of elitest.

That means black jeans and a black-and-white-checked shirt. Casual but not too casual. I pause before I walk out of my room. Maybe I should choose something Presley would hate. For a second, I consider switching my shoes for flip-flops, but my dad would see right through me.

"Bernice." I crouch and look into her tank. I'd picked her up from my old place early last week. She doesn't even bat an eye when my face looms in front of her. "Why can't Presley be more like you? Happy if you're fed, content to let me do my thing?"

Bernice doesn't answer, and I head out to my car and spend the fifteen-minute drive to my parents' place rehashing the last time I tried to disentangle myself from Presley.

It had been last summer, when my parents invited the Reillys to spend the Fourth at Gramps's ranch west of the city. I'd only gone out for the actual Fourth, and Presley had been there, ready to pounce.

Presley has a body that doesn't quit, and she made sure it was on display in her Gucci bikini top and shorts, the whole look classed up with a large sunhat and Louis Vuitton sunglasses. And yes, Meghan Trainor, she made me look.

The problem, Meghan Trainor, is that Presley spent a disproportionate amount of time working on that body and shopping for those labels. And worse, talking about them.

When she'd tried twining herself around me as we watched fireworks set off by the ranch hands, her smelling too much like wine coolers, I'd detached her arms from my waist and told her—not for the first time—I wasn't into her like that.

She'd only smiled and said, "Not yet, Josh. But you'll come around."

What the crap are you supposed to do about someone who thinks that way?

Avoid. Avoid, avoid, avoid. Evasive maneuvers at all times.

It had worked.

Until now.

I voice dial Reagan. "Are you coming to dinner?" I ask when she answers.

"Can't," she says. "I'm hosting poker night for my girls."

"Reagan . . ." I know my voice is almost a whine. But her "girls" are all other wives from her neighborhood. "I'm your *brother*."

"I heard Presley's going to be there. But don't worry, you'll be fine. Just use your big boy words."

"I tried that this summer, but it must not have worked because she emotionally blackmailed JP into making sure I'm at dinner tonight."

"Look at it as an opportunity to set the record straight once and for all. Just use your big boy words."

"I don't know the words. I have tried all of them. Zero worked."

"Good luck." Her tone is way too cheerful. "Hope you figure it out without ticking off JP and losing the firm millions in revenue."

"Thanks," I mutter as she hangs up.

When I pull into my parents' driveway in Tarrytown, I spot JP's Escalade. He keeps a luxury apartment and a vehicle in Austin for the half dozen times a year that he's in town.

I park and climb out. Usually, I love coming here. It's the house I grew up in, and it sits on an acre patrolled by my mom's three shelties, Tater, Bean, and Queso. It's two stories of light brown stone, black shutters, and white trim. It manages to look both classy and welcoming at the same time. My mom incarnate.

Queso comes racing around the front of the house to greet me, yapping, with Tater and Bean in hot pursuit. I give them scratches and head inside to deal with Presley.

"Hey, Mom!" I call out when I open the door.

"In here, honey," she answers from the front room, exactly where I expect to find her. JP and Presley are seated on a sofa across from my parents, although my mom is already up and coming for a hug.

"Hi, baby." She squeezes me tight, and I hug her back. She always smells like lemon, and it calms me, even though I can see Presley climbing to her feet to make a run at me too.

My mom steps back and tugs me over to the sofa. "Come have a seat while your dad makes you a drink."

"I'll do it, Mom." It lets me divert to the wet bar, and Presley has to sit down. "Can I get anyone anything while I'm here?"

"Vodka and cranberry," Presley says.

"You got it." I pour myself a gin and tonic and then mix her drink, bringing it to her with a polite smile. "Good to see you, Pres."

She accepts the glass, making sure her fingers linger on mine as she takes it. "You too, Josh. Can't wait to catch up."

I choose a chair where she can't join me, and the next fifteen minutes pass in small talk about the baseball team JP is part owner of and the state of the state while skirting around politics. The Reillys and my parents vote opposite, and I actually align more with the Reillys. But since everyone is super passionate about their opinions—I have a sister named *Reagan,* for pity's sake—we've all learned to leave politics alone over the years.

A buzzer sounds and my mom gets up. "That'll be the beef tenderloin," she says. "Josh, come and help?"

"Glad to." I follow her to the kitchen while I hear my dad inviting JP and Presley to the family dining room.

We do have a formal dining room, but my parents rarely use it. It's "for company." The family dining room is for friends.

In the kitchen, my mom hands me hot pads and gestures to the oven. "Go ahead and take it out," she says. "It can rest on the table while we start with salad."

It would normally be a gamble to serve filet mignon to a steak-loving guy like JP who loves his meat heavily marbled and almost mooing, but Elizabeth Brower is a dang good cook, and anyone she's fed once is anxious to repeat the experience.

I pull out the roasting pan and transfer the tenderloin to a waiting platter, then carry it out to the table and set it down. My mom is right behind me with a salad bowl, the dressings already waiting on a table that looks like it should be in a magazine about casual elegance.

She's opted to sit beside me instead of at the foot of the table, and she's put Presley across the table and diagonal from me. She's trying to create a buffer for me, and I appreciate it.

Presley makes her move after steak and before dessert.

"So how has it been at the firm, Josh?" she asks.

It's a polite question. A normal one, even, and anyone who doesn't know how Presley operates would miss this as her opening shot. But this is where she'll begin a subtle campaign to split off from our parents during dessert that will end with her backing me into a literal corner and trying to make out with me or something.

Ask me how I know.

But I have to answer or look rude, so I do, all the while calculating what her next move might be and how to derail her. "It's been good. Long hours. Spending a lot of time at the office." Subtext: I don't have time to date.

"That's admirable, son," Mr. Reilly says. Subtext: Billing lots of hours means you can support Presley in the style to which she's accustomed.

"Not too much time, I hope," Presley adds. "Need to have that work/life balance, right, Miss Elizabeth?" Subtext: As my future mother-in-law, please remind Josh to make time for me.

"I wish it were that easy," I say. Subtext: No way. "But we've got a huge case I'm on right now."

"Good thing you know the boss," Mr. Reilly says with a wink but also a slight edge to his voice. Subtext: Steve, you better give Josh time off to spend with Presley.

I stifle a sigh. This is classic JP Reilly, trying to corner my dad. Presley learned from a pro. I have to come up with something fast or my dad is going to be forced to give me time off for Presley to drive me crazy.

"It's not my dad who makes me work so much,"

I say. "I find it interesting. Anyway, good thing my girlfriend is patient about it."

My mom's eyebrows fly up, and she and my dad exchange glances.

"Your . . . girlfriend?" Presley asks, hesitating before "girlfriend" as if to make sure she won't choke on it.

"Yeah. She gets it because her job is demanding too."

Presley's eyes narrow ever so slightly. "What does she do?"

Sami's job pops into my extremely dumb brain. "Nurse."

"Why do you look surprised, Mr. Steve?" Presley asks. "Did you not know what his girlfriend does?"

My dad, caught not keeping his face straight enough, is not going to lie for me. I brace for it.

"I'm surprised to hear about a girlfriend," he admits.

He's going to blow up my escape. Unless . . . "I haven't mentioned it," I say. "It's pretty new."

"How new?" Presley asks.

"Couple of weeks, but when you know, you know." I throw that in with a smile. Let her think it's immediate and true love.

"Fascinating," my mom says. She's in no hurry to acquire Presley as a daughter-in-law, but she's not going to sit and enable any lies either. "What's her name?"

"Samantha." I keep my face as straight as possible. No need for them to know that she likes pho more than she likes me.

"A couple of weeks isn't that long," Presley says.

Her tone is full of doubt. I'm not making a convincing case. "Sometimes you don't need that long. You can know someone for years and never feel that magic, or you can cross paths with someone once and feel a lightning strike. This was like that."

"We'll look forward to meeting her soon," my mom says. That is a clear *You better put up or shut up, because you're in trouble if you're lying*.

Throwing out Sami's name was a desperate play, and now I'm going to pay the price of a very awkward conversation with Sami.

My mom changes the subject, and I work hard to keep it away from any talk of dating or relationships. As dinner ends, I make excuses to my parents and the Reillys about needing to get some work done for the next day. I jerk my thumb at my dad, like *This guy*. He frowns but doesn't contradict me.

When I climb into bed that night, I haven't gotten any threatening texts from my parents, so I fall asleep slightly less stressed; looks like they're going to cover for me.

What a misplaced sense of security.

My dad summons me to his office as soon as he gets in. "A girlfriend, Josh?"

"Why are you looking at me like you don't believe me?" Whenever you've got the weak position, play offense. He taught me that.

He doesn't fall for it. "JP and Presley don't believe you. They're insisting on a last dinner before they leave town. They want you there with this girlfriend."

"I don't owe them that, Dad. Presley will get over it."

He sighs. "Normally, I'd agree with you and say to ride it out. But JP mentioned discussing an adjustment to our retainer, which is a warning that he isn't satisfied. He thinks you're lying, and you know he'll yank his business in a second if he thinks you're not playing it straight with Presley. You've put us in the position of having to lie for you."

"I haven't," I say, guilt immediately roiling my stomach. I've forced them into a position they'll hate, unless . . . "I really am seeing someone named Sami." *A couple of nights a week on her balcony . . .*

"And this is someone you have feelings for?"

"Yes." *Feelings like it's nice to talk to her sometimes at night.*

My dad's forehead smooths. "So you were telling the truth at dinner."

"It's just so new. There was no reason to say

anything before." Also mostly true. "I would have introduced you guys eventually." Possibly true, if we bump into her when my parents visit my condo, which they haven't done yet despite an invitation.

"We'll look forward to meeting her tomorrow night." He sits back, a look of relief on his face.

"Tomorrow night?"

"Yes. You're bringing her to this last dinner with the Reillys and making it clear to Presley once and for all that you're off the market."

"Dad, Sami might not be able to make it. Her schedule is pretty hectic."

"Tomorrow night," he says. "Seven o'clock at the country club."

"But—"

"Seven. O. Clock." Then he nods at the door, and it's Steve Brower, managing partner, dismissing me.

I walk out and take the stairs down to my floor, slumping in my desk chair when I reach it.

This is bad. My parents don't like the country club. It's where they go when they—specifically, my dad—want to do some networking. It's an "I mean business" kind of place that doesn't look like a business place. Literally its only redeeming quality is that they make a good steak. But you can't stay open in Austin if you can't cook steak.

Somehow, I have to convince Sami that she wants to come to this dinner and be my fake girlfriend. And meet my parents. And Presley, who will be gunning for her.

Or . . .

I consider the options. Maybe I'll play in traffic instead.

Chapter Eleven
SAMI

The show we did last week—the one where Josh busted me—was good. No, *great*. But it was a turning point, and tonight's show was even better. It's like each of us in the band has realized we're legit—people want to see us. So we went hard tonight, and the crowd ate it up. In fact, we had no merch to sell after the show—we've never had a need—but the venue manager was irritated at having to field so many requests for it.

I pull into my parking spot at home and pound on the steering wheel, grinning like a loony tune. *He was annoyed that we didn't have merch.* Last month, we couldn't have *given* a T-shirt away, and tonight we could have sold dozens.

Tomorrow we're playing at a tailgate festival in San Antonio, providing the live music while self-proclaimed tailgate master chefs go for glory. There's no way we'll have any merchandise to sell by then, but maybe that's okay. We're basically going to be background music, so I doubt we'll have the same demand. But for next weekend, at the South Door, we better have something to hawk in the club.

It'll take money. Our usual band agreement is that we split whatever we earn from a gig five ways, but I'll talk to the guys tomorrow and see if they'll pool our check from the festival organizers and use it to pay for an initial run of band shirts. We'll just use the logo Luther's friend made for us, and I'll spend the morning researching the best and fastest way to get the shirts made before the South Door show.

I climb out of the car and practically dance into the house, a knit cap on to hide my hair because I came straight from the club. A thorough washing in the shower gets the pink out, and the steam finally relaxes me, calming the buzz.

A few minutes later, I'm in warm pajamas and thick socks but not quite ready to sleep. I step onto my balcony, wrapped in my comforter, and smile when I spot Josh's shadowy form outside. I don't know how it happened, but I've come to hope—maybe even expect—that I'll find him out here each time I step out. I've definitely been on my balcony way more than usual in the chilly January night air.

I settle into my chair. "Hey, neighbor."

"Hey, yourself," he answers. He sounds way more tired than I do.

"You okay?"

He sighs. "Sure."

"So that's a no. What's up?" There's a long silence before he answers.

"You ever lie?"

"Like *ever* ever? White lies? Stuff like that?"

"Maybe bigger."

"How big? Defrauding the federal government big? Like don't tell me anything else because I don't want to be subpoenaed in your trial big?"

"Those are the two categories of lies?" He sounds amused. "Your new haircut looks nice or federal indictment? No middle ground?"

"What's a middle ground lie to you?"

"Let's say you invent a girlfriend you don't have to get your dad's client and his daughter off your back."

"Ohhh." A twinge of sympathy flutters in my chest. "I've invented a few fake boyfriends when a dude is too pushy at a club. Like that?"

"Kind of. Except what if you also lied to your parents about a relationship because they were sitting right there when you were trying to get off the hook with Presley?"

"Josh . . ."

"You sound disappointed."

"I only said your name."

"In a disappointed way."

I stifle a laugh. "Do you hear your name in a disappointed way often?"

"You have no idea."

It's hard to imagine this cookie cutter corporate lawyer disappointing people often.

"I especially heard it a lot from myself today while I lectured me on being an idiot."

"And a liar."

"Wow, Sami. Thank you for the assist there. I would definitely have forgotten I'm a lying liar without it."

I scoot my chair closer to his side of the balcony. "You better tell me about it, so I can decide if I'm judging you harshly enough."

I listen to his dramatic re-enactment of dinner with his parents and the scheming Presley. Josh is a good storyteller and pokes plenty of fun at himself, so I don't have to.

"And that's how I invented a girlfriend I have to produce by dinnertime tomorrow or I'll break my parents' hearts again," he concludes. "Unless . . ."

His tone carries a heavy note of suggestion. "No way," I say, even as I wonder about that "again." "I'm not being your fake girlfriend." I can think of four hundred other ways I'd rather spend an evening, including cleaning the baseboards in our condo with a toothbrush.

"Way to jump to conclusions, Sam I am," he says. "I was about to ask for your nurse knowledge in thinking of sudden onset viruses or injuries that would keep me from dinner tomorrow night. Is ebola still a thing? Is that too over the top?"

"It is, yeah. Maybe stick with flu."

"Would flu also keep me away from Sunday family dinner after the Reillys leave? Because we're having brisket."

"Yes. And so would ebola."

He gives a long sigh.

"Or—and hear me out because this is wild—you could tell your parents the truth. Brisket is even better with a clean conscience."

"No way. If you met Presley, you'd understand. Nothing short of a fiancée will stop her, and maybe not even that."

"Guess you're going to have to hire a call girl."

He makes a choking sound before he manages, "What did you say?"

"Call girl. Have her pretend to be your girlfriend. I heard about a couple of girls putting themselves through college that way. You don't have to sleep with her. Just request a smart one and pay her to be your date. Then it won't even be fake."

After a pause, he says, "I can't decide if you're serious or not."

"I'm not."

"Good. Because it wouldn't work anyway. Dinner is at my parents' country club, and there's a pretty good chance that a not-small number of the men there would recognize any, uh, 'pro' that I hired. Besides, there's another complication."

"All you're doing is looking for obstacles and not solutions but go ahead. Lay it on me," I tease, tilting back my chair.

"I may have said that this girlfriend is a nurse named Sami."

I tip all the way back and land on the ground with a muffled *whumpf.*

"Whoa, are you okay?" Josh leaps to his feet and rushes to his railing, reaching toward me like he can close the gap enough to help me up.

Our balconies aren't *that* close, so I struggle to my elbows and glare over at him. "What is *wrong* with you?"

He shrinks back like he can hear the glare in my tone.

"I panicked," he said. "You're the last date I went on."

I right my chair and climb into it. "You can't hire an escort to play a nurse named Sami. What if she likes the role so much that she makes it her new alias? And word gets around? And then people get confused that *I'm* the escort?"

"That's not going to happen," he says.

"How do you know?" I demand. "Have you done this before? Do you have so much escort experience that you know how these things go?"

"Not really. But I'm not hiring an escort, so I'm pretty sure none of that's going to play out."

"I'm glad you've come to your senses." I cross my arms and pull my quilt tight.

"Sami, *you* brought up the escort, not me." He sounds exasperated.

"I'm disgusted you even considered it," I tell him.

"I didn't—" He breaks off and takes a deep

breath. "Sami? What are you doing tomorrow night?"

"Not being your fake girlfriend."

"How do you know that's what I was going to ask you?"

I turn to squint at his outline. "Is that what you were going to ask me?"

Long pause. "Yes."

"No."

"Do you have plans?"

"Yes. Not being your fake girlfriend."

"But do you have a gig tomorrow night?"

"No," I admit.

"Then you're free."

"Also no."

"You just said you don't have a gig."

"I said I don't have one tomorrow night. I *do* have one tomorrow afternoon in San Antonio until four. Factor in pack-up time, drive time, washing-my-hair time, and there's no way I can make it to dinner. But also, I don't want to go."

"I could pay you," he says, and when I suck in a sharp breath, he hurries to add, "Not like *that*."

"Do not make me put on my Doc Martens and do some stomping."

"I meant I could pay you what you would make for a show. Because you'd be putting on a performance. Downside: you'd have to eat at the country club. Also, Presley. Upside: the food is good. Also, money."

"I thought you were a good lawyer, but I guess not."

"I'm a really good lawyer." He sounds offended.

"Isn't negotiating part of your job?"

"Yes . . ."

"That bargain sucks. Food and money don't outweigh country club and Presley." Especially not after Bryce. We'd never gone to a country club. I didn't think that was a real thing except for on TV until Josh brought it up. But Bryce's family was the kind that would belong to a country club if there was one near them. But only if it was a stuck-up, snobby country club.

"That's a good point." He snaps. "Double. I'll pay you double your gig rate."

"Man, you reeeeeeally don't want to confess that you lied, do you?" But he's got me thinking. Twice as much is pretty good money, and I could easily pay for the shirts. Plus, we have songs on some of the streaming services we recorded by converting the pool house into a makeshift studio. I'd *love* to hear what we could do if we had studio time with one of Austin's better producers. This money could buy us that time.

"It's not that," he says. "I'll eventually confess to my parents. But I have tried everything to get through to Presley and JP that she and I are not going to happen. I've said it different ways. I've said it multiple times. She doesn't want to hear it."

"Maybe you're being too subtle. Or nice," I add. Josh does come across as nice more than anything.

"I haven't been subtle, but rude isn't an option. I have to get Presley off my back without JP firing the firm. She's their only child, and he's made a point of doing whatever it takes to make her happy."

"Doesn't sound healthy."

Josh sighs. "I know I've made her sound like a nightmare. To be honest, she's not that bad with anyone else as far as I can tell. But she has a blind spot where I'm concerned, and I don't know what else to do."

I can hear the high level of stress in his voice. I don't want to take advantage of that, but he's asking *a lot,* so if I'm going to seriously consider this—and weirdly, I am—I'm going to ask a lot too. "We're talking a thousand bucks here." Let's see if he blinks at that.

"Fine."

No hesitation. He doesn't even sound concerned. "Rich people," I mutter.

"What was that?"

"Nothing."

"No, you said, 'Rich people.' I'm not saying it's right that attorneys make more than nurses, but we do. And now I'm giving you a chance to take some of that money, eat good food, and do me a solid. So what do you say?"

"No." What kind of person says yes to that?

He groans and drops his head to his forearms resting on his railing. I gather my self-righteousness and my quilt more snugly around me and settle into them both.

He lifts his head again. "You're missing the most important part of this equation."

"What's that?"

"You'd get to spend the whole night sticking it to a bunch of rich people."

That makes me pause. "Hmm."

"It's really good steak."

"I do like steak."

"And a thousand dollars."

A chance to fund band T-shirts *and* potential studio time? Plus good steak?

I stand up and hold my quilt around my neck like a royal cape. "All right. I'll do it."

"Yes." It's a whisper shout as I slide open the balcony door. "You won't be sorry."

His promise follows me and my regal quilt into my bedroom as I shut the door again.

I better not be, or *he's* the one who will live to regret it.

Chapter Twelve
JOSH

I text Sami around lunch time the next day.

JOSH: Still on for tonight?
SAMI: I'm going ON stage right now
JOSH: Your work on the weekend = way more fun than my work on the weekend
SAMI: Duh

She sends me a picture of their setup, taken from the side. The drums are up, the amps are stacked, and wires crisscross everywhere. She follows that with a crowd shot, which seems to be a sea of trucks and SUVs, steam and smoke rising from their various grilling setups, and people milling around.

SAMI: Steak tonight better be better than that dude's in the green Chevy or the rate doubles.
JOSH: No chef in Austin can beat a tailgate set up!
SAMI: I take Venmo
JOSH: Not to brag, but this is what I had . . .

I send her a picture of an empty Quarter Pounder box on my desk then get back to work. Tonight will be the most expensive—and fakest—date I've ever taken someone on, but I'm still looking forward to it.

I knock on Sami's door at 6:30 and smile at Ruby when she opens it.

"Hey," she says, looking surprised to see me. I guess Sami didn't tell her roommates what we're up to tonight. "Do you need something?"

"Sami," I say. "We're going to dinner."

She runs an eye over my sport coat and slacks, a smile twitching her lips. "Is that a fact? Sami," she calls up the stairs. "Your *date* is here."

I hear rustling upstairs, then Sami appears in her interpretation of country club chic. Brown leather boots that look better suited for ladies who pretend to ride horses than stomping around onstage. Good. A skirt that falls almost to her knee, plaid, straight. Okay. Turtleneck, cream, that covers everything yet somehow reminds me she gives her sports bra a workout with every workout.

Her blond hair falls in soft waves and her makeup is understated. It's hard to believe this is the same scowling goth fairy I saw last weekend. She looks perfectly appropriate for a dinner at the country club.

"Hey," she says.

"Hey," I answer.

"You didn't say you had a date," Ruby says.

"Because you're not my mom." Sami's tone is mild.

"Or is it because I'm on the verge of better parking?"

"Nope." Sami reaches for a jacket, and I look back and forth between them, clearly missing something.

"Don't worry about it," Sami says to my unspoken question. "Let's go. Don't want to keep your parents waiting."

Ruby's eyes practically bug out. "His *parents?* Wait a min—"

"Byeeeee." Sami pushes me out the door and closes it on Ruby.

"I take it you're not telling your roommates about this deal?" I ask as we get to my car. I hold her door open then get in on my side.

"Good guess," she says.

"Would they judge you?"

"Only for charging you," she says. "They'd be one hundred percent on board with me being your fake girlfriend. They love shenanigans."

I pat the steering wheel. "It's a cliché for a former frat boy to drive a BMW. I know that. But man, I love this thing." I start the car, and she laughs.

"Somehow the fact that you know it's a cliché makes it less annoying."

I back out of the space and put us on the road toward the Rolling Hills Country Club.

"It'll take about twenty minutes to get there, so should we spend some time filling out our backstory?"

"You think we need to?" she asks. "You were smart enough to tell them we've only been dating a few weeks, right? How much would they expect us to know about each other? We probably already know it, don't we?"

"We've only hung out a few times," I say. "There's lots of stuff we don't know yet that we probably should."

"Josh." She says it patiently.

"Yes?"

"You're twenty-nine. You went to UT and lived in Brower Hall before graduating and going to Duke for law school. You were in the Fiji fraternity, and you're working at your family's firm in corporate law. You work at least twenty hours a week more than you should but still find time to hit the gym. You wear a lot of suits but you'll pick joggers every time you have a choice. You love your parents but there's some tension there. You have a special bond with your grandfather. You hate the current state politics but wouldn't live anywhere else because you love Texas barbecue too much."

She twists slightly in her seat to look at me. "How'd I do?"

"How . . . what . . . I . . ."

"Am I right?"

I shoot her a quick glance. "That was scary."

She shrugs and faces front again. "Not really. Not if you're paying attention."

"Give yourself more credit," I say. "Not that many people pay attention."

"I've gotten good at it in the last year. My job. I do a lot of listening. I've learned to hear what isn't being said too. Fill in the gaps. See the whole picture."

"You'd be a good attorney."

She snorts. "If nurse and rock goddess don't work out, I'll try detective."

"But as good as that was, Sherlock, there's still a few gaps in there."

"Tell me."

I shake my head. "No way. I want to test these bizarre powers of yours. I'm going to ask a question, you tell me the answer."

"Go ahead."

"Am I a PDA guy?"

"One hundred percent." She doesn't even hesitate.

"Correct. Did I put moves on you that I forgot about?"

"No. But you're comfortable in your own skin. People like that are usually comfortable showing affection to other people."

"I've never thought about it."

She shrugs like this isn't a big deal. She could do jury consulting, reading people before they say a word and figuring out which way they're likely to lean in a case.

"Sweet or salty?"

"Salty. Otherwise, we would have already had five different conversations about Bluebell ice cream or something, but instead I know where you like to get your tacos. Are you going to ask me anything hard?"

She sounds so smug that I can't resist throwing her off.

"Lights on or off?"

A beat of silence. "Excuse me?"

"You know what I'm talking about. Let's see how good you really are. That's not something you could possibly know."

"On." She sounds sure.

I make a buzzer sound. "No way. I definitely sleep with the lights off."

She smacks me in the ribs, and I grab her hand. "What did you think I was talking about, Samantha?" I like saying her full name. It feels round and full, and the way my tongue has to push between my teeth for a split second to make the "th" sound has me thinking about . . .

Never mind.

"That is *not* what you were talking about." She tugs her hand, but not hard, and I don't let go.

Instead, I give it a light squeeze. "We should talk about PDA for real. You're right. I'm a PDA kind of guy, and my parents will expect to see some of that. It'll help convince Presley too." I let her go. "What's your comfort level?"

"I'm not going to stop, drop, and roll with you on the dining room floor, if that's what you're asking."

"Not even if I'm on fire? That's cold, Sami."

"I'd yell at you to do it."

"That's something."

"Probably throw water on you if there's a pitcher nearby."

"Feeling safer by the second."

"So we're going to have to look like we're used to touching each other," she says.

It takes me a second to switch back to serious again. "Ideally."

"I guess that means holding hands." She pauses for a second, like she's thinking. "That'll be fine."

I hide a smile. She sounds like she's doing me a big favor. I reach over and take her hand from her lap. "Fingers laced or no?" I lace mine between hers.

"Josh . . ."

"If we get there and try holding hands while we walk to the table and we can't get it right, game's over before it starts."

She slides her fingers from mine but only to slide her hand back into mine, fingers not laced, but with all of hers curled around mine, her thumb curving around my thumb like they were carved to fit that way. "This will be fine."

I don't say anything for a bit, absorbing the way our palms feel against each other. It's too bad this is a pretend situation. I have more chemistry with her than I've had with a woman in a long time.

Speaking of which . . . "If we've only been dating for a few weeks, shouldn't we look more like we can't stop touching each other?"

She clears her throat. "I'm reserved."

I flash back to her storming that stage full-out and grin. "No, you aren't. Just imagine you're performing on stage."

"I perform from an angry place," she says, and I can hear a smile in her voice. "I don't think that's what you need for this dinner."

"Then tell me what's okay. I don't want to make you uncomfortable."

"No stupid nicknames."

I feign shock. "You mean when characters fake date in the movies and they call each other ridiculous names no one uses in real life, you don't think it sounds organic?"

"As organic as Cheetos," she says. "I'll accept honey or babe."

"I'll take those plus sweetie. What else?"

"No kisses on the mouth. No one wants to see that at dinner."

"True."

"I hate it when guys order for me, but you probably should because it'll make it seem like you know what I like. I don't eat any salad with iceberg in it, I hate olives, and I want the most expensive steak on the menu. Other than that, I'm pretty easy, food-wise."

"Now you have to give me at least five facts about you that I would only know from dating you."

She sighs but doesn't argue. "I majored in English before I switched to nursing. I'm allergic to cats. My favorite food is veggie pizza. I hate scary movies. I have no siblings. My mom is also a nurse." She hesitates. "Bonus fact: I don't know my dad, and I don't talk about it."

I take it all in and squeeze her hand. "Veggie pizza? Who hurt you, Samantha?"

She laughs, and we spend the last ten minutes of the drive talking about our favorites from TV shows to bands.

It's a light conversation, but I still feel like I know her as well as the last girl I dated by the time we pull up to the country club.

She looks through the car window and takes a deep breath while we wait for the valet.

"Nervous?" I ask.

There is the barest pause before she says, "No."

"It'll be fine. Act like the most privileged girl in Pi Phi, and you'll sail through the evening. Piece of cake."

"You're the worst." Her voice is mild, and I let

my smile widen to a grin as I hand my keys to the valet.

This is going to work. I'll get rid of Presley while impressing my parents, all in one dinner. This is definitely one of my more genius plans.

Chapter Thirteen
SAMI

This has got to be one of the dumbest situations I've ever gotten myself into. And I have a secret life as a wannabe rock star, so that's saying something.

I take a deep breath before getting out of the car when the valet opens my door. When my boots hit the pavement, I stand straight, put my shoulders back, and wish I could do a power pose like I do before we go out to perform a set.

However, since I'm not sure that's the protocol for when your life is about to become a poorly scripted romcom—without romance, no less—I wait, poseless, for Josh to walk around and join me.

He places his hand at the small of my back to urge me forward, his touch gentle, and once we're inside the country club, his hand slips down to mine, wrapping around it like we'd "practiced" in the car, palms clasped but no interlaced fingers. I can't explain it, but interlaced fingers feels too intimate.

In Pi Phi, the first Sunday of every month was movie night, where we worked through all the old eighties and nineties romcoms. One of the worst was *Pretty Woman*. Julia Roberts plays a prostitute who gets a fairy tale ending after a rich guy hires her to be his escort at some fancy stuff for a week. She wouldn't kiss her "Johns" on the mouth because it was "too intimate."

The less I think about that movie the better, but I'm feeling icky similarities here. Why couldn't I be living *Some Kind of Wonderful* instead? I'd be the best friend/drummer sidekick. Much better.

But no, I'm definitely Julia Roberts as we enter the dining room and Josh guides me over to his parents. The men at the table stand to shake my hand as he introduces me as his girlfriend, Samantha. I clench my teeth behind my smile. Of course he has to use my full, formal name instead of the unpretentious "Sami." Bryce did that too when he introduced me to his parents.

It's obvious which man is Josh's dad. They have the same jawline and build, although he gets his dark blonde hair from his mother. She nods in greeting and gives me a gracious smile. Presley nods too, but her smile is stiff. I shake Mr. Reilly's hand—he looks rougher around the edges than Mr. Brower does, his skin more callused, his hair cut more for function than fashion. But both men wear expensive-looking suits and carry themselves with the kind of confidence even money can't buy; only power can.

I try to take it all in while smiling back as

warmly as possible. Josh holds out my seat for me, and I take my place. I'd rather not be in Presley's line of fire, but it's nearly unavoidable at a round table. Josh is to my left, and he made sure to put me between him and Presley. Guess he doesn't want any Presley gropes.

"I hope we're not late," Josh says.

"Right on time," Mrs. Brower reassures him.

Her voice is warm, and her gaze is level. She's smart; you can always tell smart people by their eyes. She seems alert, assessing but not calculating, unlike Presley, whose gaze rakes over me regularly, as if trying to figure out what such a tiny package has to offer Josh when Presley is available.

A waiter approaches to take our drink orders. I get a Negroni; I don't actually know what it is, but people always talk about it in shows, and I'm happy to try it on the Browers' dollar. We chat about the weather and the Reillys' week in Austin until the server comes back to tell us about the dinner specials.

As he takes our orders, Josh places a hand on my thigh and orders for me. "I'll take the prime rib and she'll have the filet mignon in the port wine reduction."

Presley stiffens beside me.

When the waiter leaves again, Mrs. Brower smiles at me across the table. "It's nice to meet you, Samantha."

"You as well, Mrs. Brower."

"Please, call me Elizabeth. And that's Steve," she says with an affectionate smile at her husband.

I would place them in their early sixties, max. They're both seriously attractive, but I don't think either of them owes it to surgery. Nice genes, Josh.

I can't say the same for Presley. I'm not opposed to anyone getting work done, but she's had fillers in her lips. It's subtle, I'll give her that, but there's no mistaking the faint loss of elasticity that comes even when the surgeon has the lightest touch.

I kind of wish she had big, huge fillers. And lots of other obvious work. It would be easier to think of her as a caricature. A cartoon villain. But Presley has the understated glow of the very wealthy, and she doesn't overplay her hand. Her chic coral dress is a winter-appropriate satin, expertly tailored and accessorized with a simple pearl drop pendant and small, thin gold hoops.

She couldn't be more night and day from Lady Mantha's bleach-stained and frayed clothes, cheap fishnets, and neon pink hair.

It's almost like she can smell it on me—the act I'm putting on with the country club–appropriate attire I dug from the back of my closet. But I had three years of solid practice blending in with

Presleys in Pi Phi, so I keep a serene smile on my face.

"That's a great bag," I say, flicking my eyes to her purse beside her chair. "Chanel, last season, right?"

I know it's Chanel. Even a dummy knows what the interlocked Cs on the clasp mean. I have no idea what season it is. That's me being a brat.

"It's the current collection, actually." Her lips stretch as far as the fillers will let them. "But Chanel is so timeless that seasons are meaningless, wouldn't you agree?"

I give a thoughtful nod. "It's not a Birkin, exactly, but I see your point."

Her eyes narrow the faintest bit, but I turn toward Josh, who has his arm across the back of my chair. He bends toward me and whispers, "I'm a little bit in love with you right now."

I smile at the suppressed laugh in his voice. It looks like we're enjoying an inside joke, but I fight the shiver the soft caress of his breath sends down my spine.

"We don't know much about you," Mr. Brower says. "Tell us about yourself."

"Sure," I say. "I'm twenty-five, grew up in Hillsboro, went to UT, majored in nursing, and now I work at a nursing home."

Mr. Brower's eyebrow goes up. I can't tell how he feels about this, but Mrs. Brower leans forward, her expression interested. "Do you like the work?"

"I do. Most days. Sometimes it's hard, but most of the time, even on the hard days, it's pretty great."

"Why not a hospital?" Presley asks. "Is the nursing home easier?"

I can't tell if she's trying to criticize me. The question is rude, but her tone is only curious.

"I chose elder care because I realized I love spending time around the older folks. I have the temperament for it."

"What does that mean? You like hard candies and gin rummy?" She says it in a teasing tone, but she's tipped her hand now; she's definitely trying to throw me off-balance.

"Hard candies, yes. Gin rummy, no. Our residents are card sharks, honestly. The number of times I have to break up strip poker games . . ." I trail off with a shake of my head, while Mr. Brower and Mr. Reilly give me startled looks and Presley's lips tighten for the barest fraction of a second before she recovers.

Josh slides his hand around the back of my arm and gives it the lightest squeeze, which I take as an "attagirl."

Presley isn't done. "You know your filet mignon comes with broccolini, right?"

I glance over at her. "Yes. I like broccolini."

"Oh, good. I thought you might not know what it is."

I'm getting a hint of her new strategy. "Why wouldn't I know what broccolini is?"

"You're from Hillsboro, aren't you?" Her eyes are direct and friendly. But I know this kind of friendly. You don't get out of a sorority without learning how to identify and defend against this kind of friendliness.

"Yes."

"Isn't it less . . ." She pauses. It's ever so delicate. "Cosmopolitan?"

"You think we don't have vegetables in Hillsboro?"

"Of course not. I assume y'all have the basic ones." She puts a barely there emphasis on "basic."

The strategy will be to make me look like I'm out of my depth with these here fancy upper class folk. All right, then.

I smile. "It's true that it takes food trends longer to get to us there than to Austin." I turn to Josh like I'm remembering something and put my hand on his knee. "Babe, do you remember how I told you about my girls' trip to Napa for my friend's birthday?"

He nods like he absolutely remembers this conversation about a trip I never took.

"I had the best broccolini there. Sautéed with garlic and lemon, but somehow it had a nutty flavor too. I wish I knew how the chef did it. I've been trying to find a broccolini dish that good ever since." This conversation is stupid. Broccolini isn't even that trendy. Maybe that's why it's extra insulting for her to say it.

Take that, Presley. I go on girls' trips to Napa and eat fancy broccolini dishes. I know my job is only to sell everyone at the table that we're super into each other so Presley will back off, but she's fired some stealth shots, and I can't resist some light payback.

"So what do you do for work, Presley?" I'm honestly curious. Is she expected to work like Josh is, or is she more like an unpaid event planner for charity boards so she can attend fancy galas?

"I handle communications for Reilly Industries." She tucks a strand of hair behind her ear, a graceful movement made with a perfectly manicured finger in pale pink. It's pretty and I'm jealous. I have to keep my nails short for work *and* guitar.

"Oh," I say in surprise, because I am. It sounds like a real job. But she's getting on my nerves, so I unsheathe my metaphorical claws. "I assumed you were going to say a surgeon's office because . . ." I bring my hand up and almost point to my lips before letting my hand and my words both trail away, as if I've just realized that would be a faux pas. Josh's fingers press against my nape, and I can't tell if that's approval or warning. What I do know is they send a tingle straight down my spine, and I fight a shiver.

Presley's eyes narrow. "A Wharton MBA would be wasted in a doctor's office."

Oh, nice. She's got brains. I should lay off, not because she deserves it, but because I've always thought cat fights over a man are tacky, even if I'm only in this one for entertainment and not to win a guy. "Wharton? Well done." I hope she understands that's me offering a truce.

"It's not blood pressure checks in a Medicare facility, but I learned some things."

No truce, I guess.

Elizabeth redirects the conversation. "How's Cin, JP?"

I'm sure Elizabeth is very skilled at reading the subtext between women at social functions, and Presley and her dad turn to updating the Browers on Mrs. Reilly, who sounds like she's into horses, big time.

I lean over to whisper to Josh. I'm caught off-guard by the effect he has on me, and I don't know if he's aware of it, but payback is in order here. I make sure my lips brush the shell of his ear as I whisper, "Sorry."

I'm already settling back in my chair when he meets my eyes, his brimming with amusement.

"Are you though?" he asks softly.

"Of course."

His gaze drops to my mouth. He is *really* selling this fake dating thing. His hand slides from my nape but only for him to lightly brush his thumb along my bottom lip as he asks, "For which part?"

My breath catches at the friction from his touch. His eyes glint. He noticed my reaction, and my competitive drive ramps up. I can't decide if it's my best or worst quality, but he's thrown down a challenge, and I accept.

Poor Josh. Poor, poor Josh. He has no idea what he just got himself into.

I dart the tip of my tongue out, hummingbird-quick, like I want to taste where he touched me. I doubt anyone else noticed, but Josh's eyes widen for a split second, and I can't resist a smirk. And for the second time in five minutes, someone is narrowing their eyes at me.

Oh, it's on.

When the server brings out our meals a few minutes later, the parents have been talking about getting together with the Reillys this summer at their place on South Padre Island. Presley has fallen quiet, but I can't read her well enough to tell if she's pouting or regrouping. My money is on regrouping. Josh has made it clear that she's not a quitter.

I better play this up some more to drive it home. And this is a two-fer because I get to give Josh's knee a gentle squeeze. I feel the base of his quadricep jump against my palm, but I barely have time to reward myself for the point before he retaliates. His hand closes over mine on his knee, and he lifts and turns it over, palm up, to press a kiss in it. I almost drop my fork when I feel the light lick of his tongue against my skin before he raises his head. He settles it back on his leg, but about mid-thigh—much, much higher than his knee—his hand still resting over mine.

It will look like the kind of intimate gesture we've shared often, when in reality, he's got a fairly firm hold on my hand so I can't wiggle it out. I fight a smile. He's crafty, Josh is.

The rest of the night goes like this. Presley tries a couple more times to make me look uncouth. I serve it back to her. Josh plays with my hair, making my scalp break out in goosebumps. I retaliate by softly stroking his arm.

Between the two of them, I'm entertained but in desperate need of a break while we wait on dessert. Presley orders the cheese plate. I order cheesecake.

"Excuse me," I say, sliding my chair back from the table. "Ladies' room."

Josh stands when I do, ever the gentleman, and I use it as a chance to put points on the board, going up on tiptoe to brush my mouth along his jawline and murmur, "I'll be back in a minute." His Adam's apple does a very noticeable up and down, but I'm not so sure I've come out ahead on that one. The rasp of his scruff against my lips seems to have briefly made my knees weak.

I pause, pretending to cover the wobble by smoothing my skirt before I continue toward the restroom. I really hope Josh didn't notice that.

Our game has made the evening far more interesting than I expected it to be, but dining with the Reillys and Browers has only reinforced that Josh and I are a bad fit. Presley hinted at it, but I'm never going to be well-bred enough for people like the Browers.

There was a time when I'd tried to be like Presley, fitting in effortlessly with the country club crowd. I'd wanted this life, a calendar full of socializing with these people. I'd done everything I could to make myself the perfect Presley for Bryce, only to have his mom pull me aside before his family took him out for a graduation dinner to tell me I wasn't invited.

College is done now, she'd said. *Playtime is over and Bryce needs to step into the next phase of his life.*

I'd found out the next day that I was part of his "playtime" when he came over and dumped me. It was all very Elle Woods/Warner in *Legally Blonde.*

I'm not going to turn myself inside out, unravel, and try to remake myself into what they want me to be. I'd lost myself so badly after Bryce. I won't do that again.

I emerge from my stall to find Presley standing in front of the mirror, retouching her lipstick.

"I've known Josh our whole lives," she says. It's conversational, like she's commented on the weather.

"He told me. Said it was fun having another honorary sister around." She'll hate that.

But Presley is done with veiled barbs. She shoves her lipstick into her Chanel bag and turns to face me. I don't bother taking my eyes off the mirror, absorbing myself with the inspection of my eyebrow. I have good eyebrows. Great eyebrows. Well-shaped, if I do say so myself.

"Our fathers are best friends and they've always wanted to be family. They were just waiting for us to grow up so we could marry."

"Oh, like feudal dynasties? Weird. I didn't know people actually did that stuff anymore." I sound distracted because I know it will kill her to think I'm not even giving her all my attention.

"Don't play dumb," she says. "It's taken some time for Josh to be ready, but he and I are a lock. Done deal. It's happening. He'll see it sooner than later. You don't have the background. The history. *I* do."

I give myself a fresh coat of lip gloss. This is one of the rare moments in my life where I'm saying exactly the right thing, the comebacks rolling off my tongue, my brain in high gear. And it's all because I'm not invested in Josh or his future. If I were, my stomach would probably be a mess and I'd be tongue-tied, lucky to come up with even a weak "Oh, yeah?"

But not *actually* wanting Josh doesn't mean I'm going to give Presley this win. The whole point of my big fat payoff is to make her believe that Josh is not an option for her, now or ever. I have to channel some of Lady Mantha's give-em-hell attitude, but I put my lip gloss away and meet Presley's eyes.

"You do have history." I reach over and toy idly with the leather tag on her handbag. "And yet I know Josh in ways you never will." I slide my eyes up to meet hers and give her a small, knowing smile, then step around her and walk out on her soft gasp of outrage.

It was a gamble, but I suspect if Josh had slept with Presley, he would have mentioned it. And I'm very well aware that I've left her to draw the conclusion that Josh and I have gone there. She doesn't need to know that's not how I operate, especially not if it makes her mad enough to drop her Josh campaign.

An hour later, we're back on the road toward home.

"Thanks for doing this," Josh says, shooting a glance my way.

"No problem."

"Liar." He says it without any heat. "Sorry about Presley."

"She's fine," I say.

"She's the worst," he counters.

"True. But I kind of feel sorry for her." If she's been lusting after the touches, grazes, heavy-eyed looks, and even licks that Josh dished out all night, I can understand how it could be an obsession.

You know, if I was her. But I know better.

"Did something happen when you two were in the restroom?" he asks.

"We took our earrings off and brawled like ladies."

He snorts. "I mean it. She came back to the table very . . . subdued."

"I may have led her to believe that you and I have slept together."

The car does a small swerve before he straightens it out. "You told her what?"

"I didn't tell her anything. She made an assumption."

"That you wanted her to make?"

"Yes. And I didn't correct her."

"And now she thinks we're—"

"Yes."

He's quiet for a long beat. "It's not a bad id—"

"I'm not that girl, Josh."

"Right." After another minute he adds, "Sorry."

"Forget about it," I say. "But don't forget that

tonight was a show. We aren't a match, no matter what Ru—" I catch myself before finishing the sentence.

"No matter what Ruby thinks?" he finishes. "Does she think we should be a thing?"

I roll my eyes. "We're not. We gave a convincing performance. Yay, us. Presley is getting the message, and I get to go home and place an order for T-shirts. Everyone wins. Except Presley."

"Except Presley," he echoes. After a moment, he clears his throat. "I kind of feel bad."

"About?"

"Presley."

I whip my head toward him. "Are you kidding me right now?"

He doesn't take his eyes off the road, but his expression is serious. "No."

"Well, don't. Presley thinks she's entitled to you. You didn't break her heart. You hurt her ego. She'll get over it, and no doubt she'll have someone else's giant rock on her finger within a year, and she'll make a point of rubbing your nose in it. She'll talk herself into thinking she's the one that didn't want you, and you're going to be the dumped chump in her story for the rest of your life."

"When you put it like that . . ."

"I'm putting it like that because that's exactly how it'll go. And another thing—"

He winces. "Nothing good has ever followed that."

I take a deep breath because I need to get this "other thing" out before I lose my nerve. "All that stuff at the table? That was to sell the story."

"What stuff?" He sounds confused.

"The flirting."

"Can you be specific?"

"The . . . like, touching. And stuff." It sounds stupid when I say it out loud.

"Fair, but I need examples so I can make sure I don't cross any lines."

By now we're nearing the Grove, and I wish we were already home and this conversation was over. "Don't whisper stuff in my ear, for example."

"Not a go-to move of mine, honestly. No problem. What else?"

"Rubbing my neck."

"Hmm. Too bad. Those muscles felt tense, and I could help, but that's fine. I respect your boundary. What else?"

I'm distracted by the image of him massaging the stress out of my neck at the end of a long day, and I forget to answer.

"Sami?"

I blink. "Um, don't do sexy lip touching."

There's a pause. "You think it's sexy when I touch your lips?" His voice is very even.

This conversation is ridiculous. We had regular

presentations in Pi Phi about setting physical boundaries and claiming our space, but no one ever tells you how awkward it feels.

"That's not what I meant."

"Okay, what did you mean?"

There's the faintest tremor in his voice, and I shoot a quick glance at him—quick enough to catch him smothering a smile.

"Ugh, Josh. You're the worst."

He bursts out laughing as he turns into the Grove. "You made it too easy, Lady Mantha. But for what it's worth, if you want to grope my thighs, kiss my jaw, or taste me at any point, I do not object."

My jaw drops. "That's . . . you . . . we aren't . . ."

He climbs out of the car, still laughing, and even when we part ways at our back fences, another laugh escapes him.

Ruby and Ava are watching the news when I walk in, and Ruby leans forward. "Hey. How'd it go?"

"Fine," I growl, but I don't stop because I need to make sure Josh gets my point. I zoom up the stairs and march out to my balcony. He's already on his, forearms resting on the railing that faces mine, obviously expecting me.

"We are not dating, Josh. We are not flirting. We are just neighbors. Got it?"

"Sure, Sami." He gives me a lazy smile. "I got

it. Goodnight." He straightens and disappears into his place.

I step into my room and close the sliding door as an alert on my phone goes off, the sound of a cash register notifying me I've gotten money. I swipe it open, and sure enough, there it is, as promised. He's marked the transaction private, and the memo reads, "Five star performance."

I stare at it for a minute until the screen goes dark, trying to figure out what's making me anxious. It's not the money. It's . . .

I set my phone down and close my eyes, rubbing my temples as the answer dawns on me.

I'm not sure tonight was an act.

Chapter Fourteen
JOSH

Last night could not have gone better.

I roll to my back, weak gray light slipping around the edges of my blinds before my alarm even goes off. I don't need it. For one, it's a Sunday, and for another, my body clock always wakes me up anyway.

Sami Webster likes me.

That's why I'm waking up with a smile on my face.

Maybe she doesn't even know it yet herself. But her fingertips do. And her lips.

I stare at the ceiling and my eyes drift closed as I remember the feeling of her kneading my shoulder, of her hand tucked into mine, of the warmth of her breath against my jaw.

I sit up, endorphins flooding my system the way they do when I'm into a woman. I haven't had that rush in a while, and I decide to use it as fuel for a run. I'm dressed and out the door in less than ten minutes, and even when I'm met by a chilly morning, I smile. It's brisk. I like it.

It's early, barely 7:00, and the city is still quiet. I run at least a mile before I even see another person. I'll put in a full day of work, but I'll probably do it from home, and it already makes the day feel more relaxed. It's the magic of Sundays. It calls people out of bed for leisurely brunches and afternoon drives.

I wonder what Sami is up to today. She said she doesn't work weekends, and I doubt she has a gig tonight. The bar scene is pretty mellow on Sunday nights. She could have another festival to play or something this afternoon, but she didn't mention it.

If I push a few things off for tomorrow and power through our most pressing contract, I could free up a decent chunk of time. It would be worth it to get time with Sami. But that doesn't mean Sami will want to spend the time with me.

This is tricky. She wants me in the friend zone, but that's not based on a lack of attraction. I'm not cocky, but I know what I felt last night. The air practically vibrated between us, and every touch only charged it more. It wasn't one-sided. Ruby hinted that Sami has reasons for not liking a family *like* mine, but she seemed to like my actual parents fine last night.

I have enough self-respect not to try to talk a woman into dating me. I'd never want someone to go out with me because I wore her down. That's a move for losers. But this . . . this is not that. We click in every way, from our easy nights on the balcony to our obvious chemistry.

I push it out of my head to focus on my run, picking up my pace. I go for another forty minutes before winding down with a jog on the last block back to my condo, sweaty despite the cold. But also, clearheaded. I've figured out what to do about Sami: nothing.

If I'm right about the vibe between us, all I have to do is be around. Make sure our paths cross. Show up for balcony hangs. Because Sami gets under my skin in a way no one else ever has, and I don't understand it yet. But I know if she's even feeling a tenth of the pull toward me that I do toward her, there's no way her walls will stay up. Then we can figure out what we're standing on the verge of. I don't know what it is, but I want to.

Today, instead of clearing time to see if she'll spend it with me, I'll respect her space. Maybe she'll decide it's way less interesting when I'm not in it. And maybe she won't. I'll accept that. But my gut instinct says that's not where this is headed.

And no matter what, I'll be on the balcony tonight.

At home, I shower and change into jeans and a collared shirt and settle into my office. I'm a T-shirt guy by nature, but I've learned the hard way that I concentrate on work better if I'm wearing a collar. Brains are weird. Mine at least doesn't object to jeans for work at home.

It doesn't take long for me to sink into work. We're helping a drilling company acquire a competitor, and the merger involves some complicated mineral rights. I need to comb through all their disclosures for any hidden contingencies that can hurt our client. Since those things are hidden with language so redundant and boring it's more effective than Ambien, it means reading and re-reading very closely. For hours.

I break it up by getting up every half hour to run to the mailbox or do pull-ups on the bar installed over my office door. Then it's right back to the legalese. There's nothing *easy* about it.

Around lunch, my doorbell rings, and I look up from the contract, smiling. Sami. She couldn't resist coming over. Even if it's to give me another speech about no flirting, I want to see her.

But it's not Sami on my doorstep. It's Presley, and she's by herself.

"Pres. Hey." I don't bother asking her how she got my address. Either of my parents would have given it to her simply because she asked. "What are you doing here?"

"I wanted to see your new place. Aren't you going to invite me in?"

So she can mentally redecorate it with a feminine touch? Pass. Except that's not an option, so I step back and let her through. I give her plenty of room, but somehow, her forearm still ends up grazing my abs.

"It's nice," she says. "I prefer houses to condos, but this is nice."

"I can't afford a house. I had to save for two years for this condo."

She smiles as if the idea of having to save up for anything is cute. "Your parents would help you."

"They've done enough."

"Manly pride," she says, brushing past me again and trailing her fingers across my chest on her way to the kitchen. "Much better than that last borderline dorm you were living in."

I stay put. The less I give her, the sooner she'll leave. "It was an apartment." A mid-price apartment I shared with two roommates while we all worked and saved. Not a borderline dorm.

"Whatever. This is at least better than that." She walks out of the kitchen. "And how about upstairs?"

I step back and wave her up. "Feel free."

She climbs the stairs, making sure she puts some extra sway in her hips. I roll my eyes. I follow her up, running into her just as she's stepping into my office. "I spend a lot of time here," I tell her. "Probably more than my bedroom. Maybe as much as at the firm. I work a lot."

"Wow," she says, sounding amused. "It's lucky you have any time for Savannah."

"Samantha," I say, correcting her even though I'm positive she remembers Sami's name. "And yes, she's about the only thing I make time for outside of work."

"Mmm." She makes the noncommittal sound as she walks past me to my bedroom.

I wait, fighting a smile, and there it is, a sharp gasp.

"Josh? What is this?"

I stroll into the room. She's staring at Bernice, whose tank sits on a bench next to my bathroom door. Presley is backed against the foot of my bed at the far corner, as opposite as she can get from the snake.

"Who, Bernice?"

"Yes." She practically hisses it, which feels appropriate.

"You like her? I figure part of maturing is taking care of other living things."

"Most people get a dog." She eyes the tank like it's harboring something nasty, not just a three-foot pet boa.

"Snakes make great pets." I only have Bernice for five more weeks before she goes back to her owner, but I'm not going to clarify. "Boas don't even bite." I reach into the tank to pick Bernice up, sure it'll send Presley straight out of my house. "As long as you feed them regularly—"

Wait, when *did* I feed Bernice last? I don't think she's due for a meal for another day or two, but—

"Ah, dammit!" I yell as Bernice sinks her fangs into me to let me know that she is, in fact, hungry.

"Aaaaah!" Presley screams, and I swear, she looks like she's about to faint.

I can't do anything about that because I've got a boa fastened to the meaty part of my hand, her jaws clasped below the base of my thumb. Rubbing alcohol will make them let go because they hate the smell, but I don't have any.

"Pres, stop screaming," I grit out. "Boas aren't venomous. Do you have any hand sanitizer?"

She doesn't stop screaming.

"I mean it," I yell loud enough to be heard over her shrieks. "Calm down. I'm fine. Pres! Seriously, stop!" She subsides to a whimper. "Hand sanitizer?"

She gives me a blank stare before she digs in her purse and hands me a small bottle. Lemonade scented. I hope Bernice can still smell the alcohol as I squeeze a small drop on her snout. She lets go after a couple of seconds, and I finally get her back into the tank with her lid secure.

My hand throbs where she punctured the skin, and I turn to find Presley shrunken into the corner. "Pres, it's okay. I'm okay. Bernice is back in her tank."

She takes a deep, shaky breath. "Why would you have a snake?"

Is she seriously blaming me for getting bitten?

Well, okay, it *is* my fault; I obviously needed to

feed Bernice sooner. But still, not what I want to hear when I'm standing there with sharp pains in my hand.

"I'm calling 911," she says, digging into her purse for her phone.

"No," I tell her. "I'm fine. I'll go to a walk-in clinic to get this looked at. Ambulances are expensive."

"I'll pay for it," she almost yells, an edge of hysteria in her voice.

"Is your dad still in town?" I ask. I need her out of my hair.

"No, he flew home."

"No problem." I slide my phone from my pocket and order a Lyft. "I got you a rideshare to take you back to your place. Go ahead and wait outside while I get this taken care of."

"I don't want to leave you here."

I hold my hand up. It's bleeding. Not terribly, but it's not nothing. "Then come help me take care of this."

She looks like she's going to pass out again.

That's what I thought. "I appreciate the concern, but truly, getting yourself home would be the most help to me right now. I'll make sure your car gets over there later."

She hesitates, then as if realizing having me drive her car over will give her a golden opportunity to monopolize me again, she nods and hurries to the bedroom door, skirting around me and not quite looking me in the eye as she says, "Get that checked."

A few seconds later, I hear the front door close behind her.

I run my hand under the faucet in my bathroom and clean it well with soap and water. When I'm sure I've washed it as well as I can, I cut the water and grab a dark hand towel from the set Reagan bought.

Even though boas aren't poisonous, I don't know enough about snakebites to know if Presley's right and I should go get checked out anyway. I wish there was a hotline to call before I go in for a potentially overcautious visit, like with a doctor or—

Or the nurse who lives next door.

I'd give myself a facepalm if I had a free hand to do it. I'm just going to say the snake germs made my brain slow for a second or I would have thought of that sooner.

I poke my head out of the balcony door, but it's no surprise not to find Sami there. I hurry down the stairs, the towel still pressed against the punctures, and head next door to give three sharp knocks before I have to staunch the wound again.

Ruby opens the door, her eyes widening when she sees my first aid situation.

"You okay?" she asks.

"Is Sami home? I'm thinking I need her help."

"Absolutely." She waves me to the sofa even

as she heads upstairs, calling Sami's name.

Sami appears within moments, wearing loose pajama bottoms and a concerned expression. "What's wrong?"

"Bernice bit me."

Ruby looks confused.

"His boa," Sami explains, already reaching for my swaddled hand.

"Not mine. Pet sitting." It's not awful pain, but it's uncomfortable as Sami pulls back the cloth to look.

Ruby nods and whips out her phone.

"What happened?" Sami asks as she peers at the punctures.

"I thought Bernice didn't need to eat for a day or two. She thought differently. She's usually safe to handle, but I guess not when she's hangry."

"Same," Sami says without missing a beat. "You cleaned it out already?"

I wince as she touches the skin right next to one of the fang marks. "Yeah. Water and antibacterial soap."

"You just need to put some ointment on it and feed Bernice," Ruby says.

I shoot a look at Sami, who smiles.

"She's the queen of research. If that's what she found, then it's right. We should make sure your tetanus is up to date too. Hang on while I get the first aid kit."

"I got it," Ruby says.

Sami nods, and I'm glad she's staying with me. She's cradling my palm, her touch gentle as she checks and rechecks the bite.

The front door opens and a dark-haired good-looking guy walks in, pausing when he sees me on the sofa with Sami bent over my hand. "Did I interrupt something?" There's a trace of a laugh in his voice.

"Nothing like you're thinking, perv," Sami says without any heat. "Josh, meet Ruby's brother, Joey. Joey, this is the new neighbor, Josh. A boa bit his hand."

Joey cocks his head at me. "For real?"

I nod. "Yep."

"Cool story, bro. Chicks dig scars, right, Sam?"

She shrugs. "If it's not a good time, it's a good story."

Ruby walks back in with a first aid kit. "Joseph. Go away."

"Don't be like that, kiddo," he says, grinning.

"Don't call me kiddo and I won't be like that. What do you want?"

I shoot a look at Sami, trying to gain some insight into their family dynamic. She catches my eye and gives a short shake of her head. Aloud she says, "I'm going to take Josh back to his place to finish this up and make sure he has what he needs for wound care."

She stands, keeping her hand lightly clasped around my wrist below my injury, and tows me behind her to the door. Does she even realize she's still holding on to me? I'm not about to point it out.

As we're stepping out, Joey says, "Moms said to tell you—" and Ruby interrupts with "Mom, singular. There is no *s*. There is only one of her."

Joey is coming back with something, but Sami pulls the door shut on the argument.

"They don't get along?" I ask as we walk to my door.

"He's her favorite brother, actually," Sami says. "It's just how they talk to each other."

"Got it." I understand, in a way. It's kind of like when Reagan sends me a card comparing me buying my own place to getting big boy underpants. "Hey, thanks for the nursing. I owe you big time."

She opens my door and points me to the sofa. "Sit by the window so I have good light."

I obey, and she sinks onto the cushion next to me, pulling back the towel again to check.

"The bleeding is definitely slowing, but you need to apply pressure for a little longer." But she does it, creating a firm but not uncomfortable grip around the bite marks. "Does that hurt?"

I shake my head. "How do I find out if my tetanus is up to date?"

Her lips twitch. "Do what I do. Ask your mom."

"Seriously?"

She nods. "Moms always know. I never remember that stuff."

I work my phone free and send a voice text. "Mom, is my tetanus current?" I barely set the phone down when it rings with her number.

Sami grins. "What did you think was going to happen?"

I answer the phone. "I'm fine, Mom . . . small incident, no big—" She keeps cutting me off, and I give Sami an eyeroll. "With a snake . . . yes, Wade's . . . no, it was my fault . . . you don't need to do that . . . really, I'm fine . . ." She's fussing between every breath I take, so I give her something she can't argue with. "Remember my girlfriend is a nurse? And she's right here taking care of it."

Sami looks mildly startled but says nothing.

"Seriously, Mom, I'm good . . . yes, still coming for dinner . . . no, she can't. She has to work." I flick a glance at Sami, who my mom is now insisting should come to Sunday family dinner. "Yes, on Sunday . . . nurses don't have regular hours . . . She would if she could, but—"

Sami slips the phone from my fingers. "Mrs. Brower? . . . Okay, Miss Elizabeth then. He's fine, I promise. Nurse's honor." She listens intently to whatever my mom is saying. "Yes, ma'am . . . No, ma'am . . . He was mistaken about my schedule." She gives me a measuring look. "Sure, we'll do that. See you then." She hangs up the phone before handing it back to me.

"What was that all about?" I ask.

"Guess I'm going to family dinner," she says. "I'm not charging you for it, but believe me, Josh..."

She leans forward to fix me with a stare, and I have to fight not to let my eyes slip to her cleavage. "I'll find a way to make you pay."

Chapter Fifteen
SAMI

Elizabeth Brower is a hard woman to say no to. And honestly, I feel better about being able to monitor Josh's bite anyway. I doubt anything will happen to it, but since this is my first time treating a snakebite, I don't know what I don't know. I did bookmark the link Ruby sent me about nonvenomous snakebites for good measure.

"Sunday dinner" apparently means be there way before a traditional mealtime and prepare to stay awhile, but I only sigh when Josh tells me we'll be heading to his parents' place around 3:00.

I leave him after making him promise to run over if his wound does anything weird. It leaves me three hours to do some research on local producers and recording studios. As an indie group, we'll have to book and pay for our studio time, but that's not hard if you have the money, which we do now, thanks to my country club one-act show.

Finding a good producer is harder. They won't put their name on just anything. They want to know they're working with talent because their reputation is on the line too. I've spent many hours in the last few months listening to some of the local bands, and I've narrowed in on who I want; it's the same producer Night View works with, a girl named Gentry Hawk. That is one hundred percent a stage name, but who is Lady Mantha to judge? Unfortunately, she's *hard* to book.

I think the best game plan here is to book studio time to record a tight demo, kill it when we perform with Night View in a couple of weeks, and then see if they're impressed enough to recommend us to Gentry Hawk.

By the time I find a studio time that works for the rest of the band and reserve it, I've only left myself fifteen minutes to get ready for Brower Family Dinner. I'm sure it's not as formal as the country club, but with every Brower at dinner last night sporting a haircut that cost more than my Doc Martens, I don't want to be caught out.

I rifle quickly through my closet and pull out a dress that should do the job. It's a floral sheath dress, yellow flowers on a white background, cap sleeves, boat neck, and knee-length hem. It's more of a spring dress, but I like the idea of cheerful yellow flowers in January, and besides, it has the most parent-approved cut and fit of any dress I own. I pair it with black wedges and work my hair into a fast French braid. That's how I wear it for work to keep it out of my way, and I can do the whole thing in three minutes.

That gives me five to fix my face, so I opt for winged eyeliner but a soft pink lipstick. I'm finishing my mascara when I hear a knock at the door followed by Ruby calling my name.

Josh smiles when I come down, but I frown.

"You look great," he says, running a glance over my outfit.

"I look overdressed." He's wearing faded jeans and a Cowboys jersey with Nikes. "I'll go change."

He glances at his watch, his expression uneasy. "It's fine, I promise. Punctuality is kind of a big deal to my dad. I promise, you look adorable."

I try not to wrinkle my nose at this. Petite women get called cute all the time. Adorable is even worse. Like we're kittens or pixies. It's part of why I chose that name for our band: the huge performance I try to give is the exact opposite of what people would expect from a darling little pixie.

Adorable doesn't suggest sexiness or love vibes. It suggests pats on the head and cuddles. That would be fine if I were an actual kitten.

And actually, it's fine if Josh thinks of me as adorable because I don't want or need him thinking of me as sexy. So I don't argue. Instead, I say, "I'm ready to go."

We head toward Tarrytown because of course we do. It's the most affluent section of Austin. Where else would the Browers live? I grill him on his injury, but it sounds like it's doing fine.

"Let me double-check it," I say.

He shakes his head but lifts his right hand from the steering wheel and extends it toward me, resting his arm on the console between us. It reminds me of hand-holding practice last night, and I fight the urge to wrap my hand in his.

I shake it off, touching him lightly as I study the bandage I put on him earlier. It's an awkward location for regular Band-Aids, so I used adhesive cloth tape to secure a gauze pad that runs from the back of his hand to the palm. It's not weeping, and the bandage is secure.

"Looks good," I say. "Still not hurting?"

"Nope."

"At all?" I know it's been three hours, but I've stubbed toes that still vaguely throb three hours later.

"It's nothing."

"So it does hurt a little." When he shrugs, I tap lightly in the middle of his palm, well away from his bandages, to make a point. "It's okay if it hurts." Each tap is like a nose boop, a "listen up."

He glances my way. "Okay. It kind of hurts."

"Is it because a reptile punched four holes in your hand with its teeth?" He gives a soft snort-laugh. "Take any ibuprofen?" I'd told him to take at least 600 milligrams when I left him earlier.

"It's fine, I don't need it."

I shake my head and lean back against my seat,

letting go of his hand because I'm distracted by how much I like touching it. "Every other medical professional has to deal with drug seekers, and I get the guy who won't take an Advil."

"Your love is my drug," he says, his tone serious.

It's my turn to laugh. "I can't even say something like that for show. I'd never be able to do it with a straight face."

He grins at me. "Honestly, just be how we usually are but maybe with some touching, and that's all it will take."

A warm tingle dances across the top of my cheekbones when he says "touching" because some part of me is still a sixth grader. I don't know how else to explain the sudden nervous giggle I keep from bubbling up.

Needing to break the tension, I look for a change of subject. "You mentioned your grandpa but not your grandma. Did she pass?"

Josh's face loses its smile. "She did. Gramps is doing okay though."

His voice is tight, and I wish I could snatch the question back. Instead, I say only, "I'm sorry to hear about her," and ask him about if his grandfather still works at the firm. Josh spends the remaining drive telling me about how his grandfather founded the firm and ran it until he retired fifteen years ago. His body relaxes the longer he talks. By the time we pull into a residential neighborhood, he's back to the usual, easygoing Josh I'm used to.

We turn into the driveway of his parents' home, one of those big semicircle pull-through ones, paved with actual rock, not concrete, and my nerves sort of . . . wobble. He grew up in a mansion. A legit mansion—big piece of property, columns, huge double doors that a butler is probably going to answer.

They don't have to actually like you, I remind myself. I only have to make them believe that at least for right now, Josh is into me, and Presley isn't an option. I can do that. I press my hand to my stomach as Josh climbs out of the car and draw a steadying breath. I'm reaching for the door when it opens, Josh standing there with a hand extended to help me out.

I stand and barely have time to register again how mismatched we look before three dogs come bounding around the side of the house, making happy yipping noises.

"They're friendly," he says when I step back against the car.

"I'm not worried," I say. "That was just a whole lot of fur coming at me at once."

They've all skidded to a stop at his feet, nosing his legs and panting with excitement. "Meet Tater, Bean, and Queso." He bends and gives them head rubs and belly scratches, but he's badly outnumbered, so I crouch to help. He smiles at me across the dogs as one of them licks my hand.

"All right, that's enough, troublemakers." He stands and helps me straighten again, only this time, he keeps hold of my hand as he turns us toward the door. "Thanks for doing this. Again." He gives my hand a gentle squeeze.

"Sure, neighbor. Snakebite first aid. Fake girlfriending. All part of the Grove welcome experience."

He smiles but it's already fading as he looks toward the house. I can't figure out his dynamic with his parents. There's a friction there that I can't identify. They seemed watchful last night at dinner, and I had chalked it up to them observing their son with someone he'd declared he was madly in love with. Josh had seemed to be slightly on edge, but I figured it was because of Presley.

He still has that same energy about him now. It's not a sharp feeling, but it's there in the hints, like his fading smile. The deep breath he's trying to quietly draw as we start toward the house. His hand tightening around mine again, almost a spasm, like he's drawing reassurance rather than giving it.

Hmm. Interesting. I'm going to have some questions for Josh on the drive home.

We walk through the imposing double doors into a foyer of marble flooring beneath a chandelier. No butler. No Browers to greet us either, but there's plenty of ruckus coming from farther back in the house.

"Game day," he says. "We're in the—"

"Playoffs," I tell him. "I know. I follow football. You should probably know that about me." I can't resist resting my chin on his chest—possible only because of my wedge heels—and smiling up at him, eyelashes batting. "Sweetheart."

He answers by letting go of my hand and swatting my bum.

I squeak and he laughs. "You should probably know that's how I show affection."

"The price went up."

He smirks. "From what?"

"I haven't decided yet, and that should worry you."

He doesn't look sorry as he quirks his head toward the sound of cheering, and we walk farther into the house, the smell of roasting meat becoming stronger, the TV and people chatter growing louder.

"Hey, y'all," he says as we step into their family room. It's too big a space for such a cozy description, but that's kind of how it feels. There are more faces than I can process quickly, all flopped around on the large leather sectional or sprawled on the thick carpet on the floor, every eye fixed on the TV until Josh speaks, and suddenly all those eyeballs are fixed on us.

I recognize his parents right away, but there's also a couple in their early thirties, a five-year-old girl on the carpet, and a toddler boy sitting on an old man's lap, trying to feed him pretzels.

Also, I'm so overdressed. Like, there's a touch of pity in the woman I assume is his sister's eyes when they meet mine before she smiles.

I'm going to kill Josh. Something slower than boa constriction.

"You missed kickoff, son," Mr. Brower says.

Josh stiffens slightly. It's only two minutes into the first quarter, but he doesn't point that out. "Had a snakebite and all."

"I want to see, Uncle Joshy!" The girl on the carpet jumps up and hurtles toward us. He manages to let go of me and angle his body in time to scoop her up with his uninjured hand.

His mom is hurrying toward us. "Good to see you again, Samantha. That's a very pretty dress."

I don't know what to do here. Play it off? Draw attention to the fact that I realize I'm overdressed? Act like I'm coming from some other event? By the time I stammer out a belated "thank you," she's already fussing over Josh's hand.

"You had your tetanus seven years ago before we went on safari," she says. "But I still want you to go see Dr. Nicholls to be sure."

Safari? I mouth at him. I don't even know why I'm surprised. Pi Phi girls came back from school breaks all the time reporting on St. Tropez or Germany or freaking safari.

"Just the picture-taking kind," he tells me. "Gramps hunts, that's it."

"I only take what I eat," the old man calls from the sofa.

"I'm not judging," I say. Maybe I am, a little. I can't say I understand hunting, but that's why I try not to judge: haven't done it, can't judge it.

"Dinner after the game," Mr. Brower says. "Come watch."

I'd feel more in my skin if I were in my stage costume than this prim Sunday School dress. Josh leads me over to the other couple and introduces me to his sister, Reagan, her husband, Trace, and their kids, Stella and Beau. I shake hands awkwardly with the couple, and Stella wiggles her way out of Josh's arms to reclaim her spot on the carpet, no attention spared for me. Beau doesn't seem to care either, just leaning against his great-grandpa's chest as his eyelids droop.

Josh and I take the unclaimed wing of the sectional, and he settles me against his side, brushing his lips against my hair as a pretext to ask, "You okay?"

I nod.

With his head still close to mine, he presses the issue. "You seem very different from last night. You sure?"

I'm not okay. I'm nervous and unsettled. This

is way too similar to one of the worst days of my relationship with Bryce, only I hadn't known in the middle of it that it was about to become one of my worst days. Last night had been fine because I understood an opponent like Presley. I'd known dozens of her in the sorority, and I knew exactly where to poke to make her mad.

But the Browers? I don't get them. I never have. I don't understand casual references to safaris when my mom had to save up money for a weekend trip to Six Flags and a stay at Motel 6. That was the *nice* choice because it had a pool.

Josh is waiting for an answer, so I settle farther into his side, hoping he'll take it as me selling the fake dating story. In reality, I want to be less visible at this moment, with my stupid bright yellow flowers chirping, "Look at me." "I'm fine," I say like I mean it. Such a liar.

We watch the game for a bit. I do like football, but I'm not a big yeller. Josh, his dad, Gramps, and sister are, getting super invested in each play. Trace and Mrs. Brower exchange amused glances when our team misses a field goal and Reagan goes off on a rant of almost-swears like we lost the whole game. But her husband and mom don't say anything. The look says, "Gotta love her."

"Do you like football, Samantha?" Gramps asks during a commercial.

"I do, but I didn't start following it until college." My mom and I were more likely to turn on the news or a talk show if we watched TV together. I wonder if I would have grown up as vocal as Reagan is about it if I'd had a dad around.

I have a long list of wonders like that. What ifs. But I've learned to live with never knowing.

"We get nuts around here," Gramps says. "You can yell if you like."

"Thank you, sir. I'll remember that," I tell him.

During the break after the first quarter, I lean over and tell Josh we need to check his wound. I've tucked the supplies I need to dress it in my purse.

He stands and pulls me to his feet with his good hand. "Sure, let's head to the kitchen."

"Ew, Josh, no. I'm not changing a bandage in a kitchen. Find a bathroom."

"Yeah, Josh," Reagan says. "You're such a dude."

Josh ignores Reagan and slips his hand around mine as he turns toward the hall leading back toward the front of the house. Halfway down it, he stops at a door.

"Here we go." He flips a light and we're standing on the threshold of a bathroom the size of my bedroom.

I've learned not to gawk; any time I went home for a weekend with one of my sorority sisters, it was like this. I may not show it with a dropped jaw or lifted eyebrow, but I'm not sure I'll ever get used to this. Chandeliers and marble bathrooms. Real brass faucets and towels that had to cost at least as much as my TJ Maxx dress. Each.

"Sit." I point to the closed toilet lid, and he obeys, holding his hand out for me. I pull the gauze and bandages from my purse.

"You doing okay?" he asks.

I shoot a look at him. "Of course. You?"

"Same. But I grew up in this house, so that's kind of normal. You're getting a lot of Browers today."

I shrug. "It's fine." I unwind the bandaging on his hand and check the bite. "Looks good. We'll do some ointment again, but next time, just wrap it without. You'll want to keep it dry."

"Why is ointment a gross word?" he asks.

"Is it?"

"Sami." His voice is disbelieving.

"Oh, I'm Sami now?" I don't know why I say it. It doesn't matter what he calls me in front of his family.

"Yes, Sami. You're Sami. Ointment is a gross word. Tell me you know this."

I finish wrapping the wound up and tuck in the loose end. "Of course I know that. Everyone knows that."

"Are you having fun?"

I straighten and meet his eyes, his question putting me on guard. "Doing first aid on my day off?"

"Hanging out with my family."

No. I'm not comfortable in these kinds of environments. But again, it doesn't matter how I feel around his family. "Yeah. It's a good game."

His phone buzzes with a text. He slides it from his pocket and sighs. "Presley."

I fight a laugh. "You better check it."

"No, thank you."

"Please?" I say. "Consider it my payment for this unscheduled appearance."

He shakes his head but reads the text, a smile spreading across his face as he turns it toward me.

PRESLEY: My friend Conrad will pick up my car for me tomorrow. Hope your bite is better. Text me when you're done with both of the snakes in your life. I'm not waiting around Austin for you to figure this out.

"Wow." I almost flick my tongue at him, snake-like, but I catch myself in time to recognize that this is a bad idea. At least, it is if I don't want Josh to think about our flirting last night, and remember that we're behind a closed bathroom door, and have his mind move on to kissing.

Then again . . .

I get hold of myself and give him a snake-ish *hisssssss*. No tongue flicking.

He grabs me around the waist and pulls me

into his lap, settling his face into the curve of my neck and hugging me. "You are a goddess among women. I owe you forever."

I laugh—tricky, since he's stolen my breath with the feel of his thighs beneath mine and the warmth of his chest against my back. Then I loosen his arms, stand and wash my hands, and turn toward the bathroom door. "I'm going to go graze on the appetizers."

As I open it, his dad calls, "Josh! Second quarter!"

I walk out, not looking to see whether he follows. I'm not mad at him. I just . . . I need a break. I need air that smells less like wealth and expensive leather sectionals, and more like . . .

Fritos.

I follow my nose to the kitchen. Trace and Mr. Brower have small empty plates that hint of snacks, and sure enough, there's a seven-layer dip, a few jalapeno poppers, and some of the fat Fritos for scooping.

This is my kind of finger food.

I scoop up enough bean dip to equal an entire serving size, and I'm biting into a popper to chase it down when Gramps walks into the room. I hold a hand up to my mouth to spare him the sight of the mastication massacre.

"Gal, you best not be ruining your appetite," he says. "I make the best brisket for a hundred miles."

Gramps carries himself like he's tall, but age has curled his shoulders slightly, and I would bet he's not as tall as he was in his youth. He's got a full head of hair but it's snowy white, and I guess him to be around eighty-five. I'd put money on it. I'm an expert these days.

Maybe more than carrying himself like he's tall, he carries himself like he's never worried about how much space he takes up in a room. It's a Texas cowboy thing, and I like it. I'm used to it, even. I feel comfortable for the first time since I stepped into the house. Maybe it's the glint in his eye that hints at a sense of humor, or maybe it's the lines around his mouth and eyes that say they've done more laughing than scowling. Maybe it's just being around old people all day long.

Whatever it is, I relax and lean against the counter, studying him. "That is a bold claim to make in Travis County." The heart of Texas barbecue is Austin, no matter what Dallas tries to say.

"You don't get to my age by making unsubstantiated claims." He sounds smug, and I grin.

"Ninety-two?" He looks offended and I laugh. "Kidding, sir. You're eighty-five."

"Is that a fact, smarty-pants?"

"That is a fact."

He sniffs. "Josh told you."

"No, sir. Am I wrong?"

He eyes me. "Made eighty-five in October."

"Please say you're a Libra and not a Scorpio."

"You believe all that nonsense?"

"Not even a little bit."

He gives a cackle. "You're all right, girl."

Somehow, it doesn't bother me when the old people call me girl. I half expect him to offer me a Werther's.

Mr. Brower walks in and pulls a beer from the fridge. "Hey, Pops. How's the brisket?"

"Do you even have to ask?" The older man opens the French doors leading out to a gorgeous patio and yard. A smoker sits near the doors, and a delicious whiff wafts in as he examines the temperature.

Mr. Brower chuckles. "No, I don't. Can't wait. You're in for a real treat, Samantha."

"Thanks for letting me crash your family dinner, Mr. Brower."

"Just Steve is fine," he says.

Nope. I can see calling Josh's mom Miss Elizabeth but there is no way this guy will ever be Steve. I smile because I feel stiff again, and any response I think of sounds wooden and weird.

Josh calls, "Game's on," and Mr. Brower tips his beer at me in salute before heading back to the others.

"Need help?" I ask Gramps. I wouldn't mind an excuse to put off returning to the rest of the family.

"I do not." He straightens and walks in, closing the patio door behind him. "Can't let anyone else fool with it or it ruins the magic."

I stifle a sigh and head back to the game. I try to respond to any questions or comments directed at me, but otherwise, I don't say much. It's just the constant feeling that whatever I say will come out wrong. It's how I always felt around Bryce's family too; the harder I'd tried to fit in, the worse I seemed to.

Josh shoots me a few questioning looks, but I only smile and shake my head, like *I'm fine*.

The game ends and we lose, but the Brower clan takes it well since it's as deep as we've gone in the playoffs in a long time. Gramps stands. "Let's eat."

Mr. and Mrs. Brower climb to their feet and follow him into the kitchen. I start to rise too but Josh lays his hand on my arm and holds me in place, his touch light. "They're going to get everything ready. We'll serve ourselves buffet style. We'll be in charge of cleanup."

Reagan nods. "Truly, don't worry about it." She gives Josh a searching look. "Have they come by to see your place yet?"

His lips flatten into a straight line for a fraction of a second before he shakes his head. "Not yet."

She sighs. "I'm sorry."

He shrugs. "They'll get around to it eventually."

"So how's work?" she asks.

I listen as he tells her, but I can't help but feel like they had a much bigger, deeper conversation in that short exchange about his parents visiting his condo. He's been living there almost three weeks. They live fifteen minutes away. Why haven't they seen it?

I consider the interactions I've seen between them. If he had an open relationship with them, why would I need to be his fake girlfriend? And as I rethink more of their exchanges, I see slight undercurrents of tension I missed before.

It causes me to pay close attention when we settle around their large dining room table to eat. The slight curves bracketing Josh's mouth. The way his dad studies him, like he's watching for something. But for what? The way Reagan and Mrs. Brower keep the conversation moving as if they're afraid of letting quiet moments in.

I replay balcony talks with Josh as I listen, trying to hear hints I might have missed, or spaces that appear in hindsight when you're looking for them. A space like your parents not coming to visit the first place you've bought.

When dinner is over, Josh, Reagan, and Trace all stand and begin collecting plates and dishes for cleanup. I stand too, but Mrs. Brower waves me back into my seat. "You don't have to clean, Samantha. You're company."

It stings. Again, it reminds me of Bryce's family, the way his mother especially made sure

I understood I wasn't family. Maybe it's because Mrs. Brower calling me "Samantha" feels so formal. Maybe it's because she doesn't call me "honey" or "sweetie."

Whatever it is, I keep a smile on my face, and when Josh's parents and Gramps finally rise from the table, I do too and speed into the family room, sitting with his niece on the floor and helping her with a puzzle until Josh comes in about fifteen minutes later.

"I should get you home," he says, holding out his good hand to pull me up.

Once again, I'm distracted by how much I like the slide of his palm against mine, but it's not even close to enough to offset the sour feeling in my stomach, the one that has grown more acidic as the evening goes on.

Neither of his parents object. There's no "Oh, so soon?" No transparent efforts to keep Josh longer. Whenever we visit Ruby's family, they're constantly wheedling their kids to stay longer, and none of the kids is ever in a hurry to leave.

It's not my problem, I know. But I'm so glad when dinner is over, and I wonder if Josh feels that way too. But that kind of information, that's not something that's relevant for two people on their second and final fake date. Or even for neighbors to know about each other. When we get in the car, I don't bring it up. Maybe it was my imagination anyway.

Josh puts us on the road toward home and throws a smile my way. "Thanks for pinch hitting."

"Sure," I say. "But you're lucky it was brisket because I wouldn't have done it for anything else."

He laughs. "Gramps wasn't lying. It really is that good, huh?"

"It really is. I like your Gramps."

"Yeah." He falls quiet, but he's still smiling, an affectionate smile, like he's recalling a memory. "He's the best."

We fall into an easy quiet for the rest of the drive, the way we do on our balconies sometimes. His arm rests on the console between us, and I reach over and turn it so his injured hand is palm up. I'm not worried about it, but I couldn't have stopped myself from touching him if I wanted to. But I didn't want to. Probably what I need is a hug from Ruby when I get home to chase off the vibes of the Brower house, but Josh is here *now*.

I feather my fingers over the skin around the bandage. The warmth helps.

"Still look okay?" His voice has a slight rasp.

"Looks good." I should let go, turn away, think about other things. The lyrics that keep trying to be something in my brain. The show we have coming up next weekend. But I don't. I just let my fingertips play over and around his palm, straying too far from the bandage to pretend that it's about first aid anymore.

He says nothing else, only keeps his hand where it is, his eyes on the road like he senses watching me will scare me off. He's right.

When we turn into the Grove parking lot, the minor jostle of moving from asphalt to concrete breaks the spell, and when Josh pulls into his space, my hands are in my lap, my eyes fixed out the window.

We get out and walk to the sidewalk, me near our gate, him by his. Light leaks from our living room into the kitchen, but the kitchen light itself is off. Josh's condo is dark.

He flips his keys around on his finger. "Thank you again for doing that."

"I got brisket. No thanks needed."

He nods then hesitates before he steps toward me, sliding his keys into his pocket and reaching toward me. I let him, his hand closing around my wrist, a soft touch as he pulls me in, like he's making sure I know I can walk away. He draws me against his chest, the top of my head not quite reaching his collarbone. It puts me at the perfect height to hear his heartbeat, strong and steady.

"I can't thank you enough. You've bought me so much peace of mind over the last couple of days. Presley can be disruptive, and it's been so good not dealing with her. I think she gets it now."

"Glad to be Presley deterrent."

His quiet laugh rumbles against my ear. "It's more than that. You're just . . . it's been good."

I wonder what he left out in that pause. "No problem."

"I'm not sure what happened at pho, but . . ." He leans back and I tilt my head up to see what he wants. "We could pretend some more. It's pretty fun." He hooks a strand of hair that's fallen into my eyes and tucks it behind my ear.

I go still, eyes searching his in the dim lights of the parking lot. For a second—no, even less—I consider it, an image flashing through my mind of how it would feel to turn my face into his palm, to step back into the warmth of his chest. Instead, I give a small laugh and I hope it hides how much I'm rethinking my decision to go with him. I keep a smile on my face and step away.

"Nice try, Josh. But unless you can smoke a brisket like Gramps . . ."

His head drops in mock dejection. "He's a master. I don't have a shot."

I pat his arm and turn for my gate. "Text if your snakebite acts up." Then I slip into the condo, fighting the urge to check if he's watching me go.

Chapter Sixteen
SAMI

I push through the door of Nine-Nine Studios and try to figure out what to do about my nerves. I don't want to subdue them—they feed my performances. But this isn't a live performance; it's our first chance to record in a real studio. The point is *not* to sound too raw.

The guys are coming in behind me, lugging their instruments. A buzz vibrates from them, even Rodney, who betrayed his excitement by the constant tapping of his fingers on the steering wheel as we drove over.

We've agreed we need to use my *Pretty Woman* windfall to pay for the recording. They think it's a work bonus. And it's not *not* a work bonus, technically. I had to work to get it. We'll put our tailgate festival pay toward an initial T-shirt order, but we want to have some high-quality tracks to point Gentry Hawk to if Night View is willing to hook us up.

If they aren't, well . . .

I guess one of us is going to have to get up the guts to introduce ourselves to her and hope we don't put her off too much to listen to our music.

But it all starts with a good session tonight, and

three of us have never been in a real recording studio. I'm one of them. My perception has been shaped entirely by TV and movies.

A guy my age, maybe a little younger, behind the front desk looks up with a polite smile when we walk in. "You Pixie Luna?"

"We are," I confirm.

"I'm Jethro, the engineer. Let's get you set up."

We follow him to a studio. The hall is lined with band photos of Austin groups. Some have never grown past regional fame. Other photos are of bands anyone could name but from their early days. This is a good place to start, and the thrumming in my stomach says we really are at the beginning of *something*. Something more than local club gigs.

Nine-Nine has a main studio with the big soundboard and mixer, another small one next to it, and five rehearsal rooms. He directs us to leave our equipment in the hall and follow him into the main studio.

"Let's review how this is going to go," he says. "We're cutting a demo, so four songs. We're looking at ten hours, and you guys have to do it over two nights."

"Yeah. We work, and we have shows on the weekends," Luther says.

Jethro nods. "That's pretty typical. It's better if we can do it in a single day, but it's hard for anyone to make that work. It is what it is." He points to me. "Vocals?"

"That's me." We'd sent him our songs earlier in the week, and since I'm the only girl here, he's reached the obvious conclusion.

"Cool. I like your sound."

I hug the compliment close. This is a guy who hears a lot of music, so it means something to me. He has the rest of the guys identify themselves by their instruments.

Once he's matched faces with parts, he crooks his head behind him. "We'll put Sami in there. Drums there." He points across the hall. All of the rehearsal rooms are visible from the studio. "Each of those has cables running into here, so you'll be able to hear each other through your headsets but also see each other."

We'd been given the choice of laying down one track at a time, instrument by instrument. It makes for a cleaner sound. Drums and bass would come in the first day and play through their parts on all four songs to a click track. Then Jules and Wingnut would come in and lay down their melodies and I'd cap it off with vocals.

But for us, we feed off of each other. We love playing for and with each other. Bands with a messier sound, like punk bands, *only* record all together. But so do bands who have played together long enough to sound tight. We've decided we want to record with each other, not in isolation.

Jethro points each of the guys to their rooms and they go set up their amps. He spends time checking cords, plugs, and sound. It takes about forty-five minutes before he sits at the control board and says into our headsets, "Let's rock and roll."

I catch Luther's grin through the studio windows, and a prickle of energy shivers through me. Then Rodney's counting off the start to our first song, "Wannabe Man," with four clicks of his drumsticks and we're off. By the time we hit the second chorus, I can't help it; I'm dancing as I sing, "You always tried to be the big man on campus, but you've got mama's boy energy."

This feels good. It feels right. The sound coming through my headset is crisp and clear, and seeing my bandmates amps me up.

We end up needing an hour to lay down the entire song in a take we all love. Sometimes Jethro hears something he wants to adjust, sometimes one of us wants a different level on a part, but Pixie Luna all high-five when we hear the final version.

Even Jethro smiles a little. "Ten-minute break, and we'll start your next one. 'Boy, Nevermind,' yeah?"

"That's the one," I confirm.

He flicks a glance at the rest of the band. "You

guys don't mind all this fierce girl energy?"

If I were one of the Browers' shelties, the fur on my neck would be standing, but Wingnut answers before I can lay into Jethro.

"Bruh," Wingnut says, "you've heard the lyrics. Is she wrong?"

Jethro eyes me again, then gives a slow grin. "Nah. She's not wrong. Y'all kind of have a No Doubt thing happening."

"I'll take your Gwen Stefani comparisons," I say.

He shakes his head. "No. I meant the all-guy band with the female lead singer. And the energy." It's not *You're a musical genius,* but I'll take it, except he's not done. He nods at me. "Better vocals than Stefani."

I grin at him. All is forgiven. Jules snorts. "Hell, yes, little Stefani."

I punch him in the side, enough to get a small puff of air from him. "Go take your break."

We all wander off in different directions. I hit the bathroom, they go looking for water or a vape break or whatever they need, but within a few minutes we're all settled on the studio sofa, except for Luther, still outside with his vape.

I have given him every "why it's bad for your lungs" lecture I know, ending them all with "trust me, I'm a nurse," but he just tousles my hair and does it anyway.

Jethro comes back in for the next song, and

we work on it for over an hour. It doesn't come together from the jump like "Wannabe Man" did, but eventually we get a take we're happy with.

We listen to both recordings back-to-back, grinning at each other like fools. Except Rodney, but even he has a slight smile.

Jethro nods as the last notes of "Boy, Nevermind" play. "It sounds good. I'll mix these down before y'all come in tomorrow. We'll be able to finish tomorrow night."

We pack our equipment and lug it out to Rodney's van. I'm still feeling the high of hearing it all come together as I help load in the amps. Jules catches my eye, and I grin. He whoops. "We're doing this, aren't we?"

But it's not a question. Luther claps him on the shoulder. "Yes, we are, brother. We are. This is going somewhere."

"You think?" Rodney asks. He's the youngest of us, finishing his last semester at UT. Luther is the oldest at twenty-nine. But Luther always seems like he's lived twice that, and he's been active in the Austin music scene since he was seventeen. He knows it well, and his opinion here means something.

"I know." Luther says it so simply that it feels like truth.

In my bones, I feel it too. We are on the verge of something, and I'm going to reach for it with everything I have.

Chapter Seventeen
SAMI

We chatter all the way back to the pool house. Well, Rodney only drives. But the rest of us are reviewing tonight's recording session and spitballing ideas for the ones we're recording tomorrow night.

By the time we unload and I drive home, it's nearly midnight. The downstairs lights in our condo and Josh's are all off. I'm sure Ava is still up, but her window faces the courtyard. I let myself in and head upstairs to take a quick shower and change into sweats. I'm not tired yet, so I go out to the balcony.

I've been avoiding Josh since Sunday. Not hard since he's always at work. But since his car is in his spot and his lights are out, it's a pretty safe bet he's asleep and I won't run into him out here.

I settle myself into my chair, draw my knees up, and open my notes app to jot down fragments of lyrics that have been floating through my head for a couple of days. I'm halfway through a chorus when light suddenly spills onto Josh's balcony. Before I can escape inside, he's already stepping out, and I sit back in the chair I'm half-way out of.

He looks over and his eyebrows go up. "Oh, hey, Sami."

"Hey." I don't know what to say, but maybe that's okay. I'm not wanting to have a conversation.

Josh doesn't see it that way. "You're up late."

"Not really."

He settles into his chair. He's also in sweats, and he slides his hands into the pockets of his hoodie and stretches out his legs. "That's right. Night owls. Seen any other ones flying around?"

"Not tonight." Yeah. Word salad. That's me.

He's quiet for a while, and I'm wondering how I get back inside without it being awkward when he says, "So . . . you okay?"

That startles me. "Yeah, fine. Why?" Oops. Should not have asked an open-ended question.

"Don't know. You seem"—he hesitates before finishing—"stressed."

"Only for the last ninety seconds," I mumble. I don't mean for him to hear it. I really don't. But he does.

"Whoa." His voice is soft, and he pauses again before asking, "Have I done something wrong?"

This is what I get for being a smartass under my breath. If he hadn't heard me, I could wave goodnight and disappear. But not only did he hear me, he heard me say something that's straight-up not fair.

I lean over and rest my elbows on my knees and slide my fingers into my hair. "No. That was mean. I shouldn't have said it. I'm sorry."

"Then . . . why did you?" He sounds confused more than hurt.

I turn my head so I can meet his eyes. Or try to in the dim light. "I'm sorry," I repeat. "You're collateral damage. That wasn't even about you." But I realize "collateral damage" is a great title for this new song that's trying to happen, one that I realize is about Josh. It's like writing it summoned him to the balcony.

"Do you want to tell me what it *is* about?"

"No. Can I say that without sounding like a jerk?"

He considers that. "I'll allow it."

"You're being a lot nicer about it than you have to be."

He gives a sigh, one that sounds very, very tired. "I know. But honestly, I'm too wasted right now to deal with it."

He doesn't sound drunk, so he must mean "wasted" like wiped out. I'm ashamed that as soon as he doesn't want to know what I meant, I want him to start digging.

"My turn. You okay?" I ask.

Long silence. "No."

"What's up?" I ask it quietly but without hesitation. Suddenly, it matters to me to know.

"My job would be stressful no matter where I worked, but sometimes, working at the family firm makes it worse."

He sounds like the kind of tired I get when I've worked a double shift and we lose a resident and have at least a half dozen other emergencies. I know that kind of tired too well. "What happened?"

"One of those days where I was better than good but still not good enough."

"Sounds like you're being pretty hard on yourself." I keep any judgment out of my voice.

"Not when I'm the nepo hire and the prodigal son. For some people, I'll never be more than that."

Prodigal son? I haven't heard him refer to himself as anything close to that. I'm not super versed in the Bible, but I know the gist. A screwup kid comes home again. Hmm. Not a backstory I would have guessed for Josh, but I can see how it would explain some of the tension I've sensed around his family.

"I've got time and good listening skills." I make the offer quietly, no joking in my tone. It's clear whatever he's working through feels hard for him. I really am a good listener. Comes with the job. "Doesn't everybody get the luxury of mistakes sometimes?"

"Do nurses?" he asks. "Can you afford to make a lot of those?"

"Depends on the mistake, but I take your point."

A full minute passes before he stirs, resting his arms on his thighs and staring down at his clasped hands between his knees. "This is about today and about a long time before today. It doesn't paint me in a great light. You will most likely want to punch me at least four times before I'm done. And I wouldn't blame you."

"My kind of story," I say.

"I, Josh Brower, am a black sheep."

I press my lips together to keep a disbelieving laugh from popping out. Preppy frat boy, BMW-driving corporate attorney, tie-wearing, condo-owning Josh Brower is a black sheep? This should be good.

"I hear everything you aren't saying right now," he says.

That's so on point, I startle slightly. "I promise to say nothing until you explain what that means."

"You see how I grew up. Money, privilege. Stable family. All that."

"Yeah. I kind of had that figured out when I realized you lived in a dorm named after your grandpa."

"It comes with strings," he says. "Expectations. A lot of 'Browers do' and 'Browers don't.' One of my best friends from high school was a PK. Pastor's kid. He did the thing where he ran wild to prove he wasn't uptight, and I did my own version of that in college."

"You mean like partying?"

"Like it was my job," he confirms. He sounds tired, not proud of it. "The weight of family expectation hit me when I was registering for classes. My parents told me what to major in. Business and prelaw. I'd always known I was joining the firm, but that was the first time it sank in that I'd never consciously made that choice. I couldn't even pick my own college classes.

"So I acted out. Subpar grades. Academic probation a couple of semesters. Blowing off family stuff. Doing everything I could to put some distance between me and them. I sound entitled. I know I do."

I'm glad he sees it.

When I don't respond, he looks my way, and I think I see a small smile on his face. "I'm still hearing everything you're not saying."

"Not my fault," I say since I can't deny he's right about the drift of my thoughts.

"I don't blame you." He goes back to studying his clasped hands. "My parents were less than thrilled. My dad kept threatening to cut me off from everything but tuition until I pulled it together, but my grandmother would always step in. She kept telling him that I was a good kid at my core, and I just needed to grow up." He rubs his hands over his face.

The air of self-disgust clinging to him is so distinct that I'm queasy, worried he's about to tell me that it all changed because of some terrible tragedy. "Who was right?"

"Both of them. I hope, anyway."

"Then you turned it around after college?"

He makes a sound, a scoff, maybe. "It would be a better story, wouldn't it? But no. It escalated my senior year. Drugs got in the mix. I blew off my family constantly unless I wanted something. Sold a couple of watches to get high when my parents got strict with the purse strings.

"And still, when I graduated with my barely average GPA, I had a spot at law school waiting for me. The only thing I contributed to that was an excellent LSAT score. It's not a test you study for. It's evaluating logic. Analytical thinking. I took it dead seriously to pour salt in the wound, basically. Like prove I *could* do it, even while doing everything but actually saying I didn't want to go to law school.

"But even that score wouldn't have gotten me in if my dad and Gramps weren't alumni willing to make a very generous donation to the school's endowment."

I hate everything he's saying. As someone who depended on scholarships and work study to get through school, the attitude Josh is describing toward his privilege is everything I loathe about people who come from wealth.

At least now, as he's speaking from hindsight, there's shame in his voice. The guy he's describing doesn't sound like the man I've been hanging out with.

I keep my tone even as I prompt, "And then you got to law school and realized the error of your ways?" *Please let that be the answer.* Long silence. Longer silence. "No?"

A sigh. "No. You don't know how much I wish the answer was yes."

I mull that for a moment. "Okay. Now I'm in suspense. When and how does the Josh you're telling me about become the Josh I'm getting to know?"

"You mean when does my grandmother finally turn out to be right?"

"Yeah."

"I do my first year of law school. I come back and do an internship at our firm because I'm definitely not anyone else's pick. Whatever. I don't care. I do the minimum, hang out with friends. Go back for my second year. My professors can't stand me. My classmates don't respect me. And I still don't care. I'm out drinking most nights. Hungover at least half the mornings for class. High as much as I'm not. Unprepared. The more they loathe me, the less I try to hide how much I don't care about their lectures. And I mean my class lectures and my parents' lectures when my dad's buddies keep reporting back to him on what a burnout I am."

The queasiness gets more intense. I almost don't want to know what it took to turn him around from that point. Did he hurt somebody . . . permanently? Ruin someone else's life in order to hit rock bottom? OD? My hands have become tight fists as I wait for the rest of the story.

"The funny thing is, I actually liked law school. Parts of it. Maybe I just really like the law. It's so foundational to so much we do, and I hadn't really thought about how much. But I didn't like that I never got to choose it. And I didn't like myself for not standing up to my family. So I kept rebelling by underachieving. And *yes,* I know how much I was taking for granted."

There's so much self-contempt in his tone. I don't want him to grind himself down if this is all in the past. "I can respect that you recognize that."

"You're being more generous than you should." His tone is cynical, but I sense it's directed at himself.

"I'm pretty capable of deciding that for myself."

"Right." A pause. "Sorry."

"You're fine. Continue." I brace myself, sensing we're approaching the core of this.

"The semester break comes on and I don't go home for Christmas. My mom calls and asks. Gramps calls and asks. He says Grams has had a chest cold for a couple of weeks and it would cheer her up to see her only grandson. But I go to freaking Vail with one of my frat brothers to spend the holiday at their chalet. Skiing. Drinking. Harder stuff. Trying to forget I have to go back to a place I hate where everyone hates me.

"I just don't want to go home and hear from

my dad about what an underachiever I'm being. I don't want to see Gram and Gramps looking disappointed. So I party, skip Christmas, and go back to school. We're three weeks into the new semester when my mom calls and tells me that Grams has died. Turns out the chest cold was lung cancer. It never occurred to anyone that it could be something that serious, but it's some super rare kind that nonsmokers can get. She was dead less than four days after the diagnosis."

I flinch. That's bad. "That sucks."

"Yeah. The one person who never gave up on me, and I couldn't even stop in at Christmas."

He sounds so sad.

"Josh? I need to get something. I'll be back in a second."

"Okay," he says, but he sounds confused. I would be too if I shared something heavy and he was like, "I gotta go."

But when I slip inside, I keep going downstairs, out of our back fence, and in through his. When I'm standing at his sliding door thirty seconds later, I text him. *Can you come down and open your back door?*

There's no answer, but a few seconds later, a light comes on inside the condo and Josh appears, unlocking the door and stepping back to let me inside. He slides the door shut behind him and leans against it, studying me.

"I lied," I say. "I didn't need to get anything.

I wanted to give you something." I hold out my arms, offering up a hug. There are so many deaths in the nursing home that I've learned a few things about handling grief. The first is that "I'm sorry" doesn't always help everybody, but some version of "that sucks" always does.

The other is that hugs often say what words can't.

Josh slides his arms around me and pulls me against him, and I settle my arms around his waist, my ear resting against his heart again, listening to that ever-steady beat. It's hard to reconcile this Josh with the one he's been describing.

"Thank you," he says. His voice is soft, but it stirs my hair, and the tickle sends a shiver down my back.

"Of course." I've seen this kind of regret so often. Of people not stopping by often enough, and so the last words their loved ones leave with are not the ones the living meant to send them off with. Of people who would do anything to get back a little more time with an elder who slips away.

We stand like that for a minute or so, and I try to let Josh be sad and not rush in with reassurances. He holds me and says nothing. I sense that his mind is far away, probably in the past. I hope it's somewhere good with his grandmother and not in the regrets.

But slowly, so slowly I don't notice until it's

shifted, the energy between us changes. One of Josh's hands makes a gentle circle on my back, and I realize he's offering me a choice: I can react like it's comfort or like it's an invitation. I tense, but it's the stillness where you're holding your breath before a moment. A big moment.

When I respond by tightening my arms ever so slightly, his other hand comes up to stroke my hair, skimming from the crown of my head to the tips resting between my shoulder blades. This sends another shiver down my spine, one he can't miss. He does it again, and I hear the unmistakable increase in his heartbeat. It sounds much louder now as everything else fades away. The chill in the air creeping through a drafty window. The faint spill of light from his living room.

I close my eyes, and I hear only his heart, feel only the heat from his body, the gentle movement of his hands.

When the hand stroking my hair slides around to cup my jaw, he doesn't need to apply any pressure for me to lift it and turn my mouth toward his. He dips his head, slowly, and I try for sanity one last time.

"This isn't what I came over here for."

He pauses. "I didn't think it was. Should I—"

I tighten my arms again when his hand loosens slightly.

He smiles. "Good." Then he brushes his lips against mine.

A kiss like this should be gentle. Comforting. Tender, maybe?

It is not.

Maybe it's because I've heard the accelerating beats of his heart. Maybe it's because we've done so much flirting with our fake dating. But this is fire. Hot. Intense.

He deepens the kiss almost immediately, and my arms fly up to settle against his chest, one grabbing his shirt to pull him closer, the other to keep me upright, because this man, Josh, my *fake* boyfriend, has just weakened my knees. It's a disaster.

I don't care.

I want more of this kiss, of the way he tastes. His lips are warm and the right kind of dry, moving against mine so easily, like their touch creates a perfect chemical reaction, but when his tongue slides against mine, we plunge straight into physics. Explosions. Kinetic energy. Atomic-level wanting.

I give it all back. Every touch, every taste, every shortened breath. All of it. Until my wandering hands tangle in the hair at the nape of his neck, and it draws a soft growl from him. So soft it's more like a vibration.

But it slices through the hormone haze, and I stiffen. Josh stops and lifts his head. "You okay?"

I draw my arms back and brush some stray hair from my eyes. "Yeah. Yes. Fine."

He lets go of me. "Who are you trying to convince?"

"I . . . me."

He slips his hands into the pockets of his joggers and takes a comically large step back. "How's that going?"

"I think I believe it."

"That wouldn't hold up in court." He keeps his tone light, but now I see the first hint of concern in his eyes. "For real this time. Are you okay?"

"Yes. I don't . . . I'm not . . ." I scrub my hand over my face. "Sorry. I don't have any trauma like . . . that. I just . . ." This is going from bad to worse. If my AP composition teacher were here, she'd be slashing all of my verbal ellipses from the air with a vehement red pen. But how do I say, "The sound of how much you wanted me made me realize how much I want you, and I freaked out because everything else about you is what I don't want"?

I don't. I'm glad that my common sense is back, but only by one percent more than I regret it. The wishing we were still wrapped around each other part is at forty-nine percent. Instead, I say, "Sorry. You're trying to tell me about some tough stuff and I'm all over you like cheap cologne."

"I love cheap cologne." He's testing me, and his joke makes me smile.

"Nice try, but you were supposed to say I'm not cheap."

"Right, yeah, that's obvious now. Let's redo that scene, taking it from the top." He reaches for me and pulls me against him.

I do not want to step away right now. Not a single molecule in me wants any space from any of his. But I swallow hard and step back anyway, slipping my hands into his to stay connected but from a distance. "Bad idea. Terrible idea."

"We *really* see the world differently," he says, his tone dry, and I laugh. "Are you going to explain why this is a bad idea?"

"I probably should," I say. "But not right now. I'd like to hear the rest of the story of how old Josh became this Josh."

He sighs. "Back to the balconies?"

I glance around. "Let's make this a balcony. Sit."

"Uh, here?"

"Yes. Right here. On the kitchen floor."

"Okaaaaaay." But he sits.

I turn and sit too so that we're back-to-back. "What do you think? Balcony vibes?"

"In a weird way, yeah."

I wiggle a little, not because I'm uncomfortable but because I like making the touching between our backs kinetic. "I'm listening."

He's quiet for a bit, like he's wandering back to the space and time. "My grandmother's death shook me up. I was on the first plane home. I knew my grandparents were old, but you've seen my gramps. Full of energy. My grandma was the same. Their deaths seemed . . . distant. Abstract. Something way in the future. And then it wasn't.

"I've always had a good relationship with my grandparents, Gramps especially. And even though I knew he wasn't impressed with my college or law school performance, I know he's always rooting for me. I think deep down, I knew there was a point where I'd turn it around and do the expected thing. But I didn't have a timeline for it."

He falls quiet, and I drop my head back so it rests against his shoulder, my way of saying, *I'm here.*

He sighs. "You know that thing people say about how tomorrow isn't promised?"

"Yeah." It's even truer in old folk homes.

"That sunk in. Not so much for me. I don't think I'm invincible or anything, but it sunk in that I could lose Gramps just as easily. And what if I lost him before I had a chance to live up to the legacy he built for me? It haunted me from the second I got the call about my gram. It was all I could think about through the funeral and everything else.

"The night before I went back to school, I stayed with Gramps, and we had a long talk on his porch. I told him I was sorry I'd been such a screwup but that I was going to turn it around, that I know time is precious, and I would use all of mine to make him proud of me. And then I asked if he would help me get into rehab."

"Oh. Wow."

"I know. I wasn't a great guy."

I reach over my shoulder to squeeze his. "No, I meant that I'm proud of you for going to rehab. That's hard, especially to choose for yourself, not be forced into it. Most people can't do that."

He's quiet for a long moment. Then he says softly, "Thanks."

"Rehab went okay?"

"Saved my life. No doubt about it. So yeah, it was hard but good. And it stuck. I had to defer that semester, which means taking basically a whole year off to keep classes in the right sequence. I interned most of that year at the firm, waiting to pick up my coursework the following January. Then I went back to school, and I started kicking ass. Tore it up for my last three semesters."

"And you're still doing it at work?" It was pretty obvious what motivated his long days.

"Trying to."

"Trying to? Or are?"

He gave a soft laugh. "I am."

"Figured."

"There you have it. The prodigal son."

"In that story, the dad is happy to have him back, right? That's how it goes." I feel his head nod. "But that's not exactly how it's gone for you?"

"Yes and no. Gramps is proud. My parents are . . . skeptical."

"Still? How long has it been? Four years?"

"Almost exactly, yeah. But I started giving them trouble from the time I was sixteen, so I think they're waiting for me to get bored and start looking for trouble again."

"Is that likely?"

This time I feel his head shake in a "no." "I don't deserve anything I have. I got lucky. I didn't appreciate it. I'm glad I figured that out before I blew it completely. But I think until high school, I did appreciate it. Up until then, I wanted to be like my dad and grandpa. And I think that's truer to who I am now."

"But that's why your parents haven't come to see your new place? They doubt you?"

"Maybe. Probably."

"At what point will they believe you? What will it take?"

"I wish I knew. A wife, four kids, the largest book at the firm, a house with a fence and tricycles in the yard, being a senior partner. Probably all of it. I put them through hell." Regret saturates every syllable.

Everything he says only underlines why my instinct on our first date to shut it down was right—I'm not future corporate wifey material. But I hate hearing him beat himself up like this. It would bug me even more if he didn't regret it, but still, there's a point at which trying everything has to be good enough. I wish his parents could see that Josh is *there*.

"I'm so glad your gramps sees it, at least."

His back relaxes against mine. "Me too. It's a big deal to me."

We sit quietly for a while before a yawn sneaks up on me, the adrenaline of the studio session finally gone. "Man, when I crash, I crash fast. I better go."

"But you didn't even tell me all your deep dark secrets. Or at least why you shut me down over pho."

I climb to my feet and walk around to pull him to his. When he's standing, I know I should let go. I am not the kind of girl he needs to prove to his parents that he's left his wild ways behind him. But I keep my hand in his for a few moments longer before I say, "I will, Josh. But we both have superhero duty in the morning, so it'll have to wait."

"I'm holding you to that."

I know he will. And I'll put off that conversation just a little longer, because until it happens, I can pretend—at least for a while—that this thing between Josh and me is real.

Because once I explain the situation to him, we become impossible.

Chapter Eighteen
JOSH

Saturday morning, I come back from my run to make breakfast. But not at my house. I knock on the front door of the girls' place, hoping it's Ruby who answers.

She does, smiling at me. "Hey, Josh. What's up?"

"I owe Sami a big thank you, and I thought I'd surprise her with breakfast. But I'm hoping I can cook for all of you as a thank you for welcoming me."

"Twist my arm." She smiles even bigger. "What are we having?"

"Omelets. Can I cook over here? I promise to clean up my mess."

"Sure. Should I get Sami?"

I shake my head. "Let her sleep."

She was probably out late. I might have casually searched for a Pixie Luna Instagram account to see when they perform. They had a show last night, and I didn't see her on the balcony, so I have no idea when she got home.

"Mi cocina es su cocina."

"Awesome. I'll be back in a few."

"Just walk in. Come through the patio if you want."

I go back to my place and put everything I need in an empty laundry basket. Cast iron skillets, a pound of good bacon, a carton of eggs, assorted veggies, and my favorite knife. Ten minutes later, I let myself in through their patio and get to work. It doesn't take long before the smell of bacon is wafting up from one skillet while I chop onions and slice mushrooms.

"Whoa."

I glance over my shoulder to find Ava there. Man, there are no ugly women in this house. Her red hair is bigger and wilder than it usually is when I see her, and she's still in plaid pajamas as she blinks at me from the kitchen doorway.

She rubs her eyes, and I wave at her. She blinks, walks out, and returns a moment later towing Ruby. "Ruble." Ava points at me. "Is our hot neighbor in our kitchen making breakfast or did I wake up in the wrong condo?"

"That's Josh, and this is our place," Ruby confirms.

Ava nods and lets go of Ruby's hand. "Okay."

Ruby disappears.

"Hey, Ava. Ruby said it would be fine if I cooked y'all a thank you breakfast for all your hospitality."

"Ah." Her gaze roams over the counter and stovetop. "I'm vegetarian."

I wince. "Oh, I forgot. No eggs?"

"Ovo-lacto vegetarian," she clarifies. "No bacon. Yes eggs and dairy."

"Oh, good. Omelet with veggies?"

She sniffs the air. "All the veggies. And cheese. All the cheese."

"You got it."

I've chopped peppers and garlic and I'm dicing the last of a tomato when another voice says, "Whoa." A male one. I turn to see a guy I don't recognize staring at me from the doorway.

"Who are you?" His tone is suspicious.

"Josh. Neighbor. Nice to meet you."

"What are you doing here?"

I like this guy less with every word that comes out of his mouth.

"And your name is?" I prompt him, deciding I don't have to answer him. This guy screams future middle management standing there in a gray polo shirt, navy chinos, and no joke, New Balance sneakers. No dude without at least one child in their teens should be wearing New Balance. But while everything about him advertises his aggressive race toward middle age, his face looks my age, maybe younger.

"Niles. Ruby's boyfriend."

It's everything I can do to keep the surprise off my face. Maybe I shouldn't bother. It's not like he deserves my good manners. But my mother drilled into me that the whole point of manners is using them even when other people don't to keep us all civilized.

But seriously. Ruby—who is a babe—is dating this guy? This guy whose skinny arms say he hasn't seen a gym a day in his life and who's trying to hide his receding hairline with a side part that's fooling no one? *This* guy, who lacks even a single watt of the warmth Ruby radiates? I'm going to have to get the story on him from Sami sometime. But for now, I just have to deal with him.

"I'm returning their hospitality with some breakfast," I tell him. "Happy to make you an omelet. What do you like, my dude?" I don't call anyone "my dude," but I'm guessing it will bug him.

He makes the tiniest grimace before he catches himself, like even this rude dude knows that's too far.

"No, thanks," he says. "I'll just wait for Ruby to get dressed."

"Suit yourself." But I'll make him a basic omelet anyway. I don't want him rushing her through hers. Maybe shoving one in his gob will settle him down long enough for her to eat.

I have Ruby's requested queso, onion, and cheese omelet plated along with Niles's. I didn't ask him what he wanted. I made it with only mushrooms. I don't like them because they're bland and rubbery, and that seems like a good choice for Niles.

I poke my head into the living room, where Ava is watching TV, Ruby is organizing a backpack, and Niles is thumbing through an issue of *Cosmo* with a frown on his face. "It's ready. Why don't y'all eat on the patio? It's not too cold out there." It's almost sixty with no wind. "Ava, you're up next."

"Thanks, Josh," Ruby says, smiling as she zips the backpack. "Let's get it, sweetie."

Niles rolls his eyes but lets her pull him to his feet. As they pass me going into the kitchen, I shoot Ava a look, like *what is up with him?*

As if she knows exactly who and what I mean, she shakes her head and sighs.

Ruby and Niles settle themselves outside. I finish Ava's, and as I call her in, I debate whether I should have her wake Sami after all.

"Smells incredible," Ava says, accepting her plate.

"Yeah, it does." That's Sami.

I turn and find her leaning against the wall, watching us. Her eyes are slightly puffy from just waking up, and the bun on her head looks like it could be housing baby squirrels, but as she stands there in loose pajama bottoms and a tank top, she's freaking adorable.

"Thank you breakfast," I tell her. I don't clarify that I made it for all of them because it was the only way I could guarantee seeing Sami too. Our kiss was two nights ago, and I'm positive she's avoiding me. Otherwise, she would have made a point of being on the balcony instead of *not* being there. "The coffee's fresh. Help yourself. What kind of omelet can I make for you?"

"Onion, cheese, peppers, cilantro, bacon. And a side of bacon."

"That's my girl." I say it under my breath, but she stiffens like she heard me. "Go ahead and hang out with Ruby out there. This'll only take a few minutes."

She wrinkles her nose. "Is NilesQuil out there?"

I choke on a laugh. "Yes."

She sighs and disappears for a minute, returning with a hoodie before she pads out on bare feet to join them. Sami with sleepy eyes and tousled hair, fresh out of bed with bare feet and warm pajamas is something I'd like to see more of. Regularly.

A few minutes later, I have omelets served up for Sami and me. I turn off the stove and carry them outside, taking a seat next to Sami.

Niles stands as I sit. "Meet you in the car," he says to Ruby. "We need to get a move on because I have a one o'clock tee time with Kenton and Derek." Keeping an eye on me the whole time, he drops a kiss on her cheek, which seems to surprise her. Then he walks out of the back gate, leaving his plate with its half-eaten omelet behind.

"Was it something I said?" I ask as we watch him walk down toward wherever he's parked.

"No, not at all." Ruby's voice is a tiny bit too cheerful as she answers. "He's just anxious to get moving on our hike today. We're going to the falls. He wants to beat the crowds."

"I want to beat Niles," Sami says.

"Sami." Ruby's voice holds a note of warning, like she wants to head off an argument.

"I'm just saying, Charlie likes to hike. And he's not human Ambien."

"Who's Charlie?" I ask, lost.

"No one," Ruby says. "A friend from work."

Her voice is tight. I decide to try to defuse the tension. "How's your omelet, Ruby?"

She glances down like she's forgotten her plate and looks back up. "Sorry, Josh. I should have said how good it is right away. So delicious. Thank you."

"You're welcome." I watch as Sami takes her first bite.

She chews a couple times, then nods. "This is really good. I didn't know you could cook."

"Mostly breakfast," I say. "My grandmother always had me help her make it when we stayed over at the ranch."

"Transferable skills," Ava says. "If you have a good breakfast repertoire, you can make lots of other stuff too. Including dinners."

"True," I say. "But for whatever reason, breakfast is easiest to scale up or down. It's too much trouble to make dinner for one, so I usually order out." My eyes drift back to Sami as I chat with Ruby. She's taken another bite, her eyes starting to lose some of their sleepiness. Is it the coffee or my amazing cooking, aka "use all the butter"? *All* of it.

Ruby's fork clinks against her plate as she goes for her last bite of omelet, and I catch her studying me like she's trying not to laugh. Right. Because I'm staring at her roommate like a lovesick puppy while she tries to wake up and eat breakfast.

I clear my throat. "Hiking sounds good. Do you like to hike?"

Ruby gives me a knowing look. "Yes. Which is why I'm leaving soon to join Niles on our regular Saturday hike."

"Right." Warmth skims over the tops of my cheekbones. "What about you, Sami?"

"Sure. I like it okay. Mainly easy ones though. I'm not a backpacker."

"Cool. Same for me. We should do one."

Her eyebrows draw together. "Like today?"

I'd meant more in general, but I'm not dumb enough to throw away an opening like that. "Sure, today. It's going to be in the mid-sixties. Perfect weather for it."

"I . . . wasn't, um, I didn't . . ." She blinks, baby owl–style. "I'm not all the way awake."

"Well, I'll leave you two to figure that out," Ruby says. "I need to go meet Niles." She stands and scoops up both of their plates. "See y'all later." Then she's in the condo, the door sliding closed behind her.

"I'm off too," Ava says. "Gotta check on something at the lab."

They leave a big old cloud of quiet behind as Sami takes another drink of her coffee and doesn't meet my eyes. I definitely wasn't wrong about her avoiding me.

"So, Sami. Anything interesting and unusual happen in the last couple days that would make you suddenly want to avoid your good-looking and personable neighbor?"

She sputters and sets her mug down, a smile threatening to break loose. "Ahab? No."

I give her a look of shock. "You made out with him too?"

"I didn't make out with *anyone*."

"Wait, who came over to my house Thursday night? I know you and Madison are both blonde, but honestly, I don't think I could confuse you."

"I meant that wasn't a makeout."

"Fascinating. Tell me more."

She taps her finger against the rim of her mug. "It was a kiss."

I look at her for a few seconds then down at my hands, silently holding up my fingers as I count each one. She interrupts when I get to six.

"What are you doing?"

"So far, I remember at least six separate kisses." I lift the next finger. "Seven, eight—"

"Stop," she says, her voice somewhere between laughter and irritation. "All right, counsel. Don't be so literal. It was more than one kiss. I just meant we didn't make out."

"Really," I drawl, picking up my fork and knife to cut another bite from my omelet. "What constitutes a makeout to you?"

She looks disconcerted for a couple of seconds. "I wasn't expecting a follow-up question."

"I'm a lawyer. A good one," I say with a shrug. "Job hazard." But it's also entertaining as hell watching her squirm. "You were saying?"

"A makeout is . . ." She hesitates. "Horizontal."

She looks very satisfied about coming up with this technicality. "Not length or intensity? Interesting. Because I was about two seconds from picking you up, setting you on my counter, wrapping your legs around me, and seeing what I could make happen without having a crick in my neck because you're short."

She's staring at me, mouth slightly parted, like she can't believe I just went there. I take another bite of my omelet, unbothered, because I only told her the truth.

"So that wouldn't have been a makeout," I say, like I've been considering it the whole time I've been chewing. In a way, I have. But mainly because I've been imagining that missed opportunity since Thursday night.

"You raise a good point." She's staring at my mouth like she's considering a reenactment to test my definition, but then she gives herself a small shake. "I mean it's a pointless point. It was a bad idea."

To be good in corporate law, it takes predatory instincts. I let those loose in the office and keep them out of my personal life. But those instincts are genetically coded, and I feel something old and primitive spilling into my veins, the instinct of the hunt. She's looking for escape, and I can't let her find it.

"It wasn't an idea," I tell her. "There was no thinking. Only reflex. The kind that's programmed into your DNA when two compatible people strip out the BS and just do what feels natural."

A red stain is spreading up her neck, climbing toward her cheeks, but she's determined to fight me on this. "That's the thing, Josh. We're not compatible. We're so incompatible that it's funny."

"What's funny is you trying to wave this all off, like it's easy to make this kind of attraction disappear." I lean forward and lock eyes with her, food and everything else forgotten. "If you can say you don't feel it too, I'll drop it. Tell me honestly that it's my imagination."

She holds my gaze for a few seconds before her eyes fall to her plate. But she doesn't disagree.

"Eat your omelet," I say. "I'll let this go. For now. But you owe me an explanation. You're going to have to make a case for this incompatibility you're claiming. Do you have a show tonight?"

She gives me a slow nod. I can't tell if her silence is because she's mad or tongue-tied. Or maybe I gave her something to think about.

I give a single nod back. "Okay. I'll be on the balcony." Then I tuck into my omelet like our incredibly loaded conversation never happened.

She puts her fork down instead of taking another bite. "I don't owe you anything."

"I didn't mean literally."

"No, I don't owe you anything. Literally or figuratively. That's the problem, Josh. I made it clear on our only real date that I'm not interested. I didn't owe you an explanation then and I don't owe you one now. But 'no' doesn't compute for you."

"Wait, *you* came to my place. *You* knocked on *my* kitchen door. If that isn't yes, then what is?"

"It was yes at that moment. Yes can always be revoked." She stands and pushes her plate back. "I'm not hungry. I didn't ask you to come here and make breakfast. I'm not obligated to eat it because you decided to do it. I don't have to share my story because you shared yours. You've decided you want time with me, and when charm failed, you used money and your idiotic fake dating excuse to buy my time. I should have said no then. That's on me. But I've been second-guessing myself ever since. And you keep pushing."

Her words start like a shock of cold water, but they become icicles, stabbing at me, and I fight the instinct to hunch my shoulders and shelter. I listen with a blank face until she's done.

"Everyone does their own dishes around here," she says. "Thanks for the breakfast I didn't ask for, but I've reached my limit on bribes I'll take. Clean your mess before you go, please."

Sharp, sharp icicles. I don't even know what to say, and the only words that come out of my mouth are "but Madi?"

"I'll make her one later." She walks into the house without looking back. I turn to watch her grab her purse from beside the front door and walk out, the door almost slamming behind her.

I turn and look down at the ruins of breakfast. Steam still rises from her barely eaten omelet like a smoking gun.

What just happened?

Chapter Nineteen
JOSH

I clean up, which I would have done anyway, scraping two wasted omelets into the trash can.

Sami's accusations burn in my mind, and I handle it the way I always do these days: I go into the office and bury it beneath a case file thick enough to numb the sting. I work through lunch, not coming out of my office, not bothering to keep tabs on which other associates are here today to challenge me in working the most billable hours.

I stay until dinner time, at which point I pack up, hit up Torchy's for some takeout, and head home. To work some more. Redemption takes more than overtime. This is a double-time commitment.

I'm barely in my door before there's a knock. Maybe Sami to apologize before she heads out for her show? I pull it open, already frowning at the thought of seeing her, of all the things I didn't say in the shock of her accusations, but it's Ruby standing on my doorstep. My scowl fades to surprise.

"Glad to see you too," she says with a smirk.

"Heeeeeeey, Rubes," I say like she's a frat

brother I haven't seen since college. "What's good?" Like nothing is wrong. Like her roommate didn't eviscerate me on their patio this morning for daring to make them breakfast.

"That's better," she says. "I almost believe you mean it. Can I come in?"

"Of course." I step back to let her pass. "What can I do for you?"

She settles herself on my couch, so I take the recliner.

"I need to know your intentions toward my roommate."

I can't decide if she's serious or not. "She told you about this morning?"

Ruby tilts her head. "No. I haven't seen her since I left to go hiking. She was gone when I got home. What about this morning?"

"We had a . . . it was . . ." I run out of words. I'm still not sure what happened. "She laid me out."

"Did you deserve it?"

I consider Sami's accusations. I did use money to buy myself out of a tough situation, but it was with *Presley*. A "problem" I've tried to solve every way I know how while still protecting my dad's friendship with JP *and* the firm's business interests.

I wasn't trying to manipulate Sami into anything, and the proof is that when I could have put the pressure on her to come meet my family,

I didn't. I tried to get her *out* of it, because she didn't owe me that. *Sami* put herself in that situation.

"No. I didn't deserve it. She mentioned before that I'm collateral damage sometimes because of her past. I think that's what happened this morning. I'm pretty mad, to be honest."

"Because it matters," Ruby says.

I sag against the seat. "Yeah. Because it matters."

"Because *she* matters?" Ruby presses.

Ruby is a cool girl, but I'm not spilling my guts to her. Not about what I feel for Sami. Even I'm not sure what it is. Instead of an answer, I raise my eyebrows at Ruby.

She gives a slow nod. "I have brothers. Three of them. All older. As far as they're concerned, my girls are also their little sisters. They may not be thrilled if they find out our new neighbor is a player."

"What? I'm not." Anymore. In my defense, it's been years since I was.

"So you're serious about her?"

"I don't know if I'm—" I break off at the look on her face. Finishing that sentence feels like a tactical error. "I . . . like Sami."

"You like me." She narrows her eyes.

"Not like that."

Her expression smooths. "Good."

I just got trapped into an admission I had no

plans to make. Ruby is good. "You sure you never went to law school?"

"Don't need law school for stuff like this when I have three brothers. I know what's what."

Then how did she end up with Niles? I'm far too smart to voice the question.

"So, your intentions?" she presses.

"I like her," I repeat.

"And? What are you going to do about that?"

"Honestly?"

"No, lie to me."

I roll my eyes. "You've got an even smarter mouth than she does."

"Give her time." Ruby's smirk is back.

"Honestly, I have no idea. She's got me puking up my emotional guts one night, then she's running away the next. And I don't exactly have a lot of free time right now. Even if she was into me—"

Ruby brushes away my words with a wave. "You find time when it's the right person."

There is no way she's speaking from experience. Not the girlfriend who's getting squeezed in before a tee time. But her relationship is none of my business.

And actually, mine is none of hers, which she somehow keeps making me forget. "I probably need to have a conversation with Sami about this before you and I start breaking it all down."

"You're not wrong. But if you want to even get

her to have a conversation, you're going to need a game plan."

"Okay, but I try to avoid the words 'game' and 'dating' together."

"Oh, really, Mr. Fake Date Me?"

"Ruby." I shake my head.

"Yeah?"

"You're the worst."

"So say my brothers."

"Fine. What's your game plan?"

"When Sami decides to explain why she's got reservations about you, you're going to find that it comes down to a very specific issue for her: being seen and accepted for who she is and what she has to offer. The how and why she got there are for her to explain, but that's the bottom line. So that means . . ." She looks at me, waiting for me to fill in the blank.

"See and accept her for who she is? I already do that."

"Talk is cheap. You're a lawyer. What's your evidence?"

"We hang out on the balcony and talk at night a lot."

She cocks her head. "Do you now? Interesting."

That's it. After an awkward silence, I ask, "More?"

She nods.

I realize I don't have anything else to offer as evidence since I don't think Sami will be thrilled if I get into the kissing. The *makeout*.

Ruby points at me and snaps when my silence goes too long. "You see the problem?"

"I do." The fake dating doesn't make my case, and that's the only other evidence I have.

"How are you going to fix it?" Ruby demands. "I have the answers, by the way. But it's only going to count if you come up with your own."

"I need to start showing up for the things that matter to her." It gets tricky here because I can't say that Sami's got a secret identity.

"Like her shows?"

"Yes. Her acoustic sets."

Ruby rolls her eyes. "You mean her Pixie Luna shows?"

I freeze. "You know about those?"

"Of course. We all do. We take turns going and supporting her but staying out of sight. We'd go together but we'd be too easy to spot. The only question was whether you knew. I'm shocked she told you." She almost looks hurt that Sami might have brought it up with me and not her.

"She didn't. I recognized her when I had to take clients out one night. How did you find out?"

"We put it together over time. We're always in each other's rooms borrowing clothes. I think Ava was the first to notice some boots tucked out of the way that we never see her wear. I went looking for a shirt and found a shredded UT jersey. We ran across a few other things that were not Sami's usual style. There were the nights she was going to do an 'open mic,' but we couldn't find anywhere advertising open mic nights. We knew something was up, but we weren't sure what until one night Madi came home and told us that she'd seen Sami on stage in a band."

"Scary," I say.

"It's not stalking if you live with them," she says, totally unruffled. "Anyway, we kept asking Sami leading questions, trying to give her chances to confess, but she didn't. So now we make sure one of us is at every show, low-key, supporting her until she's ready to tell us."

"That's pretty awesome," I say.

"Is it? Or is it plain old showing up for someone we care about because that's what you do when you care?"

"Gee, Ruby." I open my eyes wide. "Was that a clue?"

"Who's the smart-mouth now?"

"So go to her shows. That's what you think I should do."

She stands. "Doesn't matter what I think. It matters what you decide to do, whether Sami notices, and mainly, it matters how she feels about that."

"Why doesn't she want anyone to know she's doing this?"

Ruby smiles again. "That's part of what you'll

earn from her. Good luck." She slips out the door, still smiling to herself.

At 9:00 on Tuesday night, I shut off my computer after a full day of work. I'm tired. I'd love to hit the gym and go to bed.

Instead, I change into a pair of jeans and a black button-down shirt that I hope will blend in with tonight's crowd. Then I grab my keys and head out to my car, arriving twenty minutes later at the venue listed on the Pixie Luna website as their next show. Four bands are playing and they're third. That has to be good. Means the promoter thinks only one more band will have a bigger draw.

I get my wristband at the door and slip in. The group onstage has the crowd amped up, and they bounce and flail to the beat. It turns out to be their last song as the singer announces, "Thank you! We're the Mop Buckets, and after a short break with DJ Boss, Pixie Luna will be up next!"

The crowd responds with energetic cheers.

The deejay plays some ska to keep the crowd's energy up, but I don't need it. With each minute that passes, my anticipation grows, waiting for the moment Sami takes the stage.

Finally, after about five songs while guys in black shirts mess with the instruments onstage, the deejay announces over the music, "Boys and girls and everyone in between, let's welcome Pixie Luna!"

The crowd cheers again, and the band walks out, Lady Mantha practically skipping ahead of them, energy spilling off her. Everyone takes their spot with a sense of tightly coiled anticipation about them. The drummer is hard to read, but the other three guys range from looking like they want to join Sami in her skipping or already nodding in time with a beat the rest of us don't hear yet.

Sami stops center stage, turns her back to the crowd, and takes a power stance. The drummer gives her a look, then BAM. He bangs his snares once, and they're already tearing into their first song, Sami spinning, her half mask glinting, her hair looking even darker pink depending on which lights catch it.

She performs full-out, like she's leaving everything on the stage starting with the first note, and the crowd goes nuts for it. Their bounce is higher, their flails are bigger, and . . .

I pause, straining to listen. Yeah. Some of them are singing along.

I grin. This is *awesome*. From the performance to the response, it's all pulsing. I survey the crowd, looking for any of my other neighbors, working off the instinct that they'll stay out of Sami's line of sight. I don't see anyone until I eventually notice a woman hanging out behind a column that would block her from the band's view.

I walk over, squinting. This woman has Ruby's dark hair, but she's taller. When I'm a few feet away, it hits me. It's *Ava*. In a wig. I turn before she notices me and move to a spot near the back on the other side of the room. I'll let Ruby break the news to her roommates that I know what's up, but it makes me smile that they really do make sure one of them is always there for Sami's shows.

I turn back to the stage, giving them—especially Sami—my full attention. They do a total of eight songs, every one as good as the last. Sami is incredible. She doesn't hold back, none of the reserve I sometimes sense in her showing at all. I must have seen hundreds of bands back in the day, and Pixie Luna's as good as the best ones I remember. I love this. I've *missed* this.

And even as I jump and sing along to the chorus, I wonder what it would take for her to feel comfortable enough to be this free with me. I don't know, but I'm definitely going to find out.

I can tell they're getting to the last song when she jumps out for some crowd surfing, and I hustle out to the club's entrance. Merchandise tables are set up, and sure enough, there's one with Pixie Luna shirts. "Can I get one of those in XL, man?" I say to the guy behind the table. He looks barely old enough to be in the club, but he nods and gives me the size. I hand him the cash, and then I pull the T-shirt over my regular shirt as I head back to the floor.

It's black with Pixie Luna spelled in clean lettering, bordered on the left by a moth wing. It's cool. It's the kind of shirt people will stop and ask me about at the gym.

The crowd is returning Sami to the stage when I make it back in, and the band finishes the song with a flourish of cymbal crashes as Sami throws her arms in the air like she just won a marathon.

The crowd was happy to see them before, but now they roar, and Sami's grin below her mask is huge. "We love you, Austin!" she calls into the mic, and they roar again.

When the applause finally starts to wane the tiniest bit, the band files offstage, and I head toward the backstage area. It's not a big enough venue to require backstage passes, but even if they did, acting like you're supposed to be somewhere is usually enough to get you in. When the security guy at the backstage entrance stops me, I point at my shirt. "Manager," I say.

It helps that I'm as unthreatening as it's possible to look, like at worst I'm there to sell life insurance, not stalk a band. He nods and waves me through.

I wait near the end of the hall and watch as the members of the band accept their high fives from the other musicians. I lean against the wall, watching Sami interact with everyone. She's comfortable here in a way that I don't usually see her. I would bet she's like this with her roommates, but I only see her with them when I'm there, changing the equation.

As the backslapping and hugs settle down, she glances up and spots me. She pauses, not as surprised this time as last time, but I can't read her expression beyond that. I'm on her turf, so I straighten and walk toward her.

"Great show. Even better than the last time I saw you." I stop a few feet away.

She looks me up and down. "I'd ask you what you're doing here, but . . ." Her eyes fall to my new T-shirt.

"Yeah. Busted. Throwing around my money for a hand stamp and some sweet, sweet merch."

She scratches her forehead above the mask. "I deserve that. Look, about the other morning—"

But I interrupt her by singing one of their lyrics. " 'I'm not like the other girls, the ones with manicures and pretty curls, the ones who know the right thing to say, the lacquered ones who show up and slay.' "

Her mouth quirks up on one side. "You're definitely not like any girls I know."

"I was listening to your stuff on the way over. That one stuck with me. I like the use of the word 'lacquered.' It's not used in pop punk enough."

"Rock and roll," she says, trying to find a smile.

"I also like that it answers its own question."

She quotes the third verse of the song. " 'I'm the girl who always says the wrong thing, the one you don't bring home or gift with a ring, the one who comes from the wrong side of town, but the one you can call when bad stuff goes down.' " It answers the song's title, "What Kind of Girl?"

"Is that true?" I ask. "Are you that girl?"

She lifts and drops her shoulder. "I write the lyrics."

I nod and give her a small smile. "I'm glad I got to see that. I'll get out of your uncurly hair. See you around? Maybe tonight?"

"Maybe." Her small smile is back.

I turn toward the exit, knowing that's as close to a "yes" as I'll get, but I only take a couple of steps before she calls my name.

"Josh?"

"Yeah?"

She rushes to close the short distance between us and slips her arms around my waist. "Thanks for coming."

I barely hear her above the noise from the club and the backstage clatter, but it's enough.

I hug her back, a tight hug, and when she lifts her head to smile at me, her eyes shine through her mask.

"See you around," she says. Then she turns and runs back to her bandmates, moving as lightly as the moth on my shirt.

I glance down at it and grin at the glitter smudged on it from her mask.

Sami Webster is a girl who knows how to leave her mark.

Chapter Twenty
SAMI

I don't meet Josh on the balcony.

I can't. I need to cocoon my moth self after such an intense night. The adrenaline of performing. The dopamine of spotting Josh in the crowd. The serotonin that floods my system from being in his arms for a few seconds.

It's too much. It's a pinball machine of feeling, and even if they're all good, the higher the score, the worse you feel when you eventually lose. I'm stretched too thin between band gigs and full-time work to lose at pinball.

I'm too tired to even make metaphors work. I'm too tired to write new music. I'm putting all my energy into my job and the band, and it leaves me with enough energy to sit on the balcony sometimes and, if I'm very lucky, muster the energy to half-heartedly write some lyrics while I hope for Josh to distract me.

But this is a shelter-in-place kind of night, like from a storm. A hormone storm. A hide-beneath-my-blanket, dive-into-sleep, stay-there-as-long-as-I-can kind of night.

Like I said: a cocoon.

It works out pretty well. I wake at nine, which means I've gotten a full eight hours of sleep, something I haven't done in a couple of weeks. I might have gone even longer except my phone is buzzing.

I grope along my nightstand until I find it and squint at the screen. It's my grandmother. I'm already smiling when I answer it. "Hey, Grandma."

"Hey, honey." I don't think about Austin people having much of an accent, but Letty Hancock Webster is Hillsboro born and bred, and it's in every syllable she speaks. "You finally taking my calls?"

I feel bad. A conversation with her is never less than half an hour, and I don't have extra ones of those lying around. "I'm sorry, Grandma. Whenever I have time, it's always late and I don't want to wake you up."

"You working?"

"No, I have Sundays off. I think I'm mostly going to try to recuperate from too much work this week."

"So if I told you that I'm an hour out of Hillsboro and on my way to you, you'd say I ought to keep coming?" There's a smile in her voice. She knows she's always welcome.

"Yes! Yes, come, Grandma! I need a grandma day so bad!"

"You're overdue for one, and since you plainly weren't going to have time to drive home, I'm bringing it to you."

"You are the best in the whole world!"

"You better believe it. See you in an hour. Don't eat." She hangs up.

I stumble to the top of the stairs and yell down, "Grandma Letty is coming!"

I hear the patter of feet and Ava appears at the bottom of the stairs. "She's coming today?"

"Yes. In an hour."

She whoops. "I was heading out to the lab, but now I'm sticking around."

I grin at her before I disappear into my room to strip my bed and put the sheets in for a good washing before I jump in the shower.

My grandma is right on time, knocking on the door exactly an hour later, a flowery weekend bag slung over her arm, a light cloud of her gardenia perfume trailing her into the house. She hugs and squishes Ava and me, then holds me back and looks me over.

"Too skinny. Both of you. Where's Ruby?"

"Out with Niles," Ava says.

"I'm sure Madison's still in bed too," Grandma says. She knows us well. "I'll see her this afternoon. Let's go eat."

"I'll drive," Ava says. "I have a bigger car."

It's true but it's not why she's offering. Grandma is a holy terror in her fifteen-year-old Malibu. We get into Ava's Pilot, and I breathe a sigh of relief when I get my seatbelt buckled without seeing Josh. I don't know what to say about why I stood him up *again* for our balcony chat.

"I called in a reservation at Delia's," I tell Ava. Restaurants and cafés are always packed for Sunday brunch, but the staff love us there, so they're happy to hold a table. After years of waiting tables to pay the bills, Grandma is a generous tipper, and she drilled the habit into me too.

We eat and catch up over Austin's best waffles, and as always, she's as interested in Ava's life as she is mine. She'll get the lowdown from Ruby and Madison before dinner too.

"Music is keeping you busy, girl?" Grandma asks me after getting Ava's full report. "That why you're so hard to get hold of?"

I try to give her a coded warning glance; she knows about my band, but she might forget my roommates don't. "Playing every open mic I can find."

Grandma nods. "And it's going well?"

I can't suppress a smile at all the good things happening in the last few weeks, even if it is wearing me out. "Yeah, going well."

"That's good. Now anyone want to tell me why Ruby is still with that human water stain?"

That makes me laugh and Ava roll her eyes, and we take turns complaining about Niles for the next few minutes. He makes it so easy.

"I think that's the real reason Ruby made the

bet," Ava says. "She's so bored with her own relationship, she needs the drama of everyone else's."

"What bet?" Grandma asks.

"She bet me that she can find us our perfect boyfriend by the end of the year," Ava explains. "She's starting with Sami, and if Ruby wins, she gets Sami's parking space."

Grandma fixes me with a skeptical look. "I have to plan fifteen minutes extra just to find a spot when I come and visit. You think a man is worth that kind of hassle?"

"Nope," I say, grinning. "It was an easy bet to make."

"That's my girl," Grandma says. She raised my mom by herself when her husband took off to become a survivalist in Alaska. And of course Mom raised me when my sperm donor took off and didn't come back either. They view all relationships with a skeptical eye. Or two. Or even four, when they're looking at mine.

"You sound pretty smug for a girl spending so much time with the first boy Ruby found for you," Ava says.

"No, I don't."

"Huh. So that's not where you were last Sunday?"

"I was, but that was more like a first aid situation. Had to monitor his snakebite."

My grandma does a double take. "His what?"

"Sounds more dramatic than it is," I say. "But I did feel like I should keep an eye on it. And I mean *the bite*." I cut Ava off before she can joke about keeping an eye on his snake. She always looks innocent until she lays you out with an innuendo and a twinkle in her eye.

She's not deterred. "So, it's not you two chatting out on the balcony late at night fourteen million times a week?"

Grandma's eyebrow goes up.

"Are we being loud?" I ask Ava. Grandma's other eyebrow goes up. "When we *talk?*"

"No," Ava admits. "But we've each seen you out there at least once. You're saying there's nothing going on?"

"I'm saying it would be really weird if we both sat on our balconies and didn't acknowledge each other. I promise, there's nothing spicy to talk about. Which brings us to the community center. Spill the tea, Grandma."

"Oooh, yes, please, Grandma Letty," Ava says.

Grandma can tell a story like no one else, and her best ones are about the ongoing soap opera at the Hillsboro Senior Center, where she makes even the squabbles in the knitting group sound like high drama.

She dives in and regales us with the ongoing saga of the Judy/Norman/Lois love triangle, which in Grandma's telling is way more riveting than anything we watch on TV. When we get back to the condo, Ava drops us off and heads into the lab but promises to come back for Redneck Movie Night, one of Grandma's specialties.

Madison is in the kitchen in her pajamas with full bedhead, digging a yogurt out of the fridge, but when Grandma calls, "Hey, girl," Madi brightens and shuffles over for a Letty hug.

"Redneck Movie Night," Grandma tells her. "You best be here."

"Yes, ma'am. I don't have to work until 10:00."

"Explain to me what it is you do for work again?"

Madi shrugs. "Look cute and pour people wine."

"Like a cocktail waitress?" Grandma asks.

"Kind of. We're sort of the Rolls Royces of cocktail waitressing." Madi doesn't look remotely offended by the question, but it's a sign of how much she likes Grandma that she even explains. Usually, she doesn't.

"I'm a Chevy girl myself," Grandma says. "We're doing redneck margaritas with a seventies movie tonight."

"Can't wait," Madi says.

Grandma and I spend the rest of the day poking around thrift stores where I score another prom dress that will make a perfect stage outfit. She finds three T-shirts that would make every one of the Browers blanch with the possible exception of Josh's grandfather.

The least offensive one says "Kiss My Grits," with two sunny side eggs that invite a lot of questions. Mainly, based on the placement of the eggs, I think I may have been wrong my entire life about what kissing someone's grits actually means.

We stop at the HEB for some Redneck Movie Night snacks. Grandma says she's allowed to use the term "redneck" because she is one—a proud one—and I get immunity for using it as long as it's with her. Her basic rule is that you're only allowed to use "redneck" if you know it's not an insult.

We leave the store with Funyuns, Mountain Dew and tequila for redneck margaritas, baloney and Kraft singles for Wonderbread fried sandwiches, premade potato salad, a fistful of Slim Jims, and some Skittles for the sweet.

Everyone is settled in on the sofa or floor with pillows at seven o'clock, a plate with Grandma's fried baloney sandwich in front of them (except Ava's is regular grilled cheese), a side of potato salad, and the other snacks of their choice.

"We're watching *The Sting*," Grandma announces. The pre-movie lecture might be the best part of Redneck Movie Night. She's about to go into it when Ruby holds up a hand.

"Wait, sorry, my friend Charlie just texted. Can he come over?"

"Charlie!" Ava cheers. I give an approving whoop and Madi flashes a thumbs-up.

"He can be here in ten minutes," Ruby says.

"I don't mind if y'all don't," Grandma says. "But does he have redneck credentials?"

"He loves baloney sandwiches," Ruby promises.

"Tell him to come on, then," Grandma says. "Now y'all explain to me who this boy is."

"I work with him," Ruby says. "He's a librarian too."

"We want her to marry him," Ava says.

Ruby scoffs. "That's just you, Ava. Let it go."

"I want you to marry him," Madi says.

I raise my hand. "Me three."

"Nobody needs to do any kind of marrying," Grandma says. "But if you do—"

"Get a prenup," Ava says.

"Keep your own checking account," Ruby adds.

"Keep the utilities in your name," Madi says.

"And don't spend a lot on your wedding," I conclude. She's got us well-trained.

"College girls." Grandma shakes her head, looking like she wants to either laugh or spank us. "Y'all listen, at least. But we'll see how well it sticks when you find a man who sweet talks you."

"Charlie's not a sweet talker," Ava says. "He's just sweet. That's why we like him."

"Hey, if we're having dudes over, shouldn't

you go get your boyfriend too, Sam?" Madi asks.

"Stop," I say with no heat. "I don't have a boyfriend."

"But you're gonna," Ruby says in a singsong voice.

"Am not," I answer and immediately feel like I'm in fifth grade.

"What's this?" Grandma asks.

"Nothing, Grandma," I promise.

"Mm-hmm." Her tone shows zero belief in my protest. "Sounds like your neighbor again. Let me go fix this Charlie a sandwich so we're ready when he gets here. Don't want to keep *my* boyfriends waiting."

Her boyfriends being, of course, Redford and Newman.

Charlie knocks and walks in a few minutes later. "Ladies. Thanks for letting me crash."

"Sure," Ruby says. "Grandma Letty is here. I'll introduce you. Then you need to hurry and fix your plate so we can get started." She takes him back to the kitchen and we all exchange glances with each other as we listen to the rumble of voices.

Madi rolls her eyes and mouths, *Why Niles?*

Ava widens her eyes like *I know*.

I just shake my head. We all like Charlie so much better. If he and Niles were standing side by side in the same exact outfit, Niles is probably better-looking. But Charlie is the kind of cute that grows on you, average-looking until you talk to him for a bit and then you find yourself thinking, "This is an attractive dude." He's taller and wider than Niles but wiry more than athletic. He's also got a distinct style that Niles lacks with his stupid Dockers and polos. And it seems like Charlie's eyes are always twinkling with a joke he can't wait to tell you with his wicked little smile.

I swear, the rest of us would probably all have tried dating Charlie the first time Ruby invited him over if it wasn't so obvious that they should be together—even if she doesn't see it. I don't know if Charlie does, but every now and then there's something in the way he studies her that makes me think he sees it too.

They come out trailing behind Grandma and settle into spots, Charlie settling on the floor and resting his back against the end of the sofa, careful to stay out of anyone else's space.

"Now. About this movie," Grandma begins. "This one has two of the finest men to ever grace the screen. Robert Redford and Paul Newman"— she pauses while we cheer—"in their prime. P-r-i-m-e oh my. They're playing bad guys, which is always when they're the best. I know I don't have to convince you."

She does not. She's introduced us to Redford and Newman in *Butch Cassidy and the Sundance Kid*. We're converts.

She takes her place on the sofa, me snuggled on one side, Ruby on the other.

The movie is fun, and the wolf whistling every time Newman comes on screen gets more raucous as the tequila and Mountain Dew "margaritas" flow. By the time the movie is done, everyone but Grandma and Madi have the slight flush of a mild buzz. I don't think Grandma is capable of getting drunk, and Madi says she sees too many sloppy-drunk idiots at work to be interested in that for herself.

"I'm outta here," Madi says. "I need to change and get to work. Thanks for the movie, Grandma Letty." She disappears down the hall to her room.

"Ready for our sleepover, Grandma?" I ask.

"Right after we clean up," she says.

"No way," Ava protests. "We'll take care of it. You cooked, we'll clean."

"You're really pushing the definition of cooking," Grandma says.

"We'll handle it," Ava says, her voice firm. "Go get your beauty rest."

"Thanks, Ava," I say as I get to my feet and pull Grandma up. We climb up to my room, and I notice for the first time that it takes her more visible effort than it used to as she takes the stairs slowly.

I made the bed with clean sheets when we got back from the store, so after we get into our pajamas and settle on the bedspread, she says, "Now catch me up on everything."

I flick my eyes toward the balcony door, but I can't tell without poking my head out whether Josh is there.

"Start with the neighbor," Grandma says like she's a mind reader.

"Nothing to tell, but work sucks and the band is doing awesome."

"Then tell me about that," she orders.

I tell her about the rise in deaths this month because of flu season, and how hard it's been to find CNAs that will stick around when the company doesn't pay them well enough. Then I tell her about the shows, the new merch, and the recording session.

She slides from the bed. "Let me just get my pocketbook. I need one of those shirts."

"Grandma, you don't have to—"

"Oh, but I do," she says. "I didn't start making the good money until your mama was grown, and I'll spend it how I like." She'd ended up getting promoted a step at a time from server to regional director for a major steakhouse chain before she retired a couple of years ago. Some of her poor people habits die hard, like driving a car much less nice than she can afford. But in other ways, she'll spare no expense, especially when it comes to me. She paid for my sorority dues because she said it would give me a professional network for life.

She pulls out a twenty and puts it on my nightstand. "Size medium next time I see you. And purple if you've got it."

We don't, but I'll make sure Grandma gets a purple one anyway.

"Now tell me about this recording. I got a CD player. Where can I get a CD?"

So then I spend the next ten minutes setting up Soundrack on her phone and making sure she can find our songs.

"Did you do the one that goes like—" and then she breaks into a perfect rendition of the chorus to "Wannabe Man."

I clap when she's done. "Grandma, that's so good. I love that you know the words."

"I love everything you do, pumpkin. And why are you surprised it was good? You know you got those pipes from me."

"It's true. Thank you for them." I'd grown up singing with her, which is why I did, do, and always will have a love for classic country.

"You can thank me with a concert. Get your guitar, girl. Let's sing."

She doesn't have to tell me twice. I pull my acoustic guitar from the closet and climb back on the bed, settling across from her cross-legged.

"Let's do some real punk rock," she says, and hums the opening bars to Dolly Parton's "Jolene," a song we've sung together more times than I can count. I was so proud when I finally learned the fast fingering well enough to play it when I was fourteen. Grandma grabs my garbage can and dumps it into the bathroom garbage, then settles on my bed, the small garbage can turned over and ready for drumming.

We sink into our easy harmony, and when the song comes to an end far too soon, we smile at each other, and the familiarity of making music together is another hug. The door flies open, and Ruby, Charlie, and Ava stand there, clapping.

Grandma grins at them. "Get out of here with that. I already gave you candy. You don't gotta suck up."

"Can I also be adopted?" Charlie asks, something like awe in his eyes.

"Are you as foolish as most men?" Grandma asks.

"Probably," he says at the same time Ava and Ruby say, "No."

Grandma gives him an assessing look. "Well, they'd know better than you would. Their word is good enough. You're adopted."

He makes prayer hands. "Thank you."

"Bye, Grandma Letty," Ruby says, tugging on Charlie's shirt to get him downstairs.

My phone vibrates with a text, and I look down to check it while Grandma is wishing them good night. It's Josh. I open it, curious. Well, and because I have zero power to resist a text from him.

You sound amazing. Balcony concert?

I glance toward the sliding doors again. He must be outside. It's the only way he could have heard us through my closed doors. I want to go check, but Grandma will have too many questions. Besides, she deserves all my attention right now.

"What's so dang interesting about your sliding door?" Grandma asks.

Oops. Guess I wasn't giving her as much attention as I thought.

"Does this have something to do with this Josh guy?" When she sees my guilty expression, she nods. "Mm-hmm. Tell me."

I wish there was nothing to tell her, but there is. And honestly, Letty Webster is the perfect person to set me straight right now.

"Once upon a time, a good-looking man moved in next door," I begin.

Grandma scoots up the bed and slips under the covers, tucking them under her arms and clasping her hands across her stomach. "How good-looking?"

I think for a minute. "Young Warren Beatty."

"Wow," she says. "Go on."

I tell her the rest of the story, from the first bad date to the balcony talks, and the whole fake girlfriend thing.

"How long has he been living next door?" she asks.

"Three weeks."

She whistles. "Been a busy boy."

I sigh. "I know. Busy is the whole problem. I don't have time for this right now."

"Sam, if you think that's the only issue here, you've got less common sense than I usually give you credit for," she says.

I straighten, a pinch of hurt trying to worm its way into my chest. "I just told you I'm not going to date him."

"But you want to," she says. "You need to think about why. He's a distraction right now with your music stuff heating up, isn't he?" I nod. "And you've been glancing at that balcony since we got up here like you want to climb over it to his and spend some quality time."

Definitely a mind reader. But I say, "I want to be here with you."

"Good, because I'm not going to tell you to go chasing after that boy. Even if it was actual young Warren Beatty." She squeezes my hand. "You don't see it, do you?"

"See what?"

"Tell me how this is different than Bryce." Her eyes study me, shrewd and unrelenting.

"He's . . . nicer."

"Like Bryce was in the beginning when he was trying to win you over?"

I have to admit this is true.

"Bryce was nice until he caught you. Then it

seemed to me like you spent the next three years chasing him, trying to prove you were who he wanted. But that was never going to work because people like Bryce and his family tree of jackasses measure people by all the wrong things. They can't see past the money and houses that make them feel important, and if you don't come from that, you're going to be suspected of trying to get it by marriage."

I flinch, and she rests her hand against my cheek. "Honey, none of them rejected you, because they never saw *you,* not even Bryce. They rejected who they assumed you to be. Now you're telling me that this Josh guy is chasing you, that he was brought up the exact same way, and you don't think you're in some kind of history repeating itself situation here?" She pats my cheek again before leaning back. "You have a type."

"Emotionally unavailable rich boys who want me as a trophy?"

"You said it, sister." Grandma rolls to her side to meet my eyes. "We're Webster women. It has never worked for us to count on a man. But baby"—and here she presses a kiss to my forehead—"we've never needed to. We do for ourselves. Always have done."

She's right. I don't want any of the things Bryce wanted or Josh wants. I want to be a working musician. Touring, writing music. Not a society wife. Not a country club member. And while a weekly Sunday dinner sounds nice, I've got family any time I want to go back to Hillsboro for them. Or even right here in the condo, with the family I've made.

All Josh can offer me long-term is a lifestyle I'm not made for. Bryce's rejection had been a blessing in disguise like breakups with the wrong guy always are. Maybe it had taken stepping into the shoes of Lady Mantha to understand what I really want, but I can't unknow the feeling of connecting with music fans through lyrics in a deep and real way, of feeding each other our energy in a live show, and . . . I don't want to.

I'll keep Josh at arm's length until he loses interest. Once he realizes he's more into the idea of catching me than keeping me, he'll move on. We *both* can move on. But for right now, for me, it's going to be all about keeping away.

Chapter Twenty-One
JOSH

Sami doesn't come out on the balcony. Not that Saturday night. Not any of the next several nights.

She answers texts, but we're in this strange spot where even though she's on my mind constantly, we don't have the kind of relationship where I can ask searching questions. I text her once for a recommendation on a sandwich shop, which she answers with the name of a place near our complex but nothing more.

I try again a couple of days later with a question about the best running routes near the Grove, and she responds minutes later with a link to a local online magazine that lists Austin running trails.

I get *really* personal one day and text, *Haven't seen you lately. How's it going?*

She eventually responds with a thumbs-up emoji.

I'd take it as a strong hint to leave her alone, but this standoffishness doesn't jibe with the girl who kissed me in my kitchen, or the one who sat talking with me on our balconies, or even the one who slipped her arms around my waist for a happy hug because I was at her show. The only thing I can think to do is to work even harder getting my hours in so I can cut out on nights when she's performing.

The next chance isn't until Thursday, when they're the headliner in a smaller club. This time, I wear a plain white T-shirt and buy a new Pixie Luna shirt as soon as I walk in and slip it on. I like my glittered one. I'm not washing it.

I settle into a place at the back and spot Madison before very long. Once again, I don't draw any attention to myself. I forgot to ask Ruby if the other roommates know I know about Pixie Luna. Besides, I want to enjoy the set without feeling like I'm under roommate observation.

This time when they perform, it's great, but not quite as high energy as their Saturday show. I wonder if they feed off the size of the crowd. But this crowd loves it anyway, dancing and getting into it like I've seen at their two prior shows.

I know all the words now since Sami's vocals keep me company to and from work every day as I parse them for more insight into my prickly, adorable puzzle of a neighbor. I'm pretty good at drawing conclusions, and I have some. But also, I'm trained not to *jump* to conclusions.

If I had to guess what Ruby has hinted at a few times, what I've seen from Sami with my own eyes, and most especially what I hear in the lyrics, my guess is this: she dated a guy with a similar background to mine. Prominent family, good connections, money. It went poorly. She thinks a lot of it has to do with the family, connections, and money. She thinks it'll happen again.

There are still too many gaps in all of that, gaps I want to earn her trust enough for her to fill in. Gaps I want to understand. Because I want to understand *her*.

Every time I see her on stage, I'm more sure of it. But also every time I talk to her on the balcony, or share a meal with her, or make out with her in my kitchen.

Sami doesn't stage dive this time, but a few times I notice her scanning the crowd like she's looking for someone specific. I weave from the back of the crowd to the middle, and sure enough, the next time she does her crowd search, her eyes snag on mine, and she smiles for a brief flash before she throws herself back into character and her song about why she wears big boots. (Answer: They speak louder than words.)

This time when their set is finished, I only poke my head backstage long enough to catch her eye and flash her a thumbs-up. She waves, and I disappear. I have to get back home to work a couple more hours.

There's no Sami on her balcony that night even though I check a few times.

This is a long game, something I've gotten better at playing. I'm not the guy who was used to getting everything and working for nothing anymore. I'll put in the time and watch for a signal that she's ready to figure out what this thing is between us.

Pixie Luna's next show isn't for another week, and it's a multi-band night. Big venue, mixed crowd, and they're right in the middle of the bill. It's on a Wednesday, and I have a major client meeting the next morning. It's a startup that recently secured a funding offer from a venture capital firm. VCs always try to convince startups to use the VC inside counsel. It gives them more control. This meeting will include the startup's entire board, and the VC will definitely attempt to sway them into ditching us and using their attorneys.

This is the kind of thing the firm will send a senior partner to observe, and my dad will definitely delegate that to someone he trusts to give him an objective report. I've spent two weeks preparing for this meeting and days practicing my counter arguments for when the VC makes their pitch, playing out every scenario and coming up with a rebuttal.

All of this means I shouldn't go to Sami's show on Wednesday. I should use every minute I have to prep so whoever my dad sends can bring back a report when I nail it in the board meeting. I wish I could text Sami and ask her if she wants me to be there, but I'd put a fat stack of cash on her answer being something like "Do what you want."

On Tuesday afternoon, I stare down the stack of work I've been putting off, and reality sets in; I can't take two hours off the night before a major meeting to go see a girl who tries not to see me while she plays a set of music I already know by heart. I can't.

I picture her eyes sweeping over the crowd tomorrow night, looking for my white Pixie Luna T-shirt, trying to spot my head above the sea of faces. Will she care when she doesn't see it? I've made a point of being the guy who shows up ever since losing Gram. For friends. For family. I'd do that for Sami if I was sure it's what she wants.

Do I owe her an explanation if I don't make it?

I do the only thing that kind of makes sense and send her a text. *I see you've got a show tomorrow night. Looks like a big one. Good luck!*

Around the time she gets off work, she texts back a gif of Dwight Shrute from *The Office* saying, "Thank you."

I have my answer. That's basically a "So what?" No *oh, you won't be there?* Or *you should come.* Just an impersonal gif.

Got it. Super got it. Should have gotten it about ten times before now.

Guess I'll have more time to prep for work.

I stay late at the office. Past the-gym-is-closed late all the way to only-drive-thrus-and-bars-are-still-open late. I try my luck with a fast-food salad and pull into home around midnight with a plastic container of slightly limp iceberg and grilled turkey that doesn't even have the good ranch dressing to go with it.

I'm ready to call the whole day a bust except when I get out of my car, I notice Sami on her balcony. She leans forward and peers down at me. I wave. She waves.

She's still there when I step out of my upstairs sliding door thirty seconds later.

"You didn't go inside," I say.

She doesn't pretend not to know why I thought she would. "Brain is busy."

"Would talking help?" It's all I've wanted her to do since that night at pho; open up, even a fraction.

"Not really."

"Would anything help?"

She rubs her eyes, less like she's sleepy and more like she's tired of life. "It's not one thing. Maybe if you could have a talk with my boss that would convince him I really need another CNA because I can't do all the work plus cover where we're short-staffed indefinitely. Or make sure my two favorite patients who never see visitors had family who actually turned up. Or stopped the aging process so I'm not losing a patient a week like I am right now."

She sinks in her chair and burrows into her

balcony blanket. "You could probably solve all my problems if you cloned me. Send one of me to band rehearsals at night and let her sleep all day, send the other of me to work and then come home to a full night of sleep."

"Which one is your job, and which is the clone's?"

"You can't guess?" She sounds almost disappointed.

"Of course I can. But it's so rare to see you anymore that maybe I'm making conversation just to make it because I'm glad you're out here tonight."

She turns toward me, and I think I see a smile in the dark. "I can't decide if you're a nerd because you say stuff like that out loud, or if you're so smooth that you can feed me a line and I don't realize it's a line because you're that good."

I hold up my plastic container and press it enough to make it crackle loudly. "Which category do you think a guy eating a wilted fast-food salad at midnight falls into?"

"Don't make me pity you. I need to pity myself right now."

I snap the plastic lid back in place on the salad and let it thump to the ground. "Tell me about the self-pity. I want to hear more."

"I know you work five billion hours a week, but between the nursing home, rehearsals, and shows, I'm putting in close to seventy and that feels like a lot. And it gives me no time to write."

"Write? Like fanfic? Grocery lists? Lyrics?"

"Lyrics. My *Real Housewives of Sunnyside Nursing Home* fanfic is dead forever. Didn't pay the bills."

"I'd pay money to read it."

"I bet."

We've been joking, but her tone is suddenly cool. Somehow, we're back there again, to the narrative where I'm the rich boy who uses money to get his way. I try not to let it get to me. I'm supposed to be letting my actions speak louder than my words, so I leave it alone. But I don't feel like making a clever comeback either, so I let the words hang there.

After a long pause, she sighs. "Sorry. I shouldn't have said that."

"You can say whatever you want if you think it's true. Do you?"

There's another long pause. "I probably shouldn't be talking to other humans tonight. I'm an overtired stress case."

It's not exactly vindication, but I'll take it for now. *Show interest in the things that matter to her.* "Are you going to be okay for the show tomorrow?"

She winces and rubs her face. "It's a big deal. We're supposed to sell a certain number of tickets for it, but we're not pulling our weight right now. People are mostly coming to see Night View.

And we really want to make a good impression on their producer so she'll work with us. Which means we have to be so awesome that we win over a crowd that's mostly theirs."

I stand and walk over to the railing, lean over it as far as I can. "Sami. You are awesome. All of you."

She turns toward me, and maybe it's a trick of the light, but I swear I see a flash of vulnerability I never see from her cross her face. "We are?"

Her voice is so small. It tangles up my guts. Or my heartstrings? Something in my chest and stomach. "You are," I say like there's no doubt in my mind. It's easy because I'm telling the truth.

"Okay."

"Sami . . ." I can already guess how this is going to go over, but I try anyway. "I know at least three people who would love to come see you perform."

"Good. Tell them to buy a ticket."

"You live with them. Maybe you should tell them."

She gives a small snort. "Nice one, Josh."

"I mean it," I say quietly. "I bet they would love it."

She doesn't say anything for a few seconds. Then she shifts in her chair and resettles her blanket. "Three people won't make a difference. We need way more people than that."

"You'll get them," I say. "And if you don't,

it won't matter, because you're still going to light up the crowd. Let's make a bet." It's an impulse, but I follow it, an idea brewing. "If you kill it with the crowd tomorrow, you tell your roommates about Pixie Luna."

"That's not something you can measure."

I call BS on her, succinctly. Then I add, "You know when you've killed it, Sami. Even I know when you've killed it. True or not true?"

She pulls her blanket over her head.

"Your Honor, please direct the witness to answer the question," I say.

"Stop," she says, but I hear a smile in her voice.

"Bet me, Sami. Unless you're afraid." Then I scoff. "Why am I saying it like *maybe* you're scared? You are one hundred percent certified chicken."

"Whatever, Josh."

I give a soft cluck and she whips toward me with a startled look. "That was really good," she says.

She's not getting out of this. I give another cluck, and her mouth twitches. I wait a few beats, and then I do it one more time. *Ba-kaw.*

"Oh, my Josh." Then she nearly trips over her own tongue to say, "I meant gosh. Oh my gosh."

I sit back down and kick my feet up on the railing. "I heard what I heard."

"What do you even care?" It's cute that she's trying to sound tough. "You're not even going to be there. I can tell you whatever I want about how it went. It was trash, by the way. Our worst gig ever."

"Wrong," I say. "I'll be there."

A tiny pause. "Yeah?"

I don't bother hiding a smile at the relief in her tone. "Yeah."

And I'm not coming alone.

I get into work Wednesday on time, which is late by my standards. But I was up late sending texts and emails.

I try to focus on the meeting prep, but I'm distracted by every text and email reply I get to my Sami project. It's working. I think I'm going to pull this off.

My dad would be less than thrilled if he knew the board meeting wasn't my sole focus today. Especially since he texted to ask how prep was going and I told him I had it on lock. But I know the account. I have a good relationship with the board. I've got the chops. I have to trust myself. And I will work on it some more. But tonight. After Sami's show.

I leave work at seven, hurry home, and change into my Pixie Luna shirt. When a quick look through the patio door reveals that Sami's car is gone, I run next door and knock. Ava answers and fetches Ruby at my request.

"Who's up tonight?" I ask, keeping my voice

low. "This one is a big deal. She needs fans."

"I got it," she says. "See you there."

I nod and hurry out to my car . . . and it doesn't start. It sounds like the battery, which isn't a hard problem to solve with dealer "courtesy" roadside service, but I'm in a hurry. I call the number on the card I keep in my glove box, and after a five-step phone menu and a seven-minute hold, a real live person takes my address and informs me that a technician will be there within forty to sixty minutes.

"I don't have that kind of time. Forget it. I'll take care of it tomorrow." I almost hang up before I remember to say, "But thank you for trying to help."

Okay, Lyft, then. But the app says it'll be another ten minutes before a car comes and it'll be twenty more before we get to the club.

I jump out of my car and over the neighbors' fence, knocking on their kitchen door.

Ava's face appears, startled. "Hello again," she says when she slides the door open.

"Ruby?"

She cocks her head. "I thought you were into Sami."

"I definitely am, but right now, I need Ruby."

"Coming." Ruby appears in the kitchen behind Ava. "What's up?"

"Car is dead and I need to be there ASAP. Can I get a ride with you?"

"Grab my wig," she tells Ava.

"They know I know?" I ask.

"We know," Ava confirms over her shoulder, already on the way to do Ruby's bidding.

"Let me grab my keys." She disappears down the hall and around the corner, reappearing seconds later with her keys in hand while she slides her ID into her bra. "Let's go."

We head out to the parking lot, past her condo's spots. And keep going. And going. We're near the very end of the complex's parking when she finally stops at a silver Civic and disarms the lock.

"This parking *sucks*," I say.

She gives me a huge grin that I swear looks borderline evil. "I'm working on it."

We get in and drive back in the direction of our units, where Ava stands on the sidewalk.

"Open your window," Ruby says.

I do and Ava thrusts a blonde wig at me before she waves and tells me, "Good luck." She heads back through their gate.

"Buckle up," Ruby says, grinning. "And if you don't know any Spanish swears, you're about to learn some."

"I thought Ava was wishing me good luck for Sami, but that's not it, is it?" I ask as Ruby peels out slightly and throws me against my seat.

"No, neighbor," she says, taking the turn toward the exit almost on two wheels. "It ain't."

Chapter Twenty-Two
SAMI

The last person I want to see tonight is the show promoter, but Anthony appears in the crowded backstage "green" room—it's concrete gray with old gum and cigarette burns on the wall—and scans it like he's looking for someone.

"Going to be a good show tonight," he says as he pauses at the doorway, making eye contact with us. There are members of three other bands crammed in here minus the opening one who's already out there warming up the half-full club.

There's no great way to spin this, but I have to try. We're on the verge of one of our biggest breaks, and I can't let it slip through our fingers.

I stand up and walk over to him. "Hey, man, thanks for having us on the bill. I know we didn't sell a lot of tickets, but we'll tear it up during our set, I promise."

He gives me a confused look. "What are you talking about? You met your ticket quota. Those last-minute sales sold out the show tonight."

"Our what?" Last-minute ticket sales?

But someone else has already caught his attention and he's brushing past me with a distracted apology.

At first, a wave of relief rolls through me, and I walk back to the sofa we've staked out to tell the guys the news, but then I stop.

A sudden block of ticket sales?

That has rich boy written all over it, and I fight the urge to rub my hands over my face so I don't smear my heavy black eye makeup and violently pink lipstick.

I'm sure Josh thought it would help if he bought up a bunch of tickets, but that's dozens of tickets that didn't go to actual people. This is *not* going to be a full house tonight, and it's going to be almost fifty people quieter for Pixie Luna than the ticket sales say it should be.

Once again, he's making a bigger mess by trying to solve things with money. I appreciate that he wanted to do something good, but I wish he would have asked me first. Still, I can't get mad. If he wants to blow his money like that, so be it. But it doesn't change what we have to do when we get onstage. We've got to whip up the *whole* crowd, not just the few dozen fans that bought the tickets in our allotment.

The crowd buzz builds over the next hour as the two opening acts go out and complete their sets. Near the end of the set before ours, Wingnut comes in from a recon of the crowd.

"Yo, it's wild," he says.

Anthony pokes his head in. "Pixie Luna, you're on in fifteen," he calls before disappearing.

"Good crowd?" Luther asks.

"Packed," Wingnut confirms. "Preppy but into it. Keeping the bar busy, everyone's vibing. It's good."

"I'm going to check." Preppy? I need to see this for myself.

Sure enough, when I slip past the security guard to check out the floor, it's packed with barely any room around the outskirts of the crowd.

Whoa. We really *did* have a ticket surge come through. I look for Josh, but I can't pick him out of the crowd from the floor. If he's here, I'll be able to see him from the stage.

My heart gives one hard thump, then the familiar pre-show adrenaline pumps through my veins, moving in time with the beat from the kickdrum on stage. These people are primed and ready, and whether Night View or their producer or anyone else hears our set, I'm ready to sing my face off. I will feed off this energy and send it out from the stage, and they'll pay it back times ten.

I'm practically hopping by the time I reach the green room. "Wingnut's right," I tell the rest of them. "It's a great crowd."

Jules nods. "We best get ready to swap out our equipment."

He and Rodney head down the hall toward the stage. Luther, Wingnut, and I follow, grabbing our gear from the van behind the club and bringing it in through the back. The current band finishes to loud cheers and comes off the stage with their instruments. Rodney will use the drum set on the stage, but like most drummers, he'll switch out the snare and cymbals for his own.

"Great crowd," their singer says, nodding and fist bumping with us as they squeeze past in the hall. "Kill it."

"Thanks, man," Luther says with his usual chill.

Me, I'm bouncing on the balls of my feet. The longest wait is for Rodney to configure the drums, but the club is pumping loud, fast music through the PA, and pretty soon he's back in the wings with us. He nods.

"Let's do this!" Wingnut shouts. They head onstage while I grip my mic and bounce from side to side, trying to give the energy somewhere to go while I wait for my cue.

Rodney does his four stick strikes, and the sound roars out of the amps, the deep chest-vibrating notes of Luther's bass, the snarl of Jules's electric guitar, and as they reach the end of the first four bars, I run out to hit front and center stage in perfect time to sing out the first words of our opening song: "Who do you think you are?"

We've definitely got fans in the crowd, because a cheer goes up at the sound of those lyrics. It's been a great opener for us because it's a song about everyone in your life you've ever wanted to tell off. It's an homage to an old Twisted Sister song called "We're Not Going to Take It" that Grandma used to blast when it came on the classic rock station. That song was a big old middle finger to every authority figure of the time, and this is kind of like that but more personal.

Sure, the line, "Bye-bye, dumb guy who always made me cry" is a Bryce callout, but Rodney and I wrote this together, so lines like, "Adios, chief, to the boss who gave me grief," is him checking the project manager who takes all the credit and none of the blame at his coding day job. It's more people power than girl power, and it always gets the crowd moving with its gleeful takedown of every personal nemesis we could imagine.

Jerk cops, absent dads, Kevins, Brads, and Chads . . . all of them can "Shove it, bro."

Immature? Yes.

Better even than one of those rage rooms where you smash stuff when a crowd is singing it with you at the top of their lungs? Yes. Every time. That's why we start with it.

We follow that with a more party anthem, "Here For It," and that's got the crowd bouncing and dancing.

It's not until the fourth song, "Crybaby," that we shift down to mid-tempo, and I can prowl instead of jump and run, a deliberate stalking of the stage as I sing that gives me a chance to search the crowd for a familiar face.

Ugh, for *Josh's* face. I want to see his irritating, gorgeous face.

I find him in the middle of the crowd. That's where he's hung out the last two shows, by himself and fine with it, all his attention on the stage. On me.

This time it's different. He's talking to another guy, and as I sing, a guy on his other side hits him in the arm and shows him something on his phone that makes Josh laugh. He's here with friends. And the more I watch, the more guys I see interacting with him, or with each other, but in a way that begins to reveal the size of their group.

It takes less than a minute for me to identify them as fraternity brothers. Not because they're in matching sweatshirts or anything; you just spend enough time around these guys in college and you get a feel for the vibe.

Josh packed the club with his fraternity brothers. At a minimum, the manager will be happy with their liquor sales.

I stomp across the stage in time to the beat and hit another power pose as we transition to the bridge of the song, and the crowd goes wild. The *whole* crowd. We draw a pretty even mix of genders, but thanks to Josh, it's a more guy-heavy crowd than usual tonight. And they *still* lose it, jumping, fist-pumping, hands in the air, rocking out.

I would sing every song to Josh tonight if they weren't all about how much you can't count on men. But tonight, he's the opposite of everything that went into those songs. So I don't sing *to* him, but I do sing for him. My energy amps, the crowd's rises to match it, and we race each other to the end of the song in a mad frenzy. The final chords of Jules's guitar meet a roar from the audience.

It's awesome. So awesome. It's swooping-down-the-long-slope-of-the-roller-coaster adrenaline. It's UT-winning-the-bowl-game-with-ten seconds-left-to-avoid-overtime dopamine. It's kissing-Josh-in-his-kitchen euphoria.

Whether these guys were coached or bribed or whether they're sincerely into it, it doesn't matter. It fires up the whole crowd, the whole band, and it's exactly the show I'd hoped we'd deliver on such a high-stakes night.

We finish our set with the song that's been adding thousands of new streams every day, "Walk Away," and the crowd goes crazy. The energy is insane. We rush off the stage and straight into high fives and back slaps backstage. Carlos from Night View is there, grinning.

"Hey, we came in to catch your show. You killed it."

"Thanks, man," Jules says, and they do a bro hug.

"Mighty-mite here gives it everything," Luther says.

"But so do you guys," I protest. Honestly, I can barely pay attention to the conversation because I'm already on the lookout for Josh, waiting for him to make his backstage appearance. I don't see him yet, but it's a more crowded show than usual, so there are more musicians milling around.

I turn my attention back to my band. Or try to. "You guys are so tight. You sounded amazing. And I'm going to tell you all that a million more times, but right this second, I need to go see Josh and thank him for packing the crowd. We cool?"

Luther waves me toward the floor, and Jules smiles. "Go ahead."

As soon as I step out of the hall, I'm in the crowd. Music pulses from the PA while Night View's crew sets up. The edges of the crowd are easy to thread through. I feel the brush of hands reaching for me and what sounds like compliments, barely audible over the blaring music, but I don't stop.

I press farther into the crowd, and it's getting harder to navigate. It's not the first time I've wished for six more inches of height, but I keep going, more hands thrusting my way for high fives and knuckle bumps, more shouted compliments.

I'm getting toward the center and finding the

outer ring of the fraternity nucleus. When I reach one clean-cut guy, I take a gamble. "Excuse me," I shout. "You here with Josh?"

He looks at me and his face brightens. "It's you. Did it work?"

I must have misheard him because his question makes no sense. I point to my ear and shake my head. "Josh?" I call again.

He grins and points farther into the crowd. I press on, my chest buzzing, my palms itchy, anxious to find Josh and hoping the bro-dude behind me pointed me the right way.

I tug on sleeves and shirts of everyone in my way, shouting, "Josh?" and follow their pointing fingers. I make it another ten feet when one guy I ask rests his hand on my arm and leans down to make sure I can hear him.

"You're looking for Josh?" he asks near my ear. I nod.

"You happy or mad?" He's enormous, built like he played on the offensive line for the Longhorns, but his expression is curious, a slight smile on his lips.

"Not sure, but I'm definitely going to kiss his face off," I yell back.

He grins, turns around, and gestures for me to hop on for a piggyback.

It's undignified how often short girls get this offer. But at the moment, it's exactly what I need, and I take it, immediately able to see over the sea of heads. I spot Josh and wave, but he doesn't see me, so I point my escort in the right direction and he begins weaving us through the crowd.

"Lady Mantha, you rocked," someone yells, and I grin and wave but don't take my eyes off the prize.

Josh turns and sees me, offering a tentative smile, like he's not sure if my piggyback charge means he's in trouble or not.

I give him the biggest smile I've ever given him, so big my cheeks bunch uncomfortably beneath the bottom edge of my mask, but I don't care. His frat brothers have noticed now, and as Josh starts toward me, they begin clearing a path between my new friend, the ox, and Josh.

Within seconds, we've reached each other in the pocket they've made in the sea of people, and my ride sets me down gently. The entire circle of faces around us watches like they know what's going on. Josh tilts his head and smiles at me, then says what he says every time. "Killer show."

I grin again and launch myself at him without warning, but he catches me easily against his chest as I lock my arms around his neck. "What did you do?" I ask against his ear.

"Told all my fraternity brothers that I needed to help a lady out, and they all decided it's a perfect night to hear a kickass band."

I press a kiss to his mouth, a hard one, and he gives it right back. It's the kind of kiss that makes the music fade into nothing but its bass line, which matches my pulse, and the catcalls and cheers of his buddies disappear too.

When we finally come up for air, I smooth my thumb over his lips to wipe away the glitter gloss I've left there. "Why have I not been doing this every chance I got?"

"I've been asking myself that question ever since my kitchen," he says.

I push slightly against his shoulders to be set down but tuck myself against his side and take in the crowd of guys around us. "They all came here just to make sure I had a good show?"

"They came to make sure you had a good show, so that I'd maybe finally get my shot," he says, and his soft laugh stirs the loose hair near my ear. "They couldn't resist when I told them I had to make a grand gesture."

"Ooh, is this where the music in the romcom swells and the credits start to roll?" I ask.

His face grows more serious, and he bends to make sure we're eye to eye. "That's up to you," he says. "But that's what I was going for."

It's impossible. There are too many other conflicts to resolve. But I look into his eyes, and I don't care. I don't care about all the reasons this might not work or doesn't make sense. He's shown up for me in a way that no guy ever has, and I'm not dumb enough to let this go.

"I have to go backstage," I call over the music.

"But I will one hundred percent be on the balcony tonight. I owe you about a hundred big, fat apologies. And my story."

He presses another hard kiss against my lips. "I've heard that promise several times before."

"I'll be there. For real."

He looks down at me like he's trying to decide if I mean it. "If you don't show this time, I'm going to finally take the hint."

"I should never have blown you off. It'll be late, but I'll definitely show."

"Doesn't matter. I'll wait for you."

I grin at him for a few seconds, pop up on my tiptoes to give him another fast kiss, then whirl to look for my ride.

The big guy is watching it all, smiling. I point to myself, to him, and the backstage door, and without a word, he turns and crouches, and I'm on my way back to the band.

The night only gets wilder from there. When I make it backstage again, Carlos wants to introduce me to his "friend," Nick Bautista, an exec from their record label, Bat Bridge. He wants to talk about the direction Pixie Luna is going.

"They want to gauge our dedication," Luther says after we chat with Nick for several minutes until Night View takes the stage. He'd asked how we met, how long we've played together, our collaboration process, and several things that felt . . . interview-y. "He's figuring out if we're a good bet for the long haul," Luther explains.

"I'm so glad we have you around, Luther," I tell him. "I would have thought he was chatting music to be polite."

Luther gives me a slow grin. "He's being the kind of polite that might get him a band he likes if he keeps being impressed."

Night View does a great set, and when it's time to drive everything back to Rodney's house and stow the equipment, the boys all refuse to let me.

"Nah," Jules says. "Your boyfriend did us a solid, packing the show like that. You said y'all were going to talk?" I nod. "Then we're sending you home in an Uber. You can come round for your car tomorrow."

I look at each one of them, making sure this is okay. We're all big on pulling our weight. They're all smiling. Rodney waves his hand, like *Go*.

"Thank you!" I say, already requesting a ride on my phone. Downtown Austin is crawling with rideshare drivers, and I have one ready to pick me up in three minutes.

I'm still brimming with nervous energy when he drops me off at the Grove. Josh's balcony is empty, which is a relief. He probably isn't expecting me yet, and I *do* want to talk to him, but I have another stop to make first.

I walk in through the front door to find Ava and Ruby on the sofa, both looking two blinks from sleep, but I'd texted them to wait up for me, and they have. Madi's working, so I'll have to fill her in later.

I settle on the coffee table across from them, and I realize immediately that something is up. I still have bright pink hair and I'm wearing the newly thrifted prom dress I found with Grandma.

"Neither of you looks surprised to see me dressed like this."

Ruby and Ava exchange a look. Ava clears her throat. "That's an interesting outfit, Sami. Why are you dressed like that?"

I look back and forth between them, my eyes narrowed. "How much do you know?"

Ruby shrugs. "Your show tonight was the best so far."

"And how do you know that?" I ask.

"I was there."

A flutter of disappointment whispers through my chest. "Josh told you?" I really hadn't expected him to.

Ava shakes her head. "We figured it out a while ago. One of us is always at your shows. We wear wigs and do it incognito since you weren't telling us about them for some—"

"—idiotic reason," Ruby interrupts.

"I wasn't going to say 'idiotic,' but basically," Ava finishes.

I look between them again, this time with my jaw slightly dropped. How the . . . ?

"So why didn't you tell us?" Ruby demands.

"I wasn't sure you'd understand," I say.

"What's to understand?" Ruby asks. "You're an amazing performer. We watched you all the time in college. We already knew that."

"That's the thing." I'd been trying to formulate this explanation on the way over. "In college, I did the whole hyper-sincere singer-songwriter thing. Slower. Kind of folky. Acoustic. That's what nice girls do, right?" I extend one of my feet in my Doc Marten boots. "This is not that. This is loud and fast and angry."

Ruby gives the bottom of my heel a light kick, and I put it down. "It's also smart and funny and super relatable. Yeah, it's different. But it's so . . . *you*."

I hold my breath for a few seconds before puffing my cheeks and blowing out the air. "That's what made me nervous. I know you didn't feel like it was healthy for me to stew over Bryce, but I had to get all that anger out. I wasn't over it when y'all were ready for me to be over it.

"I felt embarrassed about that, so it went into lyrics that weren't even remotely mellow enough for the music I wrote in college. I wrote song after song, shoving everything I hated about that breakup into the music. It turned into angry, anthemic rock. But it feels way safer to perform that up in front of strangers who wouldn't understand how true all the songs are."

"Are, present tense?" Ava asks. "Or were?"

Almost on instinct, I glance toward Josh's condo, like I can sense him through the wall. "More and more past tense."

Ruby nudges my foot again, and I look at her, fighting a smile when she waggles her eyebrows at me. "It's like that?"

I shrug. "It's something. I don't know what yet."

"I like him," Ruby says. "More and more every time I talk to him."

"Same," I confess. Ruby and Ava both grin. "You've really been wearing wigs to come watch me?" I couldn't let that all the way in at first because it felt too big, and even now, just the idea that they've been quietly showing up is threatening to squeeze my eyeballs.

"Ruby uses a blonde wig and Madi and I share a brown wig," Ava tells me.

"I go as Madame Fifi Lacroix," Ruby says, flipping her pretend blonde hair.

"Just Ava," Ava says. "But brunette."

"I love you guys."

"We love you too, bestie," Ruby says. "That's why we couldn't let you perform without one of us there. We've been long overdue for a "Since U Been Gone"–level jam, and that's what you do."

She pulls me into a hug. "I'm sorry we didn't give you enough time to get over Bryce. He wasn't worth a single one of your tears, but that doesn't mean we should have rushed you past the feels."

"I know you were just trying to do what was best for me."

Ava dogpiles us. There's some sniffling and cooing before I free myself and sit up.

"I guess I don't have to explain this all to Madi?"

"Nope," Ava says. "Just send her a thank you text."

"In that case, it's time for me to go have another talk."

Ruby claps her hands. "Can't wait for my parking upgrade."

I stand and shoot her a warning look. "We're not *there* yet. Pace yourself."

She points me toward the door. "Sooner you get over there, the sooner I get my space. Byeeeeee."

I ignore her and head up the stairs to my room, sending a text as I go.

Sorry, but I can't meet you on the balcony.

Chapter Twenty-Three
JOSH

I can't meet you on the balcony.

I reread the text. Is she kidding? I thought after that whole scene at the club that I'd gotten through to her. Yet here she is, blowing me off again.

That's it, then.

A sinking feeling starts in my stomach just as my phone buzzes again.

Come down to your kitchen.

That wins a small laugh from me. She definitely knows how to push my buttons.

I walk into the kitchen to find her standing at the sliding door, shivering, and I hurry to unlock it. "It's below forty out here."

"Yeah," she says with a slight chatter of her teeth despite the oversized sweatshirt she's wearing. She's ditched the mask and her hair is still pink but in a messy bun now instead of her two wild pigtails. "That's why no balcony."

"Fair." I pull her into my arms to warm her up, but mainly because I want to feel her against me again. I keep her there until her shivering stops. "I'm glad you're here."

I can't tell whether she's nodding against my

chest or cuddling in farther, but either way, I hold her closer.

After a couple of minutes, I feel her sigh followed by a mumbled, "Now I have to talk."

"You sound like I'm about to start pulling out your nails with pliers. Is it that bad?"

She gives a small, snuffling laugh. "No. It's just that the more I think about this, the dumber I feel for making you jump through so many hoops."

"Hey," I say, holding her away from me enough to meet her eyes. "That is absolutely valid, and you should."

She swats at me, and I catch her hands, grinning. "I make my own choices. I wouldn't have kept trying if I didn't think you were worth it."

A soft breath escapes her. "You ready for my drama?"

"Not quite." I scoop her up, bride style, and she gasps and then giggles as I carry her into my living room, settling us into the center junction of the sectional. I lean back against it, and she slides off my lap enough to settle next to me with her legs still draped over my thighs. I look down at her and raise my eyebrows. "Now talk."

She responds by wiggling and fidgeting, finally drawing up her legs so her feet are wedged under me like I'm bracing her for sit-ups. Then she tucks her arms into her sweatshirt, leaving the sleeves empty, rests her chin on her knees, and begins.

"I'll try to keep this short, but interrupt if you have questions." When I nod, she continues. "I grew up in Hillsboro with a single mother. My father left before I was one and I don't remember him. Mom grew up with a single mother. My grandfather ran out on my grandma when my mom was three, and she doesn't remember her dad either."

"Dirtbags." That's the nicest word I can come up with.

She shrugs. "I guess. We did all right. My mom raised me the same way Grandma raised her: don't count on a man, do for yourself, work hard, and you'll never have to depend on anyone. Grandma worked as a waitress forever then eventually worked up to regional manager for Pickle Patch."

"They make a good breakfast."

"Facts," Sami says. "My mom became a nurse. It can be hard hours, but there's always work, and I liked that I could earn well with a four-year degree. College was barely affordable; a masters or law school? Forget it. So I worked like a dog through high school, got scholarships, and went to UT. I had it better than a lot of people in my town, but I'd always look around at the kids whose parents were together, whose dads were lawyers or doctors, or even jobsite superintendents, and I'd think, 'It would be so much easier to have a family like that.' And

I think I started looking for that in college. Not consciously."

She stops to rub her cheek against her sweatshirt-covered knee, and it reminds me of a cat, one that will dart away if I make any sudden movements. I say nothing and wait for her to pick up the story.

"I met Ruby, Ava, and Madi our freshman year, and I adored them. Ava and I probably clicked the most because we both love life science, but all of us got along. Madi, though? Next level. She comes from major money and probably has the biggest brain out of all of us."

"I don't know her well at all," I say, "so I shouldn't judge, but something about that surprises me."

"Madi doesn't let anyone know her, really. Even after all these years, in some ways, we barely do. But Pi Phi really wanted her to pledge, and they were constantly recruiting her. Her mom was Pi Phi. It doesn't look good if a legacy doesn't want to join. I overheard them one night when they came over to the dorm to sell her on pledging. They talked about the sisterhood, the opportunities to give back, the way you have a lifelong network of women who will look out for you personally, socially, professionally."

She peers up at me, her eyes tired. "Can you imagine why that appealed to me?"

"Because it was a much bigger net than just your mom and grandmother?"

She nods. "Don't get me wrong, my mom and grandma are *everything*. But having that much backup built in? I'd never experienced anything like it. When the sorority girls left, I started bugging Madi to pledge. I told her we should both do it, and it would be fun.

"Eventually, she was like, sure, okay, and we went through rush and made it through every round. We both got bids. I accepted mine. Madi didn't."

"For real?" A lot of girls at UT would give up a future firstborn for a Pi Phi bid. Their grad network is impressive and can open doors from Austin to New York and DC.

"Yeah. I found out later that she only agreed to accept the bid if they offered me one too. Told them we were a package deal." She shakes her head, and I catch a smile on the half of her face I can see. "So Madi. Lunatic."

"Were they mad?"

"At Madi. And some of the girls held it against me, but mostly they were mad at her for rejecting them."

"Did they treat you okay?" The Greek system is not nearly as dysfunctional as movies and TV shows like to make it out to be, but sometimes sororities can be harder on their members than frats are.

"Eventually. In some ways, it helped that I didn't live in the sorority house. That kept costs down for me, and when I explained to my grandma why I joined, about the professional benefits I was banking on down the road, she was all over helping me. She knows that a lot of professional success comes down to who you know and not what you know. She made sure I had enough for the real dues plus the unofficial ones. The new mandatory T-shirt for every event, the matching outfits they wanted, the specific brand and cut of white jean, or the specific sandal."

"At this point, rock goddess Sami is as normal to me as sweatshirt Sami," I tell her, tucking a strand of hair behind her ear. She shivers and goose bumps pop out along her neck. I smile. She's into me. Maybe as much as I'm into her. "It's hard to imagine you being matchy-matchy with your sisters."

"It wasn't hard at first. It was amazing to be part of a group like that. But over time, it started to wear thin. Especially once I'd committed to nursing and realized I probably wasn't going to need their connections to get hired. But I stuck it out because of Bryce."

"That bastard," I say, mostly to make her laugh. It works.

"Yeah, basically. We started dating my sophomore year. He was the guy that half of Pi Phi wanted, and he picked me."

I couldn't blame him, but I did want to punch him, and I wasn't even exactly sure what he was guilty of yet.

"He came from a super wealthy Dallas family. Graduated in geology with a plan to go straight into an MBA at Rice so he could start working for his family's oil business." She lifts her head and rests it on her knees so she can look me fully in the face. "I'll spare you the details because I'd only want to know about your exes in the most general terms, but let's just say I was gone on him. Saw our five-year plan, getting married after business school, the whole bit."

I definitely hate this guy.

"What I didn't know is that his family didn't like me. At least, they didn't like me for him. Felt like I didn't come from a similar enough background to understand their lifestyle and future plans for their precious boy. His mom told him I was fine for college, but when we graduated, he needed to move on to a more suitable relationship. So that's what he did. He dumped me the day after graduation. I heard through the grapevine a few months ago that he's engaged to some girl from Dallas."

"So basically, you find everything about UT frat boys from wealthy families triggering."

"Basically."

I pull her back into my lap and nestle her against my chest. "I get it. I get why on the surface, I seem the same. But I'm not like him. I'm not that guy."

She presses into me. "I know. There were red flags I only saw in hindsight. I've always written music. It was a thing with my grandma and me. My mom told me it was fine for fun but in no way a career, so I'd perform at coffeehouses and small places for open mic nights. Singer-songwriter stuff, very different vibe. He came to one or two and told me it wasn't bad, but he'd rather we put in time with friends since the Austin scene was too competitive for me to get anywhere."

I kiss the top of her head. "I'm not that guy," I repeat.

She tilts her head up to return my kiss with a soft one, pulling away far too soon. "I know. You've shown up for me in the ways that matter."

I kiss her again, a longer kiss, one that tells her how much I want to be her guy. She eventually draws away with a tiny growl that nearly undoes me. It's like the rock goddess has turned kitten in my arms.

"There's more. Let me tell you the worst of it, and then we can be done with it forever."

I wonder if she knows how the word "forever" lands when it's coming out of her mouth. Probably not, but I've never been able to talk about "next month" with someone I'm dating, so I wonder why "forever" doesn't make me sweat.

"Lay it on me," I tell her. "I'm ready."

"I didn't take the breakup well. Not only did I not see it coming, I'd bought into the life plan most of the Pi Phi girls had. Everything in my future involved Bryce. We were going to make the family I never had. We'd have two kids and the perfect suburban house. And probably an actual Suburban. Soccer mom. Dance mom. Whatever. His family was always nice to me, and I thought I was enough of a catch that I didn't see any speed bumps."

"You're more than enough." It's true, but also, I know a dozen guys like Bryce. I can see it all playing out like a slow-motion catastrophe that takes her down before she even realizes she's in the middle of it.

"I know that. But I was so hurt at the time. I felt like I was never going to be good enough for anyone except someone who came up as rough as I did. Eventually, I was fine with that. But I had no idea that I was such an issue for his parents until they told him that playtime was over."

She shifts and slides her legs from my lap so she can fold them beneath her and kneel, bringing her almost eye level. It makes it easy to see that hers are burning, not with hurt but determination. "The only thing I'm madder about than not seeing it coming is taking so long to get over it. I think it's because my mom would never get mad about my dad. Even when things were the toughest and my grandma would say he was a lowlife who should be paying child support, my mom would just tell her it was pointless to be mad. That was her thing. Don't get upset. Just fix it. So it didn't feel okay to be mad about Bryce."

I can't hide my smile. "It seems like you got there eventually." She has no problem reading Bryce for filth on stage, even if she's not using his name.

An answering smile peeks back at me. "Right? I started channeling it into lyrics. But they didn't fit my usual vibe. And when I found the right rhythms and melodies, the music started pulling things from me in ways it never had before. I reached out to some guys I knew from gigging, and we started jamming together. And we knew we had something. Putting it out there as a performance was cathartic, but I didn't want anyone I knew to see me because if they knew my situation, they'd see too much in those lyrics."

"So Lady Mantha was born."

"Yeah. It kind of started with the tattoo, actually. When I finally hit the point about a year ago that I wouldn't take Bryce back if he begged, I wanted to commemorate it, so Madi came with me to get my tattoo. I picked a luna moth because it means transformation."

"Oh," I say, realization dawning. "I thought it was a butterfly."

She shakes her head and turns slightly, pulling up her sweatshirt in the back to reveal a tank top.

"See how it's green with those markings on the bottom of the wings? Luna moth. And that's a purple chrysanthemum. It symbolizes loyalty to myself. I've spent the last eighteen months figuring out who I am and what I want."

I reach up and trace the moth. She goes still when I touch her, and it's not until I lift my finger that she breathes again.

"You're kind of killing me here, Josh." Her voice is low.

"Am I?" I ask, lazily. I can feel it in the almost-physical vibration of the space between us. I can feel it in my lungs and fingertips and the way my muscles tense. "How can I make it better?"

It's a dangerous question, and I know it. She turns to face me again with a glint in her eye that tells me I'm about to pay in the best possible ways.

"Well," she says, tapping her bottom lip slowly to make sure I can't take my eyes off her warm, full mouth, "I guess you could kiss me better."

I reach up and draw her tapping finger down, entwining it with mine and using it to pull her ever-so-slightly toward me. "I think I've given you the wrong impression, Lady Mantha. I'm here for Sami. In fact, I'm all in for Sami. The question is whether she's got the guts to step into this. To be all in. To see what we've got here."

Sami leans forward until she's close enough for me to feel the puff of her breath while she keeps her eyes locked on mine. "I don't know who this Lady Mantha is, but I'm right here. And no one has ever called me a coward."

"You're saying you're not my fake girlfriend anymore?"

"I'm saying I'm not your fake girlfriend anymore."

But I want to be totally sure we're talking about the same thing. "You mean you're my real gi—"

She cuts me off with a kiss that would have leveled me out if I weren't already sitting. She comes up short of breath for a second to make herself clear. "Yes, Josh. I'm saying this is real. No more talking."

I grin and shut up. I'm a lot of things but stupid isn't one of them.

I finally walk her next door in the wee hours with swollen lips and beard burn. When I stagger upstairs to my room and make sure my alarm is set to go off in three hours, I still don't regret it.

She's unexpected. Definitely not part of the plan.

And exactly what I want.

Chapter Twenty-Four
JOSH

It's an all-eyes-on-me situation.

Maybe this is how it feels for Sami. Every person in the room, staring at you, waiting for the next thing that comes out of your mouth.

She likes it. Wants it. Thrives on it.

I . . . do not.

NewTekk is looking at me. As in their entire executive board. Their expressions range from confused to concerned.

One person looks flat-out thunderous, the senior partner from Brower sitting next to me, Roger Jardin, who looks like he wants to reach over and press on my windpipe until I'm no longer breathing.

"Josh," Roger says with the careful enunciation of a man who is trying to sound like nothing is wrong, "what are we looking at here?"

The NewTekk board president looks from the screen—where the CFO has just shared the single greatest professional mistake of my life—to me.

"Mr. Brower gave BitGenesis the evidence they need for their lawsuit," the CFO says.

I don't know what my face looks like. It feels like all the blood has left it. And I didn't start out great this morning, circles under my eyes and my face puffy from only grabbing a couple hours of sleep after seeing Sami home, post-DTR talk.

"Is that what this is?" Roger asks.

It's obviously what it is. It's all right there in the conveniently magnified email header.

From: JBrower@BrowerMoore.com
To: RJardin@BrowerMoore.com,
    Darvesh@NewTekk.com
CC: LPeele@Ogilvy.com,
    TonyWoods@bitgenesis.com

That screenshot says I have screwed up very badly. I've sent the plaintiff suing NewTekk for intellectual property rights a copy of an employment contract that strengthens their claim.

This is the meeting I'd been prepping for since last week. Dotting every *i*. Crossing every *t*. Preparing to demonstrate that we are excellent counsel.

This is nothing short of disastrous.

I'd gone into the office an hour early as usual, ordering my coffee with a triple shot of espresso along the way. It was enough to give my hands a tremor all morning, but not enough to keep me alert. Not if I made a mistake like this as soon as I got to my desk.

Not *if*. I *did* make this mistake. I'd meant to copy that email to Tony Workman at NewTekk, and the email autofill had supplied the wrong address. The *worst* wrong address.

All those hours of prep. Of billable hours equaling thousands in income for the firm, and a single mistake might cost the firm any future NewTekk revenue. Darvesh, their board president, has doubt written all over his face. Roger's lips have flattened to a straight line as they all wait for an explanation.

I open my mouth to give them one. Darvesh leans forward slightly, waiting. I don't know how I can feel like my face has drained of blood *and* like it's pounding through my ears at the same time, but I do. I do. It's so loud, I can't think over it. Nothing comes out of my mouth.

Roger jumps in, showing the smoothness that got him to partner. "Ladies and gentlemen, Josh and I are going to have a quick debrief and come to you with a solution. If you'll excuse us a moment."

Darvesh nods, but the look he gives me is loaded with disapproval.

I follow Roger out of the conference room. He pauses where we'll still be in sight of the NewTekk board.

"Look at me like you're considering what I have to say thoughtfully, not like I'm going to tear you a new one," Roger says.

I rearrange my expression to my best active listening face.

"Keep it like that for the next few minutes because I'm absolutely going to tear you a new one." And he does, for the next three minutes. He is a master, keeping his expression thoughtful, pausing a few times to say things like "do you understand me, you entitled little puke?" I nod and fight to keep my expression even each time. He's right. I have no excuse. None.

"There's only one way out of this," he concludes, "and you better pray it works, because if it doesn't, I may not be able to talk your father into firing you, but I will absolutely get you blocked from the partner track for the next two votes. *Minimum.* Got it?"

I want to say, *It was a stupid autofill error.* I want to say, *It's the first major mistake I've made since I started working here.* I want to say, *You've had it out for me since I started.*

But I can't say any of those things, because when it comes down to it, he's right. There's no excuse.

I nod. "Got it."

"Good. Here's what we're going to do. We're going to go in and acknowledge that this was a careless mistake on your part. We will inform them that you are being reassigned, and I will be handling their business from this point forward. We will also be waiving your billable hours for the next month as you transition everything over to a new *senior* associate. Understand? Smile and nod if you do."

I smile and nod. It's the only thing I *can* do.

When we walk into the boardroom, I stop to face the NewTekk board. "My apologies for the oversight on the email autofill. This is not the standard our firm holds itself to, and we will not be making that mistake again."

Darvesh nods in acknowledgment, and I take my seat as Roger continues the reassurances. "I'll be overseeing your account personally from this point on, bringing twenty years of experience with tech firms with me. As a sign of good faith, we will not be billing you for Josh's hours during that transition."

It's a substantial savings—over ten thousand dollars.

I hold my breath, hoping they accept the terms, hoping that I haven't just blown a massive hole in the bottom line of the firm's profits.

Darvesh and Tony Workman—the board VP and the guy who *should* have gotten the email—turn and confer. They each look at the other three board members, and when no one raises more than an eyebrow, Darvesh nods. "We accept. We'll stay with you so long as there are no more oversights."

"Understood," Roger says, and I know it's galling him to be reprimanded like he's a first-year associate.

The rest of the meeting continues with Brower and Moore as the NewTekk legal counsel, but this isn't even close to over for me, and I try not to fixate on how my dad is going to take this. I force myself to stay focused by digging my nails into my palms every time my attention wanders, either to the coming reckoning with him or just due to tiredness.

It's no surprise when within five minutes of returning from a lunch grabbed at the sandwich cart on the sidewalk, my secretary informs me my dad is on the line.

I take a deep breath and answer. "This is Josh."

"My office. Now."

"You look like hell," he says when I walk into his office three minutes later.

"I'm fine, Dad." Or I will be as soon as we get this verbal whupping over with. I deserve it, but I'm not looking forward to it.

I take a seat and brace myself. When he used to read me the riot act during college and law school, he could go for an hour without a word from me, pulling up all past sins and warning me against future ones. The memory exhausts me, and a yawn escapes me before I can stop it, but I try, clenching my teeth together halfway through it and causing my jaw to lock and my face to temporarily contort.

"Am I boring you already?" His voice is acid.

"No, sorry. I tried to stop it." I hope he sees that I'm already responding differently to him than I have in the past. I owe him humility; I'm not going to smart off.

He peers at me, leaning forward to study me. "You've got circles under your eyes. Why are you so tired?" He doesn't ask it with concern; there's a tone I don't recognize in his voice.

"Insomnia," I say.

"Is that the name of the concert you went to last night?"

That's not at all what I expected him to say. "What are you talking about?"

"Reagan called this morning. She was worried. Said she was scrolling through Instagram or something and saw you tagged in a post. She said it's a video of you and a bunch of friends at a concert. Those run pretty late, don't they?"

"Why is Reagan monitoring my social media?"

"She's not. She just happened to see it and called your mom. Said it was a long time since she'd seen you out partying on a weeknight, and she was feeling stressed because it made her think of the bad old days. Wanted Mom to have me check on you. According to Roger, your sister was right to worry."

"That show is not why I'm tired."

"You're sticking with plain old insomnia?"

I don't say anything. I'm not going to double down on the lie.

"You embarrassed the firm this morning, Josh. And when it's you, it's a direct reflection on me. I had to fight the partners of my *own* firm to hire you, convincing them that your last year of law school was proof you were ready. And now this."

All of it stings. I screwed up, but he's making it sound like it was inevitable. "I made a mistake this morning," I say, but before I can finish, he jumps in, describing my error in much more profane terms.

I press my lips together and take a deep breath through my nose. "That's fair," I say. "I didn't sleep enough. I made an autofill error, not an operational or process error. This is my first mistake in three years. *Three,* Dad. I get my work done well and on time. Early, when I can pull it off. I come early. I stay late. I've never made a procedural error, never gotten a document wrong. No one has been able to criticize my work ethic or my work product."

"Until right now. Until today, when you decided that you would stay out and party on the night before an important meeting, the first you've been given lead on since becoming a third-year. And that choice—a choice that never once served you well in college—nearly sank a huge account for us."

There's nothing to say here. If he doesn't want to weigh that against three years of near perfection, I can't make him. Instead of arguing, I say, "Yes, sir. I understand."

He sits back, studying me like he's waiting for another protest. I meet his eyes and say nothing.

Finally, he sighs and scrubs his hands over his face. "Only our relationship is saving you right now. Some of the partners never wanted you here, and if you make a mistake of this magnitude again . . ."

"I understand." I have only the barest hold on my emotions right now, and that's all I can say. The exhaustion of so little sleep, the stress of the meeting this morning, the disappointment—and worse, resignation—in my dad's eyes, like he always knew it would come to this, is more than I can handle at the moment.

"I have another meeting." He nods at the door, dismissing me.

I walk across the huge expanse of his carpeted office, his look of *I knew it* gnawing at me. At the heavy walnut door, I hesitate, turning before I open it. "Dad?" He glances up, looking almost as tired as I feel. "I'm sorry."

I think I see a tiny flicker of surprise cross his face before he simply nods, and I slip out the door.

A conversation like that with my dad used to send me straight into a streak of bad behavior. Doubling down, I guess. I'd head right out to the clubs and bars and stagger back to my dorm near dawn or sometimes not at all. Didn't matter that he didn't see me do it; it was enough to know it would make him angry if he did. Those choices always ended up showing up in average grades or blown commitments.

I can't screw up this day any more than I already have, so instead of staying until ten o'clock, I leave at five-thirty to get home when Sami does. I want to see her. I need to see her.

When I pull into my space, hers is empty. No problem. It's about ten degrees colder today than it has been for the last week, but I head inside, drop my backpack, and collapse on the sofa to text her. *Hey. I'm home already. Come over when you get here? I left the back door open.*

Instead of a text back, a few minutes later I hear the sliding door and pull myself upright as she comes in, still in scrubs. They're pink, and she looks adorable.

"Hey," she says, walking toward me. "You're home early. Everything okay?"

As soon as she's within reach, I pull her into my lap and settle her against my chest. "It is now." Her hand rests over my heart, like she's monitoring its beats. The tension drains from my body as it becomes more aware of her softness.

"Want to tell me about it?" she murmurs after a while.

"I blew something important at work. My dad

wasn't thrilled. I got a lecture like I haven't heard in a long time. It sucked. The end."

She tilts her head back to meet my eyes and reaches up to brush at my hair like she wants to push it out of the way, but it's not long enough for that. Warmth spreads through my chest as I realize she's just looking for new ways to touch me. "You going to be okay?"

I sigh. Probably. After some sleep. But if I say that, Sami will insist I go to bed and leave, and right now, she is the only thing in this crap sandwich of a day that is good and right. "I reset the clock today," I tell her. "I wiped out three years of perfect behavior with a stupid mistake. So tomorrow, I start over on day one."

She stirs, like she wants to put some distance between us. "You've been coming to every show. You don't have to do—"

But I'm already shaking my head. "Let me decide how I want to spend my time, Sami."

She stills, settling back against my chest before I feel her nod. "Okay. But you should know, I'm prioritizing the band right now. Things are starting to simmer, and I can't take my eye off it. It's okay for you to prioritize work too."

I consider her words. "Does that mean we're only going to spend time with each other by luck?" Because that isn't what I want. The last long-term girlfriend I had was in high school, and I don't know much about how dating works as a mature adult, but I know I want something more from Sami than being fit in where she can. At the same time, I understand her priorities, because I'm going to have to do the same thing if I want to show my dad I'm taking my job seriously.

"No. We're going to have to choose it." She toys with the top button on my shirt. "What if you pick one show a week to come to? One that fits your schedule best? And what if we set aside Saturday mornings for each other? And what if, on nights I can make it home from rehearsal early enough, we spend evenings together when we can, watching TV or . . . you know. Whatever."

The button slips through its hole and her hand slides inside to feather across my collarbone.

"Whatever, huh?" I ask, my breaths turning shallow. "You've got a deal."

Chapter Twenty-Five
SAMI

Three weeks of bliss.

I'm not sure if that's short or long, but to me, it feels like forever. I've never had three perfect weeks before. But as if our conversation on Josh's sofa that night somehow got the universe on our side, everything lines up perfectly.

Pixie Luna keeps picking up shows, doing three a week, including a big one when Night View asked us to fill in for them after their bus broke down in Houston and they couldn't make it back in time.

Josh comes to weekend shows, using the other nights to work late so he can make time for us on nights I only have rehearsal. At least one of my roommates is always at the other ones, always down by the stage, dancing her face off, always coming backstage afterward to assure me we're awesome.

Saturday mornings have now become the high point of my week. We've done everything from spend an entire morning snuggling on his sofa, watching old cartoons and eating our favorite childhood cereals, to driving out to Fredericksburg for breakfast at a place he remembered trying and loving with his grandpa.

Even Ruby's smirks don't bug me. I haven't lost the bet yet, but I'm beginning to think if I did . . . she's right: I won't care because I'd be coming out way ahead.

Last week, Josh and I went to the Museum of Ice Cream. I can't wait for it to warm up so we can hang out at Barton Creek and soak up the spring sun or even hang out by our own pool and do nothing but share earbuds and read or listen to a podcast together.

But this morning, I have an extra special activity planned: brunch at Delia's and an announcement. I've never taken a date to Delia's before; I've never wanted to taint it with memories of an ex.

"Have you eaten here before?" I ask Josh as we pull into the parking lot behind the restaurant.

"No," he says. "Is it your special place or something?"

"Yes and no," I say as we climb out of his car. "I come here with the besties whenever we're all around on the weekend. I've never brought a date before."

He stops and fixes me with a stare across the roof of the car. "I'm not your date."

I grin. "Boyfriend, then." It doesn't even feel cheesy to say.

"Dang right."

After we order, he gives me a smile, but his

expression is questioning. "What's up? You're practically wiggling in your seat."

"Is it that obvious?"

He shrugs. "I know you."

The simple way he says it makes my breath hitch. He does. He makes me feel seen. Maybe that's why I'm breaking the news to him before anyone else.

"The president of the record label for Night View came to our show last night."

His eyes widen. "I should have gone."

I wave that away. "We didn't even know this guy—Nick—was going to be there. But we went hard like we always do, and I guess it impressed him."

The corner of his mouth twitches. "How much?"

"He's considering signing us."

His full grin breaks out. "Yes! That's awesome, babe."

"Babe" also doesn't sound cheesy to hear, and it really should. "It's not a done deal yet," I say. "But that's the other big news. He wants us to open for Night View at Southwest Fest to see how Pixie Luna does with bigger crowds. And it'll be on the *festival* stage."

His eyebrows shoot up. Getting a shot on the festival stage is as good as an anointing in terms of declaring which indie bands will ascend to glory. It's practically a guarantee that they're going to explode. It's meant to launch Night View into the national spotlight, but it could be amazing for us as the openers.

"The festival stage?" he says in a whisper shout. "The *festival* stage?"

These are the times I love that Josh used to spend so much time on the Austin music scene; I don't have to explain why this matters. I only nod.

He collapses against the back of his chair, a dopey smile on his face. "The festival stage. My girl is a literal rock star."

"Maybe," I say, and when his eyebrows shoot up again, I actually giggle. "Okay, probably."

"Definitely. This is incredible. We have to celebrate."

"That's why we're here." I gesture to the restaurant around us.

He glances around. "I'm glad you shared this place with me, and I can't wait to try the food. But did you bring me here because our schedules are too packed to go out at night?"

"Yeah, but it's cool. I love this place."

"I'll love it too," he says. "But this is life-changing news. The kind of news you make time for. If our schedules weren't an issue, where would you want to go to celebrate the best news ever?"

I shift again, this time slightly nervous. "It hasn't happened yet."

He leans forward and meets my eyes, picking up my hand and lacing his fingers through mine. "It will."

We stare at each other for a few seconds before I give him another grin. "Yeah, it will."

"So, the celebration of your dreams," he prompts.

I think about it, an image forming in my mind. "Spencer's. A fancy dress and their best wine." I've never been. It's the kind of place girls from Hillsboro don't go. I'm not sure even brisket-eating Browers from Austin would fit in at Spencer's. It's absurd. Over the top. And so is the idea of my band getting signed.

"Done." He's already pulling out his phone. "I'll get the first available reservation, and we're going."

"You don't have to do that." Now I'm embarrassed, asking for something so over the top. I'd meant to give it to him as a point of reference, a vibe, not a hint.

"I would have suggested it myself if I'd thought it was your thing," he said. "That was our family special occasion place."

"Why wouldn't it be my thing?" I tense, bracing for whatever he's about to say. There's no answer he can give that won't offend me, and I need to prepare not to overreact.

He shrugs. "I don't know. You usually like way cooler stuff. But even if it's kind of old school, it's delicious. We can make fun of the stuck-up people while we eat. I saw the governor last time we were there."

Oh. I guess there was *one* answer that wasn't going to get him in trouble.

He looks up from his phone. "There's one opening on Tuesday night at eight. Kind of late for dinner, but would it work?"

I nod. "It'll work."

And I mean: this will work. He will work. We will work.

I don't know how, but somehow, even with our crazy schedules, long days, and workaholic tendencies, it will. I can't believe the knowledge doesn't send me flying out of Delia's in search of a getaway.

Instead, I reach over and take his other hand, lacing those fingers together too, and repeat, "It'll work."

Not that I'm telling Ruby. Yet.

"You look amazing," Josh says when I open the front door to his knock Tuesday night. He takes my hand and has me do a twirl to check out the gold dress I'm wearing. It's a satin slip dress, but the open back really makes it, and he gives a low rumble of appreciation when he sees it, the fabric dipping well below the middle of my back, the hem grazing my knees.

"You do too." He's wearing a black suit with

a gray and black tie against a gray shirt. It looks sharp. "Silver and gold."

"I'll take second place to you any night," he says.

"That's not what I meant," I protest.

"But it's what's happening, and I love it."

"You love what?" Ruby asks, emerging from her room.

"My *dress,*" I say with the tiniest warning.

Ruby does her smirk. "Looking good, kids. Have fun. Bring me four-hundred-dollar leftovers."

My eyes widen. "Josh, it's not that—"

He rolls his eyes. "No, it's not that much. But if it were, I'd still pay it. You deserve it."

I'm in wickedly high heels, and I don't have to stretch quite as high as usual to press a kiss against his lips. "You're smooth."

We take his car and use the valet at the restaurant. Spencer's is the kind of place that *only* has valet parking. Josh gives our name to the hostess, who smiles and welcomes us. "We'll have that table for you in a couple of minutes."

We stand near the entrance to wait, and I take in the surroundings. Dark wood. Low lighting. Marble floors. Glimpses of white linen tablecloths beyond the hostess stand.

"Josh?" A woman's voice says in surprise.

We look over to see his mom coming from the direction of the restrooms.

"Mom?" He looks equally surprised. "What are you doing here?"

"Your dad landed a big client, so we're celebrating."

"Oh," he says, his voice slightly subdued. "That's great."

"Come and eat with us, honey. We'd love to have y'all. Hey, Samantha. You look so pretty."

"Hey, Miss Elizabeth. It's good to see you."

"Come on and follow me. We were about to order." She turns, but Josh catches her elbow to stop her.

"That's okay, Mom. We won't crash your dinner. You enjoy yourselves."

"Don't be silly," she says, turning back with a slight frown. "You're not imposing. Come on," she repeats, and this time when she heads into the dining area, Josh meets my eyes with an apologetic look.

"It's fine." I mean it, and I tuck my hand into the crook of his arm to prove it. "I like the idea of you eating together." He missed their last Sunday dinner. I've tried to stay out of it, hoping time will smooth things over between Josh and his dad, but this is too good of an opportunity to pass up. "Besides, it's not like we have to fake anything this time."

He smiles and presses a soft kiss to my hairline. "True. Come on, real girlfriend. Let's go eat some expensive food on my dad's dime."

We wind our way through the tables after his mom, who has flagged down a server to request two more chairs.

After a couple of awkward minutes of stiff handshakes with his dad and making small talk while we wait for the staff to accommodate our new table situation, we all settle into chairs and busy ourselves with the menus. I don't know about them, but I already know what I want. I've been studying the website and daydreaming about lobster since Sunday morning. Looking at the menu is just an excuse to buy some time before we have to make polite conversation again. Maybe this wasn't such a great idea.

"You should get the New York strip, Samantha," Mr. Brower says. I still can't make myself think of him as Mr. Steve. "It's outstanding. Best in Texas."

"I was thinking I'd get the Maine lobster," I say. "It sounds amazing."

He gives me a slight frown. "Everything here is good, but the strip is something else."

One of the things I'd figured out months after my breakup with Bryce was that I'd made mistakes too; the main one was bending and folding myself to fit in with his family. That's how I'd come out of that relationship feeling so lost.

I draw a quiet, steadying breath through my nose and smile. "Maybe another time. I've got my heart set on the lobster."

Mr. Brower leans forward, like he's ready to argue his case for the New York strip. "Trust me, Samantha, you'll re—"

"Sami," I say.

He draws back. "Pardon?"

"Call me Sami. Everyone does." I'm keeping *all* my pieces, and I've never fit Samantha.

Miss Elizabeth clears her throat, a small sound that still catches the attention of the Brower men. "The Maine lobster is lovely, Sami. You'll enjoy it. What about you, Josh?"

She made the tiniest pause before my name, so slight I'm not positive I heard it, but I appreciate her nudging her husband to back down.

The menu discussion continues until our server arrives to take our order, and when Mr. Brower selects a bottle from the wine list, he quirks his eyebrow at me as if to ask, *Do I have your permission?*

I smile. "I'll trust your judgment here."

"So, Sami," Miss Elizabeth says without a pause this time. "How's work?"

"Which job?" I ask.

Josh shoots me a quick glance, and I tense, waiting for him to redirect the conversation from my music ambitions, but instead a smile turns up his lips. "She has two," he explains to his parents. "She's got a band called Pixie Luna, and they're the hottest thing in Austin right now."

I smile at him before looking at his parents. "That's a slight exaggeration."

"It's not," Josh says.

His parents trade a fleeting look that I'm not sure how to interpret, but I'm pretty sure it didn't say, *Let's start planning their wedding.*

"A band," his mom repeats, but her voice is fainter than before. "What kind of music do you play?"

"Rock," I say. "Maybe pop rock would be a good way to explain it." Sensing they need a minute to process all this, I give them a smile. "If you'll excuse me a moment, I'm going to run to the ladies' room."

I step away and take my time in the restroom, retouching my lipstick on smiling lips because Josh stood up for me. Josh told them I have an awesome band. Josh didn't try to nudge me into my perfect Pi Phi mold to fit with his parents.

Josh isn't Bryce.

I'm still floating on that high when I return to the table, and I give Josh a searching look. He gives me a single head shake but a half smile and stands to pull out my chair for me.

"Thanks for not running," he murmurs into my ear as I take my seat.

"You're stuck with me now," I say in an equally low voice. He answers by pressing another of those kisses against my hairline. I'm coming to love those. They say, *Now isn't the time and place, but I need to touch you anyway.*

A lull falls over the table, and the set of Josh's jaw tells me that whatever they discussed while I was gone, he won't be the one to break the silence now.

Finally, his mom clears her throat. "How's the nursing home?"

"Good," I say. "But hard. We've got staffing problems because the management company won't raise the pay for the CNAs. It's hard with all the Pixie Luna stuff."

"Maybe more balance would help," she says.

"Cut back on some of your shows," Mr. Brower suggests, because of course he does.

Our food arrives before I can respond, so I spend the next few minutes eating and feeling sure I made exactly the right choice with my lobster. "This is so good, Josh," I say. "Thank you."

"You deserve this and more," he says. "I'm glad you like it." There's an apology in his eyes, and I bet he's trying to say he's sorry that his parents somehow became part of this deal. "We came to Spencer's tonight because Sami's band was offered an opportunity to play at Southwest Fest."

His parents nod. Even the old folks at work know what that is.

"Not just an invitation to play," Josh continues. "To play on the festival stage, opening for another band whose label is interested in signing them."

This meets with a few seconds of quiet before his mom smiles and says, "Well, all of that sounds very positive, Sami." She says it indulgently, like she might if Reagan's daughter asked her to watch how fast she could run in her new shoes.

"It is," I say. Josh's jaw looks tight, like he's biting back words. "In fact, if the opportunity is good enough, I may put in my notice at the nursing home to concentrate on music full-time."

His eyebrows go up in surprise. "Yeah? Are you in a financial position to do that?"

"I won't know until I see the offer, but I've been researching standard terms for these kinds of agreements. It's possible. I mean, I'd still have to work for a nursing service to fill in on shifts and supplement what we earn through shows until things take off, but . . ." I can't fight a smile. "Yeah, I think I'll be able to do it."

"Wow," he says. "That's huge. Congratulations, babe. You are doing the damn thing."

I hold up the wine glass, filled with the cabernet Mr. Brower ordered for the table. "I'm doing the damn thing," I repeat, and the crystal sends out a sweet chime when we toast.

"Are you sure that's a good idea?" Mr. Brower asks.

"Dad . . ." Josh's tone holds a warning.

"You have to be realistic, son. Saman—er,

Sami"—he corrects himself when my eyebrows go up—"you're looking at very longshot odds. Is now the time to give up a steady career in a high-demand field?"

It's not actually a question despite his inflection at the end. He's *telling* me that I shouldn't be considering it. And while it's true I haven't brought it up with my mom because she'll have the same reaction, *he* is not my dad. He gets no say. The Browers don't get to mold me into a more ideal girlfriend for their son with passive-aggressive comments and fake concern about my nursing career by trying to nudge me away from a music career.

"I have no one depending on me but me," I say, calmly taking another bite and letting them consider that. "Now is the perfect time to try and fail."

"Or succeed," Josh says, once again ignoring his parents. "And you will."

"But Josh," his mom says, "aren't you worried about all the travel, and . . ." Her voice trails off when he lifts a hand and signals for our server.

"We'll be taking the rest of our meals home," Josh tells him.

Wait, he's going to walk out on his parents?

They're both staring too, frozen. His dad pulls himself together first. "Wait a minute, Josh."

"I'll wait as long as it takes the waiter to bring

our to-go boxes," Josh says. "You might even get more than a minute."

"You can't just walk out because you don't like the advice we're giving," Mr. Brower says.

"Not when you're giving it to me, no. But you're trying to tell Sami how to live her life, and you don't know her well enough to do that. You don't know what she's capable of, so your opinions don't count here. This is a night for us to celebrate an invitation she's worked hard for, and we're going to do that without any wet blankets, please and thank you."

Mr. Brower gapes as the waiter arrives to box my food for me, and I don't say anything until the server is done and Josh stands as a signal that he's ready to leave. I'm torn between wanting to give him a standing ovation and quietly slipping out in hopes that his parents will forget I'm the reason they're having this argument.

I decide silence is the best option here and follow him from the restaurant.

"So that is a thing that happened," I say carefully when we're settled back in his car and he's pulling out of the parking lot.

"Yep." He sounds neither annoyed nor pleased.

"Are you okay?"

He turns onto the main road before reaching for my hand. "I don't want you to stress out or feel responsible for what happened in the restaurant."

"I kind of do. Don't get me wrong, it's amazing

that you stuck up for me. But I don't want you to be in a fight with your parents because of it."

He sighs and gives my hand a squeeze, his eyes staying on the road. "It's not exactly because of you. A disagreement like that was coming anyway. After I screwed up that meeting a few weeks ago, I realized that despite years of good behavior, they'd just been waiting for it to happen. And if I'm perfect for the next ten years, when I do finally make a mistake, they're going to say, 'Knew it.' I don't think I can change the way they think about me. So why bother?"

I turn his hand over and gently trace lines along his palm, appreciating the light calluses from lifting at the gym, memorizing the lines and their branches as they crisscross his skin. "Those are sad words, but you don't sound sad." His voice sounds more . . . detached. Is it his way of not feeling hurt?

"I'm not. I was pretty upset when it happened, but I've had a few weeks to think about it, and . . . I don't know. I don't think I'm mad or even hurt. All I know is that they're not going to believe I've changed. I spent too long refusing to. And if they're not going to expect more of me, I'm going to quit trying to figure out how to give them what they want, because I don't know what that is."

His words worry me. "You shouldn't give up on them, Josh," I say quietly.

"I'm not." He shoots me a quick look with a reassuring smile before he puts his eyes back on the road. "I'm not cutting them off or pushing them away or anything. But I'm going to do the things that make *me* happy. Maybe that means cutting down to sixty hours a week at the office since three years of doing eighty-plus hours didn't make the point." He slides me a rueful grin. "I kind of do like the work. Or at least, I don't mind it. So I'm not going anywhere; just re-evaluating."

I wrap my other hand around his and stare out of the window for a minute. "You kind of screwed me up, you know," I say, my voice low.

There's a long pause, then a neutral "how?"

"I haven't been able to write an angry breakup song for nearly a month."

He laughs and his shoulders lose their tension. "Sorry."

"But, Josh, also . . ."

"Yeah?"

"You're the best guy I've ever known."

He gives a low whistle. "That is saying something when you have guys like NilesQuil hanging around all the time."

I give his hand a light pinch. "Stop ruining the moment."

"Yes, ma'am." He's still smiling.

"And I don't want you to be in a fight with your parents."

By now, we're turning into the Grove parking lot. He doesn't answer until he's parked the car and cut the engine. "Whatever is going on there is a me and them thing, and it doesn't have anything to do with you. They might try to say it does at first, but if anything, you've given me clarity, okay? I'm not going anywhere, and they can choose to believe the evidence or not. But I'm not the entitled kid I was. And watching you chase down your goals has been making me think about mine."

He turns and draws me toward him, meeting me over the console. "You're true to yourself, Sami. I'm learning from that."

I'm still worried about how he left things with his parents. There's some fixing that needs to happen, but when his lips touch mine, and his sweet kiss turns searching, it drives out every thought except him. The cute boy next door has turned out to be made of all kinds of layers, but this one, this melting, magical kissing thing he does?

This one is my favorite.

Chapter Twenty-Six
JOSH

I made it sound simple to Sami after dinner last night, but it's not. It's hard to be at a standoff with your father when he's also your boss. He can call me up to his office whenever he's ready to talk, regardless of whether I am, and that's what he does when he gets into the office this morning.

"Have a seat, son," he says when I walk in. Or orders, really. I do, not saying a word.

"When Reagan told us you'd been out partying the night before you blew it with NewTekk, I thought, 'Here we go again.' But you sat right there and told me things were different, that you care about your job and this firm, and it was a one-time screwup."

"It was." Maybe he was listening. Maybe he believed me. Maybe this isn't going to be the lecture I was dreading all the way up the stairs to his office.

"I've seen you blow it too many times to believe that, but your mother did. She told me to give you a chance, to watch you over the next few weeks and see which Josh we were getting in the office: before-law-school Josh or after-law-school Josh. The jury was out until last night."

I cross my legs at the ankles and slide my hands into my pockets. No matter what he says next, at least it'll look like I don't care. "What's the verdict?"

"That I was right not to believe you."

The words land like punches. *Not.* Jab. *To.* Cross. *Believe.* Hook. *You.* Uppercut.

"Your evidence?" I keep my voice calm, like this whole conversation is merely interesting, an anonymous case like the ones he used to have me and Reagan analyze with him over dinner.

"Your girlfriend." There is no mistaking the disapproval when he can't even bring himself to say her name. "You had us believing at first. Steady career, Pi Phi, dressed the part, held her own at dinner with the Reillys. Instead, she's the same wild tail you've always chased. Tattoos. Rock band. It's ridiculous. When are you going to outgrow this?"

My hands clench at his disgusting reduction of Sami. "Don't talk about her like that."

He snorts, but he sees something in my face that keeps him from doubling down. "She's not the problem," he says. "She's the symptom."

Like that somehow excuses his words.

I fight to keep my voice even. "I get it, Dad. I understand that I can't do anything to change your mind, so I'm not going to try. I'm going to do my job. I'm going to do it as well as I've been doing it. I'm going to keep supporting

Sami because she is talented like you wouldn't believe."

I lean forward. "Remember how I used to go out to the clubs all the time in college? And in high school any time I could sneak in before that? You always thought it was about drinking. But it wasn't. It was about the music. It was about how I connected with it, about how it could make me feel when other things couldn't under the weight of your expectations."

The need to make him understand when I know he can't is so strong that I surge to my feet to pace.

"From the second I saw Sami onstage, before I even knew it was her, something in me came back to life. I've felt like *myself* for the first time . . ." I pause to consider it. "For the first time ever. I am a guy who wants to help this firm grow. I want to contribute to the family business. I want to be worthy of the opportunities I've been given. But I also want to be real, spend time around live music, show up to support my girlfriend who is a next-level talent. I'm not going to choose, so if that's what you were hoping to hear . . ." I shrug. *Not going to happen.*

"I know you feel like you gave me a chance here after law school," I continue, "but you didn't. Not really. You've been waiting for me to fail since I started. I screwed up. I know it. But it won't happen again. I'm going to figure out what I have to offer here, and I'm going to give my best on every account you assign me to. But I will *also* be there for Sami."

It won't be easy. I'm going to have to cut hours by about ten a week, and my dad will only see that as further proof I'm slacking, not that I'm balancing the ways to show up for people in my life. But he was never going to see the truth anyway.

"Josh, you can't be at the clubs every night drinking and at the firm every day trying to represent us to clients who pay us more than your yearly salary to be the best in the business."

I rub my hand over my face. This is pointless. "I'll be at Sami's shows, Dad. As often as she has them. I will also be at work, prepared and on point. You let me know if you have any future concerns about my performance."

Then I walk out, closing the door on him calling my name.

"I hate that y'all aren't getting along," Sami says.

We're sitting on my balcony, Sami tucked between my legs and resting against my chest, a blanket wrapped around both of us as we watch for owls and bats.

"It's whatever," I say. "I was stupid to think I was going to change his mind by coming to work at the firm." I give a short, unhappy laugh. "Not that anywhere else would have hired me."

"Is that still true?" she asks. "You don't think another firm would take you now?"

I think for a bit. "Maybe? I think I've impressed enough people over the last three years that I could make the jump to another firm."

"Would you ever want to?"

I resettle her against my chest. "I don't know. I never thought I'd like business law, but I do. Not always what I'm doing with the firm, but I've gotten to work on some interesting things. I wish there was a way to make it so every case I get is interesting. Like talking over contracts with Luther and learning how deals are negotiated in the music industry. But I'm not at a point where I get to pick and choose, and I don't think that magically happens when you switch firms."

"Could you ask your dad about bringing on more music clients?"

I shake my head. "To do right by them, they really need experts. It would mean opening a whole new area of practice for the firm, not picking up clients here and there. More likely, it would mean going to another firm where they have an established entertainment law practice."

"Would it make things better or worse for you not to work with your dad?"

"Asking the hard questions tonight."

She shrugs, and I like the friction of her small shoulder against my shirt. "I know what it's like to be in a job you want to love or even used to love, and now you don't. If making a change will fix it, make a change."

"Another rough day at Sunnyside?"

"We lost two patients. And I couldn't get a family member on the phone for either of them to let them know. I had to do two bed-to-wheelchair transfers because we were shorthanded on support staff again, and now my back is killing me. I had another pointless phone call with the regional director today, arguing for higher CNA and orderly wages."

She sags against me. "I hate that I'm burning out, but I'm burning out. They warned us about it constantly in nursing school. I don't want to be a statistic, but it's starting to feel inevitable."

I consider this. "Could you still get a nurse to cover you if you take a few days off to relax and work on music?"

She twists to watch me over her shoulder. "With enough notice."

I pull her back against me. "If I could find you a secluded place to work, free of charge, so you could sleep and eat and write music for a few days, would you want to?"

She stiffens slightly. "Josh, I don't think I'm ready to—"

"I won't be there," I clarify. "I have to work. But there's no reason both of us need to burn out. Take a break. Give your music some uninterrupted attention." I squeeze her shoulders, and she relaxes again. "You're getting signed soon. You'll want new songs to give them."

Still, she hesitates.

"It's free," I add. "It won't cost me anything."

She turns around to draw me into a hug. "You're so good to me. That's really thoughtful. And yes, time to work on my music would be so good right now."

"Even if you can't write any more angry breakup songs?" I tease.

"Even though you've ruined me," she agrees.

"Then plan on it. Three days next week, you in a quiet cabin with your guitar."

A gust of wind slices over the balcony and she gives a hard shiver. "I swear it's getting colder instead of warmer the closer we get to spring. Let's get inside so I can thank you properly."

I press my hand to my chest, scandalized. "Sami Webster, are you trying to *make out* with me?"

"Yes, definitely."

I scoop her up and race into my place before she can even finish the word.

Chapter Twenty-Seven
SAMI

I turn on the road Josh indicated on his directions. *GPS won't get you there,* he'd said. That's how I'd found myself taking a barely paved access road from Highway 290 and bumping along it for two miles before I took "the first left past the old rundown barn," went another mile, and now I'm taking what should be my final turn on what's less a road and more a gravel path to get me to my destination.

I crunch and even lurch a couple of times over the rough driveway before it makes a slight turn, and there ahead of me is the small cabin Josh told me to watch for. "No wi-fi or cell service but you can text. Gas stove. Electricity. It's outdated but it's comfortable, and no one will bother you."

It's tidy on the outside and having the small place to myself makes it worth the two-hour drive from Austin. Josh told me it wouldn't be locked, and sure enough, I walk right in with my small suitcase and the bag of groceries he told me to bring.

The cabin is slightly musty, like it's been shut up for a while, but it's way too cold to open doors or windows to air it out. We're hovering just above forty in Austin, and it had only gotten colder the farther north I drove.

I set the suitcase down and go to the woodburning stove with its box of matches on top. I'll get that going and this place will be cozy and smell like warmth and crackling wood in no time. It doesn't take long to get it going, and once the fire is burning merrily, I shut the grate and explore the rest of the small space.

The main part of the cabin is filled with a table for four on the right, situated in front of a small kitchen. On the left is a sofa, the woodburning stove, a fireplace, and a rocking chair. I find only two more rooms: a bathroom with a toilet and small shower, and a bedroom with a double bed, an armoire, and a chest of drawers with very little room to maneuver around them.

It's tiny. Simple. Perfect.

Josh is always doing things like this for me, figuring out what I need and finding thoughtful ways to provide it. I'm learning that, by nature, he's a problem solver. I'd apologized to him a couple of nights ago again about accusing him of trying to buy what he wanted when he proposed the fake dating thing, but he'd only shaken his head.

"You were right. It was such a habit I didn't see it. But Ruby set me straight, and I've been trying to think of solving problems in ways where I don't just throw money at them to fix them."

Somehow, Josh has gone from "just another Bryce" to possibly the perfect man. I only wish I could find a way to do the same thing for him. He's brushed it off any time I bring it up, but I know the tension with his dad weighs on him. I wish I knew what to do to fix it.

The best I could come up with was to refuse to come to the cabin unless he finally promised to go to his Sunday family dinner. Without me. I'd hoped it would make it easier for them to talk if Josh didn't feel like he was going to have to defend me at any moment.

When he got back last night, he'd texted to tell me he was coming to our show. When I'd asked how dinner went, he'd only answered, "Fine."

It was the kind of fine that meant it definitely wasn't fine. But he'd done it, and now I'm here in this tiny, perfect cabin, and the next thing I do is crawl into the bed and sleep.

When I wake up, I'm truly rested. There's something about not having anyone waiting on me that relaxes me like usually only a week of vacation can. I don't have rehearsal. I don't need to be at the nursing home. I don't even need to be on hand to try one of Ava's kitchen experiments or give Madi an opinion on her outfit. Josh has given me space to breathe, and I draw in a deep, grateful lungful.

Then my eyes pop open and I'm scrambling for my bag, because just like that, a lyric pops into my head, and I want to write it down and chase it. *I asked for breathing room, but you only held me close. I thought I needed space to run, turns out I want you most.*

I tap out the rhythm on my knee with the pen. It's not perfect but it's the start of something, and I settle in, letting the words come, crossing out, rewriting, and straightening two hours later with a finished song. The lyrics, anyway.

I climb off the bed and stretch. The room is cold, and I scoop up my notebook and head to the main part of the cabin. The weather has been so chilly lately, but here in this room, the warmth from the woodburning stove washes over my cheeks and into my cold fingertips. That sends another snatch of lyrics through my head, a possible metaphor about winter and fire and hearts that might not be too trite if I work with it some . . .

Hours later, I crawl into bed beneath the quilt, my brain tired, the cabin warm, and my notebook bursting with new snatches of melodies and lyrics.

Tuesday, I feed myself oatmeal and treat myself to a walk outside. Even with my fleece jacket, it's too cold for me to stand it long. I check my phone, and while it doesn't show cell service, it does show the temperature: a brisk thirty-six degrees. Whew. Texans aren't built for that kind of cold. The walk doesn't even last ten minutes before I'm inside, shivering in front of the woodstove.

Today, I'll spend more time with the guitar, pulling the rocking chair close enough to the heat that I can noodle around without my fingers getting stiff. Around lunch, I have a song knocked out and recorded on my phone, and I start a pot of water boiling for pasta before I slip on another pair of socks and explore the cabin.

Josh had said only that it belonged to a family friend who never used it and wouldn't mind me being there. It definitely doesn't look like it's used much, but as I look for clues about the owners, a suspicion begins to grow. The style in here is old. Ranch old. Hand-tied quilts and antique furniture old. *Grandparent* old.

No framed pictures decorate the house, just a single cross-stitch on the wall asking to "bless this mess." But the built-in shelves to either side of the fireplace hold books and worn-looking game boxes for Parcheesi and Candyland, so I try there next for clues. Eventually, on the fourth book I pull from the shelf, a Louis L'Amour hardback cowboy story, inside the cover a masculine scrawl reads, "James Brower."

This must be Josh's grandparents' place. I wonder why he didn't just tell me that?

But I know the answer. I wouldn't have taken him up on the offer. I've caused too much trouble in his family already.

I pull out my phone to call him but remember I don't get a signal here. I text instead. *This is your grandpa's place?*

His answer is immediate. *Yes.*

You should have told me, I type.

Would you have gone?

I stare at the question. *No. But that's my choice.*

Gramps will be glad someone is there. No one's used it in at least two years. Trust me. It's fine. Getting things done?

I think of the two completed songs, feel the itch in my fingers wanting to get back to my guitar. *Yes,* I text back. *A lot. Thank you.*

He answers only, *Of course.*

My phone says it's dropped another two degrees, so I feed more wood into the stove, bring the blanket out to the rocking chair, and settle even closer to the heat to work.

By the time I realize daylight has faded enough for me to be working mainly by the glow from the potbelly stove, I've worked through another couple of songs. One came fast, but the other one took most of my time. I stand to stretch, but when the blanket slips to the ground, I shiver.

A glance through the window reveals that the morning dew never evaporated; it clings to the sparse grass outside, frozen into ice pearls.

I check my phone again. It's twenty-nine degrees! My genes were bred for heat, not this. Brrr. I text Josh. *How cold is it there?*

A minute later, he answers. *High thirties. Weather map says it's below freezing up there?!*

"It ain't tropical," I mutter before I confirm with a yes and the phrase "wood burning stove" punctuated after each word with the prayer hands emoji.

Maybe you should drive home, he texts. *That's too cold to be out there.*

Maybe. Any other time, I'd take him up on the offer to return to my snug condo, but I'm supposed to have one whole day left to work, and I don't want to give it up. *I'll be fine,* I text him. *Wearing all my socks and a trendy quilt muumuu.*

I go to run some water for hot cocoa, but when I turn the handle, nothing happens. It worked fine earlier when I made pasta. I try the shower and kitchen faucets too, but none of them come on either besides an anemic drip from the bathroom sink.

The pipes must be frozen. This has never happened to me before, but every now and then, the local news will go nuts reporting about a freak cold front and talk about pipes freezing. What do they always say to do? Maybe leave the faucets running slightly so the pipes don't burst? I have no idea if that still holds true if they're already frozen, but I go around and turn them all slightly on just in case.

The only warm spot in the house now is the six-foot radius around the woodstove, and I'm going to have to pull the sofa over to it and sleep there if I don't want to freeze tonight. With the way this cold is getting in around the old windows and beneath the door cracks, there is no way even sleeping in two sets of clothes beneath the quilt will keep me warm in that bed.

I should have listened to Josh. I pull out my phone to text him. *Never mind. You're right. Too cold. Packing up to come home.*

Don't, he says, followed by three siren emojis. *Roads are icing over and closing. Stay there. Do you have heat?*

Dang. We haven't had a central Texas ice storm like this in so long, I'd forgotten how brutal they can be. *Enough,* I say. *And I think there's enough wood.*

So sorry, he texts. *Didn't think it would get so cold up there. Check in with me every hour? Please?*

I text a thumbs-up. As soon as I press send, the light I'd turned on blinks out. "Uh oh. Please don't be what I think this is." I shuffle to the bathroom, blanket firmly tucked around me, and flip the switch. Nothing. "Great. Electricity is out too." I don't know who I'm talking to. Maybe the mice I hope aren't hibernating in the walls.

I finish pushing the sofa near the woodstove and curl up in the corner, turning into a tight ball to conserve warmth. It's tolerable as long as I stay near the woodstove. If I leave it for even a minute, the bitter cold starts seeping through my layers and turning my nose red and runny. Maybe my eyes even start to sting from feeling ever-so-slightly sorry for myself for being stuck in the middle of nowhere without electricity or company and very little heat.

My phone buzzes with a text from Josh. *Gramps is coming to get you. Don't freak out when you hear his truck.*

I start to type back, *When?* But my phone dies and I groan in frustration. I can't even charge it now.

Minutes start ticking by, and I try counting them in my mind, but I lose track after about twenty. I have no idea if it's an hour or an ice age later when I hear the sweetest sound in the world: tires crunching over gravel. Headlights bob through the cabin's front window, then stop, followed by footsteps on gravel and across the porch, and a knock at the door. It creaks open and Josh's grandpa sticks his head in, cautiously, like he doesn't want to scare anyone.

"Samantha?" he calls.

"Sami," I say, and his eyes fall on me where I'm curled and shivering in the corner of the sofa.

"Poor mite," he says. "Josh called and asked me to come check on you. Looks like the power's out?"

I nod. "And I think the pipes froze too." My voice wobbles.

"Aw, honey, he should have told me you were coming up. I'd have been over here much earlier to check on you. Let's get you over to the big house. It's only about twenty minutes from here but I've got a generator. Truck's warm, so you can leave the blanket, but why don't you gather the rest of your things while I put out the fire?"

"Yes, sir," I say, climbing from the sofa and doing a shuffle run to grab my overnight bag from the bedroom. I sweep the few skin products I brought from the bathroom sink into my bag too, then hurry back to the warmer living room to pack up my guitar.

"Fire's out," he says. "Let me take your things and you make a run for the truck. That fleece jacket won't keep you too warm."

I don't even bother arguing. I shove my feet into my Vans—trickier than usual with three pairs of socks on—and run for the truck, crawling into the warm cab with chattering teeth. It's a nice truck, a Chevy with leather seats and seat warmers doing the Lord's work on my frosty buns, blessed heat roaring from the vents.

He opens the back door on the extended cab long enough to set my belongings inside then shuts it tight and climbs into the cab faster than I'd expect a man his age to move.

"Thanks for coming, Mr. Brower," I say. "I didn't want to be a popsicle."

"Call me Grampa Jim," he says. "And I'm sure

glad Josh sent me over. Let's get you warm and fed."

An hour later, we're in a sprawling hacienda-style ranch house, and I've warmed to normal human temperatures, but I stay near Grampa Jim's fireplace with the bowl of chili he served me, letting my phone charge.

"Doing all right now, girl?"

"Yeah. But I'm fairly sure there's a part of my lizard brain that will never forget that I almost froze to death, and it's going to panic every time the temperature drops below freezing now."

Grampa Jim chuckles. "Lizard brain. Funny. Josh said he sent you up here on a retreat. Hope staying here won't cramp your style."

"No way," I say. "You're way better than being frozen to death."

He cackles at that, and I love it. I can't wait until I'm old enough to cackle when I laugh. "Glad I'm good for something. You got anyone else worried about you?"

"Probably not," but I reach for my phone to turn it on, just to be sure. "I'm sure Josh caught my roommates up on your rescue mission, so everything should be fine." But when my phone vibrates to life, it keeps buzzing with incoming messages. I wake it up and scroll. "Oh no. My mom and grandma have been calling. My mom's power went out so she went to my grandma's house to stay with her, and they're freaking out that they can't get hold of me."

I start to dial before I remember that there's no service out here. "Shoot." I set my chili down for faster texting so I can reassure them.

"I got a landline," Grampa Jim says, rising as he speaks. "Too far out for cell service, but the power outage usually doesn't affect phone service. Hang on."

He returns shortly with a cordless phone. "It's still charged. Do I need to explain to you how to use it?" His eyes twinkle as he asks. This is a favorite way for my residents at Sunnyside to tease me, poking fun at what my generation doesn't know about older technology, but we have office phones, so I'm fine.

I demonstrate by dialing my mom's number, and Grampa Jim gives me a nod before he disappears in the direction of the kitchen.

"Hello?" my mom says, sounding suspicious. Of course. She wouldn't recognize the number.

"It's me, Mom."

"Sami, honey, are you okay? We kept trying to get hold of you, then your roommates said you'd left for a few days, and they couldn't get hold of you either."

"I'm fine, Mom. A friend loaned me his cabin to get some music written, and I lost power, but his grandfather brought me to the main house, and he's got a generator and water and everything."

"Oh, thank goodness. She's fine, Ma," she

calls over her shoulder. "She's on the phone."

Once I answer a dozen questions, my mom sounds satisfied that I'm truly safe and well. "So where are you again? In a hermit cabin writing music?"

"Yeah." I don't love her incredulous tone. She's always enjoyed listening to me and Grandma sing together, but she gets weird when I start talking about doing music on my own. "I've got a new band, and it's doing really well, but I've been so overwhelmed with work that I haven't been taking much time to write new music."

"So, a friend—a man—set you up with a cabin so you could do that?" she asks. But it's not really an ask. Her tone is demanding that I fill in all the blanks.

"My neighbor, Josh. I've been seeing him. He's a good guy. Supportive. He's seen me edging toward burnout, so he pushed me to take some time off."

"From your job?" Her voice is skeptical. "Shouldn't you put aside music for a little while if you're feeling maxed out?"

I stifle a sigh. I understand why that's her instinct. As a single mom, she could only ever consider the practicalities. But I'm just single, not a single mom, and I have more options. I'm beginning to realize that every day. The pure peace of just making music for two solid days is still humming through me.

"Mom, what if I told you that there's a pretty good chance I'll have an opportunity to quit the nursing home and focus on music full-time? I could cover all my expenses, picking up nurse sub shifts through an agency if I need the cash, and I can make something of this band."

She's quiet for several long beats. "I'd say you didn't go to college for music. You went to be a nurse. So be a nurse."

I hear Grandma in the background fussing at my mom. "Give me that," she says a second before her voice comes on the line, loud and clear. "How you doing, honey? You safe?"

I reassure her with an update about the very nice Texas ranch house I'm sitting in now, toasty and full.

"Good, good," she says. "Now what's this about music and nursing?"

"Things have been going pretty well for the band," I tell her.

I hear my mom call in the background, "You *knew* about this?" Her voice is indignant.

Grandma covers the receiver, but I hear her response anyway. "Yes, Gina. And how you're acting right now is exactly why I knew, and you didn't. Now hush."

She speaks normally into the phone again. "Sorry about that. You were saying about the band?"

I catch her up on the opportunities looming,

and she oohs and aahs at all the right moments. "To sum up, if things go well at Southwest Fest, I could end up with a record deal and maybe even go on an official tour instead of slapping together club gigs wherever we can talk people into booking us."

"That's amazing, honey. I sure am proud of you."

"Grandma? What if push comes to shove, and I have to choose?"

"You mean choose between music and nursing?" she asks. "That's easy. As long as you can pay the bills, do what makes your heart most happy."

There's a scrabbling sound and a grunt and my mom gets back on the line. "You do not quit a stable nursing job to play rock star," she says. "Hobbies don't pay the bills."

"But this one will," I tell her. "And it's not a hobby. These past two days have been . . ." I don't know how to explain it. A gift, even with the dropping temperatures and the drafty cabin. To sit and think only about music and not what impossible feat the nursing home director would ask me to accomplish?

Bliss.

I don't finish the sentence before there's more scrabbling and Grandma's back. "Listen to me, Sami. I'm older and wiser. If you get a chance to do this music thing full-time, you do it. You understand?"

My mom is squawking protests in the background, and it wouldn't surprise me in the least if my grandmother is holding her off with a hand on her head, the way brothers torture younger siblings in TV shows.

"We love you," Grandma says to be heard over my mom's fussing. "Glad you're safe. Call when you're home."

I hang up the phone, smiling. Grampa Jim walks back in. "Good call?" he asks.

"Good call." I study him for a few seconds. I know better than most that not every old person is wise, but I have a pretty good sense about who to listen to. The wise ones know a lot. "Could I ask your advice on something?"

He turns toward me and fixes me with his eyes. They're the same shade of blue as Josh's, and they shine with the same intelligence. It would be a stupid person who underestimated this man just because he has white hair and liver spots.

"Depends," he says. "Try me."

"It's about Josh."

He considers that. "Still depends. I'm not in the business of telling my grandson's business. But you can still try me."

"Josh is the best guy I've ever dated," I say, and he smiles.

"I approve of your opening statement. Continue, counselor."

"It took us both a minute to get past some old

ways of thinking about things, but aside from my roommates, I've never had someone so thoroughly in my corner. But I'm worried I might be causing problems with his parents, and I don't want him choosing me over them."

"You think his feelings might be strong enough that he would do that?"

I hesitate, playing over the things he's said and the words that are still unsaid. Neither of us has talked about love. But he does for me the things I do for my roommates because I care and want them to be happy. I don't know what you call that if it's not love. "Yes, sir," I answer. "I think his feelings might be that strong."

"It bothers you, this idea that you could be an obstacle between them?"

"Yes." As much as Josh has talked about figuring out his own path, about how he's accepted that his parents will never see him as changed, it hurts him. He doesn't say it, but I see him talking himself into believing that it doesn't.

"What makes you think he's going to be forced to choose?" Grampa Jim asks.

I can't quite pin down his tone. He sounds kind of like one of my college professors using the Socratic method to lead me toward an answer. "They think I'm pulling him back into his old life. Partying. Not caring. Blowing off responsibilities. But I'm not," I say before he can ask. "Josh really does love the law. I'm not sure he's found exactly the right fit yet, but I think he likes being part of the firm, likes being a Brower. I won't make him choose, and if he tried, I'd cut him loose."

"Is that a fact?" He takes a sip from his mug, and I swear he's trying to hide a smile.

I don't back down. "Yes, sir. It's a fact."

He sets his mug on the arm of his chair and nods. "If I've got this right, Josh has been going out of his way to show his support for you. He refuses to quit the firm even though my stubborn son is practically taunting him to do it, and your worry is that he'll try to choose you over them?"

"That's . . ." It sounds so presumptuous when he says it, but . . . "Yeah, that's it, basically."

"You think that taking care of Josh means pushing him away so he doesn't try to do that?"

"Ye—wait, no." I stop and think. "Maybe? I don't know. It almost made sense in my head until you said it that way."

"Sounded kind of dumb, did it?" This time, there's definitely a smile playing around his lips.

"To be honest, I was going for noble."

He flat-out laughs. "You really are something, Samantha Sami. I think what you're trying to do is figure out how to show up for Josh the way he's shown up for you, but you're overshooting the mark by quite a bit."

"So what do I do?"

He smiles. "The last couple of months are the

first time I've ever seen Josh go after what *he* wants. When he was screwing around in college, that was a reaction against what his parents wanted. Then when my Catherine died . . ." He trails off in a sigh, and I don't try to fill the silence.

Eventually, he stirs again. "Catherine's death shook Josh. He went the other way, trying to be exactly the son Steve and Elizabeth wanted. And now it looks like he's leaning toward another extreme, which is the false binary that he must choose between you and them. If it's not true, show him it's not true. If you take yourself out of the equation, you're only reinforcing that belief."

"I'm trying to make sure he doesn't shut them out," I say. "I made him go to family dinner."

"We appreciated it," Grampa Jim says. "It's good that you see he needs his family. But maybe it's not him that you need to convince. It's possible my son is pushing our Josh because he wants to have some control over when he gets hurt instead of waiting for Josh to blindside him."

"Like when someone picks a fight so they can force a breakup they believe is coming," I say. That's Madi's MO every single time.

"Exactly."

"So, prove to Miss Elizabeth and Mr. Brower that Josh doesn't have to choose between us, and make Josh believe it too?"

"Basically," Grampa Jim says.

"But how?"

"That I don't know. But I've faced down a lot of shrewd people in boardrooms and across negotiating tables in my career, and you could hold your own with any one of them. It'll come to you."

"But I want a plan," I say, my voice verging on a whine.

He chuckles again. "Trust your gut. And your grandma's. From what I heard on this side of that call, you've both got good instincts. Especially since yours led you to take a chance on that grandson of mine."

My jaw drops. "Grampa Jim, are you telling me to drop out of nursing to be a full-time musician?"

His smile crinkles his eyes. "I looked you up on Soundrack." Then holds up his hand, pinky and index finger extended. "Rock on."

Chapter Twenty-Eight
SAMI

Josh is waiting for me when I drive home Wednesday night. Grampa Jim had asked if he could be my audience while I worked out some more music, so instead of packing up to go home early, I stayed and played for him, working out lyrics while he made me a turkey sandwich for lunch.

I leave him with a hug in the late afternoon so I'll be on familiar highways by dark. I text everyone who will send out a posse for me if I don't make it home today that I'm on the road and will be home by dinnertime.

The whole drive home, I think about Jim Brower's advice. *Show up for him the way he's shown up for you.*

I can't sit in on Josh's board meetings. I can't coo over his paperwork. I do know what he needs, maybe because I need it too: our parents' faith in us. Their belief that we can succeed, and the knowledge that if we fail, they'll be there to bandage us up and send us out to try again.

I would love for my mom to be on board with the possibility of a career change for me, but Josh? Josh needs to know his parents have any faith in him at all.

When I pull into my spot at the Grove two hours and no answers later, Josh charges out of his kitchen like he's been watching for me and throws me over his shoulder as soon as I step out of the car.

"Josh," I half shriek, half laugh. Mrs. Lipsky emerges from the breezeway just then, her mail in her hand.

"That's the way, son," she says. "Too much political correctness these days. Sometimes you just gotta handle your woman."

"I'm too sexy for my shirt," Ahab announces as Mrs. Lipsky heads back to her patio.

"Put me down, Josh," I say, pounding on his back.

He ignores me and barrels through my back gate and into my condo. "Fists of fury is here," he calls. "I got her." He doesn't set me down until he reaches the living room, where he deposits me between Ava and Madi.

Madi pokes my arm. "Not an icicle."

Ruby comes out of her room and yells, "Cuddle puddle." In seconds, we're a wiggly mass of limbs, and when they finally let me up for air, Josh is standing there, arms across his chest, grinning.

"I'm fine, y'all," I say, blowing an errant lock of hair out of my face. "Still have all my fingers and toes. Now let me up."

"No way." Josh swoops down and picks me up

again. "Cuddle puddle." And he collapses onto the free cushion of the sofa to wrap me in a huge hug while my roommates cheer.

The end of the week is insanely busy. I work Thursday and Friday all day, then come home long enough to change before heading out for Pixie Luna shows. It's much nicer to get ready at home, no more smuggling my secret identity outfits like I'm on *Mission: Impossible*.

Saturday morning, I'm so wiped that Josh tucks me into my downstairs sofa and we do cartoons and cereal again, this time with Ruby and Ava before NilesQuil shows up and drives Ava to leave with mumbled excuses about checking on things at the lab.

Once Niles and Ruby leave, Josh shakes his head as the door clicks closed. "That dude *kills* me. If I find Ruby a guy who likes to hike but doesn't do it with the hiking stick lodged up his—"

"Josh." I shake my head. "We've all tried."

"Why?" he says, totally confused. "She has to know she can do better."

"We all have theories," I say. "Mine is that she's looking for someone with the complete opposite energy of her brothers, but none of us really knows. She insists she loves him."

We both make scrunch faces at the same time and laugh.

Josh heads back to his place at noon to work until he comes out for our show. I spend the afternoon working on music, another new song, this one about risk and reward.

Having a full day of rest leaves me almost jittery with unspilled energy by the time we hit the stage, and even Rodney grins when I open the first song with a howl. We go hard through the entire set, sweat stinging my eyes and dripping off Luther and Rodney, the crowd pulsing hard enough for us to hear the thump of their feet on the wooden floor above our amps turned up to eleven.

It's a fun show, and I feel the worry about Josh and his parents fall away while I'm on the stage, catching Josh's grin in the audience every few minutes as he and Wyatt—my piggyback-ride-giving giant, who now comes to most shows—dance.

They stop backstage to give me hugs after our set before they take off, which is why, when I meet Josh on our balconies later, I have major news to drop on him.

"You're not going to believe what happened after you left," I tell him.

He turns his chair to face me and settles into his blanket. "Tell me."

I settle into my own chair facing him. "Turns out that Big Time Records is interested."

He shoots up straight in his chair. "Big Time Records as in Big Time Records?"

I laugh and nod. It's a label you say in the same breath with Capitol or Interscope. "They sent an A&R guy. Said he'd been hearing the buzz and now he gets it. Saw us on the Southwest Fest lineup and wants to see how we connect from the festival stage and start talking a deal."

He clasps his head, his mouth hanging open. "Holy . . . that is major."

"Right?"

"What are you going to do?"

I shrug. "I don't know. We don't have any actual offers yet. Just maybes. Right now, the plan is to deliver the best performance of our lives on that stage and see if either label ponies up."

"I mean, this is amazing. Not surprising but amazing. But those labels are totally different vibes. Bat Bridge is indie. Big Time is corporate. Deep pockets. Scrappy upstarts. You're going to have a lot to think about because they're both going to want you."

"Maybe," I say, but the buzzing in my chest knows it's true even if I'm not saying it out loud. "Guess the guys and I have our research cut out for us."

"How would you feel about me looking into it?" he says. "I have a lot of practice trawling through legal databases; I could see if either of these companies has pending lawsuits or a legal trail you should know about."

"What if I say yes but only on the condition that you consider whether you'd want to do this for real. Like work in music law. What do you think?" I ask.

He shakes his head. "Sami . . ."

"Just think about it. That's all. Please?"

"Okay. You drive a hard bargain. Now can I do some investigating on these labels?"

"Knock yourself out. It'd be good to have a lawyer brain on the case. But I'm not paying you."

"In money." He waggles his eyebrows in such an exaggerated way that I can see it even in the dim light.

"Ew, Josh."

That makes him laugh. "Tonight was the best I've ever seen you guys, but that's what I think every time I see you. You're going to be an unstoppable force by the time you hit the festival stage."

"Thanks," I say.

"I mean it." He sighs. "I wish your mom would come watch you. If she did, I think she'd worry way less when you go full-time."

"I haven't decided I'm quitting Sunnyside," I remind him.

He rests his arms on the railing and settles his chin on top of them. "Haven't you?"

I bite my lip, trying not to let a premature smile escape, but it does anyway. "I will if we get a deal we can all live with. Or more importantly, live on."

He grins back. "Then you're definitely quitting."

We talk for a bit longer before the chill drives us inside. It's ten degrees warmer than it was earlier this week, but not quite fifty degrees is still cold.

I rinse out my pink hair dye in the shower, Josh's words looping through my head. *I wish your mom would come watch you. She'd worry less when you go full-time.*

I shut off the water as an idea strikes, my stage mascara still running down my cheeks as I replay his words a few more times.

That's it. That's how I show up for Josh: we tag in our grownups.

I'm up with the dawn the next morning, hoping that Grampa Jim is an early riser like most of the Sunnyside residents. He'd made sure I had his number before he sent me off on Wednesday with a promise to call him if I had any trouble on the icy roads.

The phone rings, two times, three times, and I'm about to hang up and try back at a more normal hour when he answers. "Hello?"

"Grampa Jim? It's Sami."

"Sami-girl, everything okay?"

"Okay with the possibility of greatness. I've hatched a plan."

He gives a chuckle, and I imagine him moving toward the edge of his seat. "All right, then. Let's hear it."

I lay it all out for him, then ask, "What do you think?" His job is to get his son and daughter-in-law to Pixie Luna's festival stage performance. I'll get my mom there. In both of these scenarios, the grandparents involved will be more than happy to apply any and all emotional blackmail to make it happen.

Once they get our parents there, the rest is up to me and my band. We'll deliver a show that makes them all believers. We have to. My mom needs to know that this isn't a long shot. And Steve and Elizabeth Brower need to know that Josh has chosen someone who is excelling in her field, even if that field is music, not law or even nursing.

If they see for themselves that Josh isn't going back to his party boy ways, that he's still putting in the time at work, that he's still demonstrating excellence, that he's still showing up for family stuff, that he's not choosing me over them . . . maybe they'll believe.

And in case that's not enough, I'm going to engineer a way for them—especially Mr. Brower—to see how much Josh is learning about the legal side of my industry. Then maybe, just maybe . . .

I don't even want to articulate it in case I jinx it.

"You're hanging an awful lot on a single performance," Grampa Jim says. "You sure you want to take that on?"

Not at all. But it's the only plan I've got.

The next two weeks are basically my training montage. This is the part of the movie where every hour I'm not at work, I'm at rehearsal. We're practicing not until we get it right but until we can't get it wrong. We have four shows before Southwest Fest, and we go harder for each one.

Josh and I touch base when we can over more bowls of cereal, tired Saturday mornings while we binge shows that don't require anything from us; there are a lot of very average sitcoms in rotation.

That's not to say things between us have cooled. The boy can melt me with a look, and it takes nothing at all for him to send me up in flames. The graze of his hand against my back. The touch of his fingertip trailing over my cheek. Maybe that's why I keep us in my living room so much; it's a safety zone, and I need things between us to go slowly while everything else in my life is moving at warp speed.

Even if all those touches and looks and long, hot kisses before we separate are driving me fricking crazy. It's the best kind of crazy. Melt-your-bones crazy. Tie-your-stomach-in-knots crazy.

The closer Southwest Fest gets, the more

nervous I get. We've got one last show to practice, the Tuesday before the festival, a midsize venue with an audience of about two hundred. When we take the stage, I smile out at the crowd, recognizing faces.

It's not just Josh or even Ruby, who has brought Charlie because Niles finds our shows "loud." It's the faces of people who have made a point of coming out for Pixie Luna for weeks, who have found us over the last few months, and now our shirts dot the crowd as they roar to greet us. To *greet* us. We've won crowds over by the end of a set, but now they roar in anticipation.

Like we have at every performance for weeks, we open up another artistic vein and let it all flow, pouring everything we have into it. This? Is magic. It gets better every time. I sing "Dumb Boy" for Ruby and hope she knows that's who Niles is, "Treat You Right," a song that's gotten better every time we do it because it's become more and more about Josh and no longer a hopeless plea like it was when I'd written it about trying to keep Bryce.

We tear through the rest of our songs, ending on "Here For It," a love letter to every fan in the audience, reminding them of what they deserve.

When we finish, they are *wild*. We wave and laugh and finally leave the stage, but the club manager meets us in the wings. We can barely hear him over the screams as he shakes his head and points to the stage, saying, "Encore."

Luther and I grin at each other. Jules and Wingnut fist-bump. We all turn to look at Rodney, who says, "Bad Reputation"? It's one of our favorite covers, a Joan Jett and the Blackhearts song that we do for fun in the band, and we run back out, slip into our places, and grin at each other as the screams surge with the opening notes.

This time when we leave the stage, the manager smiles at us. "I'm glad I knew y'all when," he says with a wink, then he heads back to the club floor. We were the last act of the night, and it feels amazing to send people home on that kind of high.

Josh is waiting when we step backstage, and I fly right into his arms. We're all so busy high-fiving and congratulating each other that it takes a few minutes before I realize there's a man waiting for an opening, leaning against the wall like he's been there for a while. I recognize him. It's the A&R guy—Jonny?—from Big Time and he's got a woman with him. She's dressed right for the club, but something about her screams authority.

Maybe it's the expensive haircut or her perfect makeup application, but it doesn't surprise me when I tell him hello and he steps forward to introduce me to Marisol Navarro, the president of the label.

"Nice to meet you," I say, shaking her hand.

"Incredible show," she says. "I was wondering if we could head over to the Driskill Hotel bar to talk."

"Uh, sure. Let me check."

I turn my back and mouth to Josh, *Big Time Records*, pointing behind me. His eyes widen as I walk over to the rest of the band. "Boys, Big Time is back tonight, and the president is asking to meet with us. *Be cool.*"

I say it in time to stop Wingnut from whooping or doing something equally uncool. He gives me a sheepish look and shuffles his feet, but he's grinning.

"Not us," Jules says. "They don't need the whole band. You and Luther can handle this."

Luther scans their faces. "You sure?"

Rodney nods.

"We'll pack up," Wingnut says. "Call us when you're done. We'll wait at the pool house."

"Is this real life?" I ask Luther.

He reaches out and squeezes my shoulder. "It is. We've earned it. You ready?"

I take a deep breath and nod. "Let's introduce the rest of you to the president before you take off."

They follow me back to Jonny and Marisol, Luther bringing up the rear. He hangs back to talk with Josh until I make the rest of the introductions, then steps forward to shake hands too.

"It was nice to meet you," Jules says. "We're

going to take off and get everything back to the studio"—I smother a smile at the pool house's promotion—"but Sami and Luther will keep us posted."

"Your man needs to come with us," Luther tells me in a low voice. "We been talking. You okay with that?"

I look over at Josh, who watches me with raised eyebrows, like he knows what Luther told me and he's waiting for a verdict. "Absolutely." Guess he took my condition seriously.

An hour later as we sit in a quiet corner of the hotel bar, Josh is asking questions about royalty rates, "three-sixty" deals, rights retention, profit participation, and all kinds of things I wouldn't have thought to ask. I've always depended on Luther to know this kind of stuff while Jules handles booking shows and I've handled lyrics, sound, and image. Now I regret not having dug into the business side of things more, because there are whole sections of the conversation I'm not following.

The label people pay the tab and get to their feet, shaking hands with all of us.

"We'll look forward to making this official," Marisol says.

"Possibly," Josh counters. "As we told you, you're not the only label interested right now. My clients will need to hear the other offer before they make a decision."

She nods. "Big Time Records wants to be in the Pixie Luna business. I know a winner when I see one." She and Jonny smile and take their leave.

Josh waits until they're gone before he takes his seat, looking at me with those same raised eyebrows.

"Your clients?"

He shrugs. "I'm fairly sure the price is right, and I can promise you I've done the research."

I fight a smile. "What are you billing me?"

He taps his cheek, a clear request for a kiss. I laugh and comply. Luther grabs him and gives him a loud, smacking smooch on the other side. Josh sits back and grins. "So I'm hired?"

I look at Luther. "Your call. I don't want everyone thinking I hired him just because he's hot."

Luther smiles. "Your man knows his stuff. Impressive as hell. You're hired. But Sami will have to keep up the payments, not me."

Josh toasts him with the glass of water he's been nursing. "If you want, I can meet with the rest of the band before Southwest Fest and explain the pros and cons of going with Big Time versus an indie label. I'm positive Bat Bridge will make an offer. Y'all are going to have a big choice to make."

"Can you come tomorrow night?" Luther asks.

Josh nods but gets to his feet again. "I'll be there, but for right now, I need to get home or I'll be worthless at the office tomorrow. You want to come with me, Sami?"

"Yes, but I better stay and go over some stuff with Luther."

Josh nods and gives me a kiss, one that tells me it's probably for the best I'm putting a tiny bit of space between us tonight. "See you tomorrow," he says, then he dips out.

Luther and I look at each other, and a slow grin spreads across his face. "I know you're all in for this band, but you didn't have to go out and date a lawyer to get us a good rate."

I laugh. "I didn't even know he knew all of that."

"He's sharp," Luther says. "We should let him negotiate for us, and if he's as good as I think he is, he'll be able to negotiate a good enough deal to make his commission more than worth the while."

I flop back against the booth seat. "Is this real life? Is this happening? Are we about to sign a record deal?"

"Indeed, mighty-mite," he says with a shake of his shaggy head. "Indeed we are."

Chapter Twenty-Nine
JOSH

Saturday. Show time.

Last night, I had the extreme honor of meeting Grandma Letty in addition to getting a nerve-wracking introduction to Sami's mom, Gina.

Grandma Letty loves me. Miss Gina is much harder to read, but we ate a dinner cooked by Ava on the patio together—the roommates, Webster women, and me—and it went okay. Miss Gina didn't laugh at my jokes, but when Sami and I were on our balconies talking for a few minutes like we often do before going to sleep, Miss Gina had poked her head out.

"Josh," she'd said.

"Hey, Miss Gina. Sorry to keep you awake."

"You weren't. My mom and I will ride with you to the festival tomorrow." Then she'd disappeared inside without waiting for an answer, and Sami had grinned.

"You're in," she said. "Don't blow it."

So now it's early afternoon, and I'm knocking on the door next to mine to escort my girlfriend's mom and grandma to her rock concert. The other girls will drive over to the Arbor—the amphitheater—together.

Grandma Letty takes the front seat of the BMW. Gina looks at the blue-and-white crest on the grill and almost sniffs but not quite before she climbs into the back.

"Have you watched Sami perform before?" I ask them as I put us on the road, hoping to keep any awkward silences from falling.

"Not with the band," Grandma Letty says. "But I've been listening to their songs. *Streaming* them. I know they're going to be good. I can tell. I spruced up my shirt."

She has indeed bedazzled the Pixie Luna T-shirt stretched across her chest.

Miss Gina is dressed in tan slacks and a neatly tucked plaid blouse. "She was always good when she played in little cafés." She says it in a way that suggests that's where she thinks Sami should still be performing.

The Southwest Fest main stage is going to be quite a change of gears for her.

The festival stage is an amphitheater built each spring for the festival. Between the stands and general admission, it holds three thousand people. Today is crisp but not too cold; it's blue and sunny, the temperature hovering around sixty, perfect for the last weekend before spring.

Sami got one free festival pass, which she gave to her grandmother; she'd bought her mom's ticket, and the rest of us had sprung for our own, but she was able to get ten VIP show passes, good only during the Pixie Luna set.

I choose the expensive parking so Grandma Letty won't have to walk far, although I suspect she could probably outdo any of us. She practically vibrates with the same energy Sami has before taking the stage.

We make our way inside the festival amphitheater. We're a half hour early, and it's not hard to find the VIP section with Ava's bright hair marking the spot. What I absolutely don't expect to see is the familiar set of my grandfather's shoulders. I pick up my pace to reach him, and I'm even more shocked to find him standing with my mom and dad.

"Hey, y'all," I say as we reach the group. It looks like Sami's tenth pass went to Ruby's brother, Joey, who has somehow provoked a screech of outrage from Ava, who lunges toward him as he dances out of the way, holding something out of her reach.

I turn back to my parents. "I didn't expect to see you here."

"Sami invited us," Gramps says. "She's my buddy now."

"Gramps made us come." This is my dad, his voice cool with a slight undertone of irritation.

My mom simply leans up for a kiss and pats my arm. I busy myself making introductions, under no illusions that any of them will remember each other, but it gives me somewhere to channel my nerves as the amphitheater fills faster and faster.

When the seats are full and the pre-show noise of the crowd is drowning out the classic rock pouring from the festival PA, my dad leans over and calls, "Is this thing going to start soon?"

I nod. "Pixie Luna opens," I call back. "They're first."

As if on cue, roadies walk onstage to check the amps. I recognize Jules's guitar and Luther's bass. Rodney himself is up there in a black roadie T-shirt, checking the cymbals and positioning the snare. When they've fiddled and tweaked for a few minutes, they disappear again, and the recorded music fades out.

An announcer comes over the PA, welcoming everyone to the festival stage, and the crowd cheers. He gives the usual spiel about restroom locations, first aid stations, and thanks to the sponsors. Then he pauses, and pitching his voice even lower, he says, "And now for the show. Ladies and gentlemen, this band has been together less than a year, but they've dominated the Austin music scene like they're veterans. Please welcome Pixie Luna! For those about to rock, we salute you!"

It's a smart thing to say as the crowd roars their approval of the AC/DC lyric, and the band runs out to the opening licks of the song. Rodney is now in a Foo Fighters shirt. Sami is in a green mask the color of her tattoo, a shiny purple prom dress over fishnets, and Doc Martens, with her pink hair in two buns near the top of her head.

The sound guy turns down the AC/DC instrumentals and now we can hear Luther plucking his bass and Jules picking out a melody this crowd doesn't know yet, but I smile. They're opening with "I'm Not Your Prom Queen."

"What's up, Austin?" Sami yells into the mic before she flings her hands into the air to wait for the answer, and the audience cheers back. Then she holds the mic close to her mouth, takes her wide-legged power stance, and calls, "This is for the girls who tell it like it is!" Then Rodney bangs the snare, Jules's guitar growls, and they're off. Miss Gina's mouth falls open.

Sami's energy is contagious, and it's perfect symbiosis. Not once, not even during their midtempo songs, does her energy or the crowd's come down. She pushes them harder and higher, and they're ready to lose their minds during "Boy, Nevermind."

Grandma Letty is down by the rope with my neighbors, bouncing and dancing; Miss Gina is standing slightly apart, smiling; and I try not to notice my parents too much because I don't trust myself to act right if they're standing there looking bored. I make sure my back is angled to them.

When Pixie Luna finishes and Sami calls, "You've been fantastic, Austin!" they have to stay on stage for several more minutes as the crowd cheers.

Finally, the announcer comes on the PA and says, "That was Pixie Luna, people, and now you know why we put them on the festival stage. We'll let them catch their breath and take a short break while we wait for your Saturday headliner, Night View!"

Only when Sami is off the stage do I walk toward my parents. Gramps slides an arm around my shoulders. "Son, I'm sorry to tell you this because I know you like that Sami, but"—he takes a dramatic pause before finishing—"that's too bad because I'm going to marry her."

I laugh and hug him, a good, manly back-slapping hug. "They're good, aren't they?"

He shakes his head. "Better than good."

I turn toward my parents. "So, what did you think?"

My mom is smiling, but before either of them can answer, a man walks over, his hand outstretched for a shake.

"You Josh Brower?" he asks, as I take his offered hand.

"I am."

"Nick Bautista, Bat Bridge Records. Luther says you're the guy I need to see if I want to sign them, and I do. I hear you're talking to Big Time too. They offer you a three-sixty?"

I shoot my parents an apologetic look and

answer his question. "They did. What is Bat Bridge bringing to the table?"

"Fifty-fifty, and only fifteen years on rights to the masters."

He has my attention. In the music industry, major labels often offer a three-sixty deal, as in 360 degrees: a full pie, and they get a slice of every part of it. Their deep pockets mean artists get access to the best studios, producers, and music video directors as well as a high chance of being put on a tour opening for an arena band. But the label also keeps the recording rights, period.

Indie labels only take fifty percent of the recording profits and usually ask for a twenty-five-year exclusive on the rights. They'll often pair their newer bands with established bands for tours, but they're smaller shows and they can't always pay the biggest producers what major labels can. The difference is that their bands get more creative control and keep all the profits from touring and merchandise sales. It can add up.

We discuss all this, and I hear him out, aware that my parents are waiting for me, and finally I close out the conversation. "I'll take it to the band, Nick. It'll be their decision."

"Just promise me you'll give me a chance to counter whatever Big Time offers. They can wave a lot of cash, but they don't nurture their acts the way Bat Bridge does."

"Will do," I say, shaking hands with him before he leaves.

I turn to my parents. "Sorry about that. What did you think of the band?"

They exchange glances. My mom says, "We get it. She's the real deal."

"We still have concerns," my dad says, "but yes, Josh, we get it."

I smile. If wanting them to see the magic of Sami was the only thing I have on the line, I'd be grinning like a maniac. But ever since the meeting with Big Time on Wednesday night, an idea has been growing, one that feels risky but right. I'm about to lay it all out for my dad when a whirlwind of pink and purple flies from the artists' area and cannonballs into my arms.

I gather Sami up, holding her against me, and feeling the energy still pulsing through her body. "You were incredible, babe," I tell her.

She pushes against me until I let her down and grins up at me. "Yeah?"

"Yeah. But bad news," I say, still grinning.

Her eyes narrow. "What is it?"

"You're going to have to choose between two record deals. Bat Bridge wants to sign you."

She pushes her mask up, her eyes wide. "Yeah?"

"Yeah."

"YEAH!" she shouts, and runs back toward the artists' section, probably to tell the rest of the band. Halfway there, she runs back, flings her arms around my grandfather's waist and yells, "Hey, Grampa Jim." Then she rushes over to my parents, tiptoes to plant a kiss on each of their cheeks, and disappears again.

I grin as I watch her go, but her mom catches her before she makes it past the rope again and sweeps her into a giant hug. Guess her mom is a believer too now.

I turn back to my parents. "You were saying you have concerns." My dad nods and starts to speak, but I hold up a hand. "Wait. I want to say something, and it's not going to make you feel any better."

My mom's smile fades, and my dad gives me a slight frown.

"I've really enjoyed working at the firm, but—"

"Hey, Josh," Marisol says, stopping to shake my hand as my dad's frown deepens. "You're a hell of a negotiator. Look forward to sparring with you soon."

"Same," I say as she waves and makes her way over to the band.

"You were saying?" my dad prompts me.

"I enjoy working at the firm, and I learned a lot from the cases I've been on, but . . ."

His mouth tightens, and my mom looks worried. "But what?" she asks.

"But I've been learning a lot about entertainment law, specifically the music industry lately. It's fascinating, and there are plenty of artists right here in Austin who need someone watching their back." I'd heard enough stories from Luther about bands who had signed all their rights away, too excited about getting a deal to ask tough questions. I take a steadying breath. "So anyway, that's what I want to do. Entertainment law."

My dad's face doesn't soften. "So you've found a different firm?"

I shake my head. "No. That's the thing. Sami's told me more than once that I'm entitled, and maybe that's how this will sound, but I want it all. I want to date Sami *and* I want you to like her. I want to practice entertainment law *and* I want to stay with the firm." I hesitate, then spit it out. "I'd like to open an entertainment division at Brower and Moore. At first, it'll just be me, and it'll just be music, but Austin has a huge film industry too, and I'd like to expand in that direction as quickly as possible."

My dad gives me a long look, his face inscrutable, before turning to Gramps and exchanging looks with him. Gramps's expression doesn't give anything away either.

"Let me get this straight," my dad says, turning back to me. "You want to stay with the firm but practice whatever law you think is interesting? And make a whole division out of it?"

"Basically." When he doesn't say anything, I add quietly, "I'm hungry for this, Dad."

Something flickers in his eyes, and my mom slides her hand through his. "Josh?" he says, a twitch of a smile at the corner of his mouth.

"Yes, sir?"

"You start Monday."

Gramps chuckles and Mom pulls me into a hug. "We like her, Josh. Sami is good for you."

Then my dad takes his turn. "Proud of you, son." We stay in the hug for several long moments, and I swear I hear him sniffle before he pulls away.

"Your Sami is something," Gramps says. "She made me promise to stick to your parents like white on rice so I could make sure they could hear you talking business with the record people. Sent me pictures of the executives so I knew who to keep an eye out for."

"Sami set us up?" my dad asks, clearly surprised.

"She surely did," Gramps confirms, grinning. "With my help."

My dad shakes his head, but he's smiling. "Was a new division her idea too?"

I start to shake my head, but then I pause. "Now that I think about it, I think my sneaky girlfriend may have planted a few seeds on that one."

"Now I really like her," he says. "We're going to head home now, but you and Sami better be over for Sunday family dinner tomorrow."

I grin. "Yes, sir."

His gaze goes to Sami, who's only visible by her Doc Martens in the middle of a group hug from her band. "You seemed lost for so long. We only ever wanted you to find your way."

I follow his gaze to my girlfriend's combat boots. "I have, Dad." For maybe the first time ever, I know exactly what I want. *Who* I want. Now all I have to do is tell her where I stand.

Chapter Thirty
SAMI

"Bestie brunch in ten!" I call from the foot of the stairs so everyone can hear me. "Well, besties and Josh!"

I've made waffles and bacon, homemade whipped cream, sliced strawberries, fresh blueberries, and strong coffee. I text Josh to come over. I'd spent all day with him at Southwest Fest, checking out different acts. Then he'd come back to the pool house with us and laid out the terms of each label deal. We'd all talked it through, deferring to Josh's research and Luther's experience before making a choice.

"What are we celebrating again?" Ava asks, coming in. "I know there's a million things to choose from, just wondering if it's anything specific."

"I'll tell you when everyone is here."

Ruby is next, followed by Josh hopping the low fence to come through the patio door. Ava has to go up and nag Madi, who eventually shambles into the kitchen, eye makeup smeared but not looking too grumpy as she sniffs the bacon.

When everyone has served themselves waffles and settled into the patio chairs, I stand at the head of the table. "I have an announcement," I say.

"Could you stand up?" Madi asks, and everyone laughs as I throw a napkin at her.

"That joke gets as tired as a ninety-two-year-old on Sunnyside movie night," I say, my tone as dry as unbuttered toast. "Now settle down." I wait until they do. "I have called you together to announce that you are looking at the newest artist on the Bat Bridge label."

Josh grins while the girls cheer and holler their congrats. I laugh and answer all their questions. Yes, we'll be going on tour but not until summer, and I'll keep working until then. We picked them because we like the creative control. Yes, Josh is an absolute shark in negotiations.

"Don't worry," he tells the girls. "I've still got a few things to pin down so Pixie Luna gets the best end of the deal."

"That's my man," I say, grinning. "Now eat up, because they might not admit it, but I make the best bacon in the house."

Josh plucks a piece from his plate and takes a bite and sighs. "Perfect crunch. I freaking love you."

The table goes silent. Josh freezes. My mouth makes an *O* but no sound comes out.

"What did you just say?" Ruby asks, her eyes gleaming.

Josh puts his bacon down and swallows.

Then he gets up and walks to where I'm sitting. Leaning down, he says softly in my ear, "I'm madly in love with you, Sami Webster."

I turn to meet his eyes. His big, blue eyes, with those lusciously thick lashes. "You've put me in a very difficult position," I say in a stage whisper. He gives me a questioning look. "If I say it back, I lose a bet to Ruby, and she gets my parking space."

He crouches beside me, resting his elbow on my chair arm, his chin in his hand. He looks from a grinning Ruby to me. "Tough one," he says, his voice sympathetic. "Do what you have to do."

"I'll be right back," I say. Then I disappear into the condo for a second and return with my keys. "I love you, Josh Brower," I say as Ruby whoops and Ava and Madi clap. "And now I have to go move my car."

Josh scoops me up and gives me a kiss that soon makes Madi beg for mercy. "Knock it off," she complains. "I can't take that much sugar in the morning."

"That was a sucker's bet," Ava says as the other person with designated parking. "You're pretty great, Josh, but not worth the permit."

He lifts his head to grin at her and slides his hand into mine.

"You better watch yourself," Ruby tells the other two. "I'm coming for you next."

That starts some trash talk, and as I turn toward

the back gate, Josh digs his own keys from his pocket with his free hand. "I'll come with you. I need to move my car too."

I blink up at him, confused. "Why?" He's parked where he always is, right next to me, directly in front of his condo.

"Because, Sami. I have *two* assigned spots, and the other one is right there. I just never really thought about it." He points to a space that's always empty on the row behind ours, only ten feet away. "Now that one's mine, and this one is yours forever now." He takes my other hand and touches his forehead to mine. "Just like me."

Epilogue
SAMI

I snuggle against Josh's side, watching the sun set behind the Austin skyline as we share the wicker love seat on my balcony, purchased specifically for this purpose. It feels good to be here with my man, my besties somewhere downstairs, probably arguing about the details for the upcoming pool party. But that's only because Ava keeps insisting on going as low-key as possible, and Ruby and Madi aren't having it.

I've been home from tour about a week, but there's a part of me that still expects to wake up tomorrow morning and climb onto the bus to drive to the next stop. It's way better than the van we were in for our first tour last summer, but still. Nothing can beat being home, surrounded by all my favorite people. And barbecue joints. That's not unimportant.

I slip my other arm around Josh's waist and squeeze. This is infinity times better.

"Still exhausted?" Josh asks.

"Not really. Content, more like." It had been a long tour. Almost four months compared to last summer's first tour of eight weeks. "This is the first time since we got back that I feel like I'm truly starting to decompress. I was even thinking about pulling out my guitar."

"Wow," Josh says. "You are feeling better. What are you going to write about?"

My guitar comes out when I have a song idea. "I don't know. Maybe how perfect it feels to sit on a balcony with you, watching the sun set on a late September night. It doesn't get much better than this."

"Hmm. Let me see if I can make a case for an improvement." His voice holds the trace of a laugh.

"Go ahead, counselor." No doubt he'll head inside and return with a bowl of ice cream. The man gets me.

Sure enough, he gently disentangles himself. "You relax. Give me a couple of minutes, and I'll be back."

"Cookie dough," I say.

"Sure, cookie dough." He disappears into my room, and I nestle further into the love seat. It's a perfect Austin evening, and I fully soak it in, feeling every single one of my blessings as I do. A successful tour with our second album, which went gold five months after release. It means I can work on music full-time now, and I'll have to figure out what that looks like when I'm not on tour.

Things with Josh are better than ever. He joined us on the road several times when he could work remotely, I came home when I could, and we had lots and lots of FaceTime. He'll have to hire a new associate soon to help him handle the business he's bringing into the Brower and Moore entertainment law practice. Big Time Records even uses him quite often because they were so impressed with his know-how in their negotiation for Pixie Luna, even though they lost. Maybe even *because* they lost.

Grandma and my mom came to three different shows on the tour, and my mom wears her Pixie Luna shirt and sings right along with Grandma.

And now I have more than two favorite Browers: Grampa Jim is going strong, but I've gotten to like the rest of Josh's family quite well. Maybe I even love them. I know for sure I miss their family dinners when I'm on the road. And Mr. Brower told me once that he liked our song "Hills and Souls" "quite a bit." He almost blushed when he said it.

My friends are healthy, happy, and thriving. And I'm about to eat a bowl of ice cream with my favorite person in the world.

He's taking longer than I expected, and I hear some giggling and a shushing from the patio below me. "Rube? Is that you?"

Dead silence.

Huh. Weird.

I straighten, trying to decide if I want to go down and evaluate the shenanigans, because that was a shenanigans giggle if ever I heard one. But before I can even decide, Ruby's voice calls to me from the sidewalk.

"Hey, chica, I want a private performance!"

I stand and walk to the railing, smiling down at her. "Sorry, you can't afford me now."

She grins. "What if it's all of us?"

Ava and Madi step out next. "Yeah, private show!"

"Hear, hear," Mrs. Lipsky calls from her balcony.

"Yes, rock star. We want a show." That's Hugo, Jasmine grinning beside him.

Something is definitely up but I have no idea what. Do they really want a show? Should I go in and grab my guitar? I bite my lip, trying to figure out what I should do here.

Madi heaves a dramatic sigh. "You're such a diva now. I guess you need a bigger audience."

Next, Grandma and my mom join them from under the patio, and my jaw drops. "What in the world?"

Ava shakes her head. "Still not enough, I guess. Come on out, y'all."

The entire Brower clan fills in beside them, from Grampa Jim all the way down to Reagan's kids.

"Josh?" I say, a quaver in my voice. I have an inkling of where this might be going.

"Wow, give her a huge audience and she still

wants more," Ruby says. "All right, if that's what it takes."

She waves her arm toward Josh's back door, like she's beckoning someone. The band soon appears, Rodney holding a set of bongos, Jules with his guitar strapped in place.

"*Now* can we get a show?" Madi asks, like she can't believe I'm being this ridiculous.

"I . . . yes?" I say.

"Too late," Ava says. "Looks like we'll have to do it."

Jules looks to someone I can't see, his eyebrows raised, and then gives a nod before he starts picking out the melody for "Row, Row, Row Your Boat" while Rodney plays a soft beat on the bongos. Luther points a flashlight at me, spotlight style, even though it's not full dark yet.

Then, like we're at a freaking campfire or something, my roommates and family start singing words that are definitely not the actual lyrics.

"Sam, Sam, Sami girl, you two make quite a team. Why don't you make it permanent, and he'll give you a ring."

My heart pounds as the band and my neighbors start in with a second round. "Sam, Sam, Sami, girl, you should reward his scheme, Josh has worked so hard on this, we think you sense a theme."

Finally, the whole Brower clan takes the third

round, the other two rounds continuing softly so I can hear. "Sam, Sam, Sami girl, you've grown in our esteem. We love you like you are our own, so join our family."

Mr. Brower—no, Mr. Steve—is singing. Not just singing. *Grinning*.

Tears pop into my eyes. Just as I'm about to call for him, Josh steps out, standing on the sidewalk in front of the semicircle the rest of them have formed. He waits until they're done singing, smiling up at me the whole time, his eyes soft.

When they finish, he goes down on one knee, and Grandma, my mom, and Miss Elizabeth all hug each other.

"Sami, I love you," Josh says. "You probably get sick of hearing me saying it, but it's true. You've had over eighteen months of evidence, and now it's time for me to make my closing argument. You're my favorite person in the world. You're my best friend, and I'm better for knowing you. I would love for us to keep growing together, and I can't imagine my life without you."

He extends his hand to show a ring box, and he opens it. "This belonged to my grandmother. I think she'd be thrilled if you accepted it."

There's a soft amen from Grampa Jim.

"Samantha Marie Webster, will you marry me?"

I swallow around a very big lump in my throat,

and my voice cracks and wavers when I ask, "Do I get ice cream if I say yes?"

There's a rumble of laughter and my mom's scandalized, "Sami!"

But Josh laughs. "You get ice cream no matter what."

"Well, hang on. I have to think."

Then I turn around and run into the house, down the stairs, and out through the back door to launch myself at Josh with enough force that I would have bowled him over completely if his dad didn't catch him.

"Yes, Joshua Steven Brower. Yes forever!"

As he stands to sweep me up into a kiss, Luther leads everyone in a rousing chorus of "For He's a Jolly Good Fellow."

And surely he is.

Acknowledgments

Special thanks to Shawn Larsen, Ryan Clinton, and Dean Gloster for answering legal questions. Thank you to Ryan Clinton and Jenna Speyer for Austin info. Thank you to Jay Tibbitts, drummer for The Strike, for the band and music questions. All errors are my own! Thank you to Jenny Proctor, Brittany Larsen, and up-and-coming rom-com writer Emily Branch for their speed reads on this and their insightful story recommendations. Thank you to Jeanna Stay for the eagle-eyed editing. Much appreciation always to Jen White, Tiffany Odekirk, Aubrey Hartman, and Teri Bailey Black for listening to scenes over and over until I get them right. Thank you to the Zoom crew for keeping motivated and the fun talks every day. Thank you to my Facebook reader group for all the suggestions, poll answers, and cheerleading! Thank you to Kenny and my kiddos who do so much to help and support me, and for whom I do this all. My kiddos especially have helped make this book possible as they've stepped into their business roles. Smart cookies!

About the Author

Melanie Bennett Jacobson is an avid reader, amateur cook, and champion shopper. She lives in Southern California with her husband and children, a series of doomed houseplants, and a naughty miniature schnauzer. She holds a Masters in Writing for Children and Young Adults from the Vermont College of Fine Arts. She is a three-time Whitney Award winner for contemporary romance and a *USA Today* bestseller.

Center Point Large Print
600 Brooks Road / PO Box 1
Thorndike, ME 04986-0001 USA

(207) 568-3717

US & Canada:
1 800 929-9108
www.centerpointlargeprint.com